Praise for The Viscount's Forbidden Love:

"This is a compelling and emotional journey: watching these men finding themselves, each other and finally a way to navigate a world that won't accept them and their love. Their feelings for each other never waver, and there's some really tantalising spicy intimacy near the end of the story... A beautiful romance and a fitting end to this original series!" Goodreads review

"A slow burn romance with lots of angst and tension... I feel that Ms Wakeford wrote this story with real sensitivity and with a sense of reality of the time." Goodreads review

"A Compelling Forbidden Love Story... The attraction and tension between the two were palpable and continued to build as the book progressed." Goodreads review

"What a finish for this exhilarating series. Extremely well written... Can't wait for more by this fabulous author. Curl up and enjoy this book and the rest of the series, you will not be sorry." Goodreads review

"Very angsty, and I love angst... This was emotional in so many ways... It really was a beautiful story of forbidden love." Goodreads review

"I enjoyed this well written story of forbidden love. The characters were complicated yet delightful. I enjoyed the romance and steam, but most of all, the happy ending." Goodreads review

The Stanton Legacy

Interconnected steamy historical romances set in England and America from the 1830s to the 1860s following two generations of the powerful and wealthy Stanton family.

Book 1: The Viscount's Scandalous Affair

An illicit affair set in late regency London between two unlikely lovers whose emotional and bumpy journey into love ends in a happily ever after.

Book 2: The Vixen's Unlikely Marriage

A steamy romance set in Victorian England featuring a marriage of convenience between two unlikely characters, a beautiful vixen and a virtuous clergyman, who nevertheless find themselves falling in love.

Book 3: The Bluestocking's Secret Obsession

A slow-burn but steamy friends-to-lovers romance set in Victorian England and America in the Civil War.

Book 4: The Viscount's Forbidden Love

An MM romance set in Victorian England with plenty of heart, angst and steam—and it does have a happy ending.

Spin off novellas:

Mr Templeton Finds Himself a Wife
Miss Stanton Meets Her Match

THE VISCOUNT'S FORBIDDEN LOVE

A Historical MM Romance

BOOK 4
THE STANTON LEGACY

M.M. Wakeford

First edition.
978-1-7395071-4-5

Cover designed by Sweet 'N Spicy Designs

www.mw-author.com

Contents

Stanton Family Tree

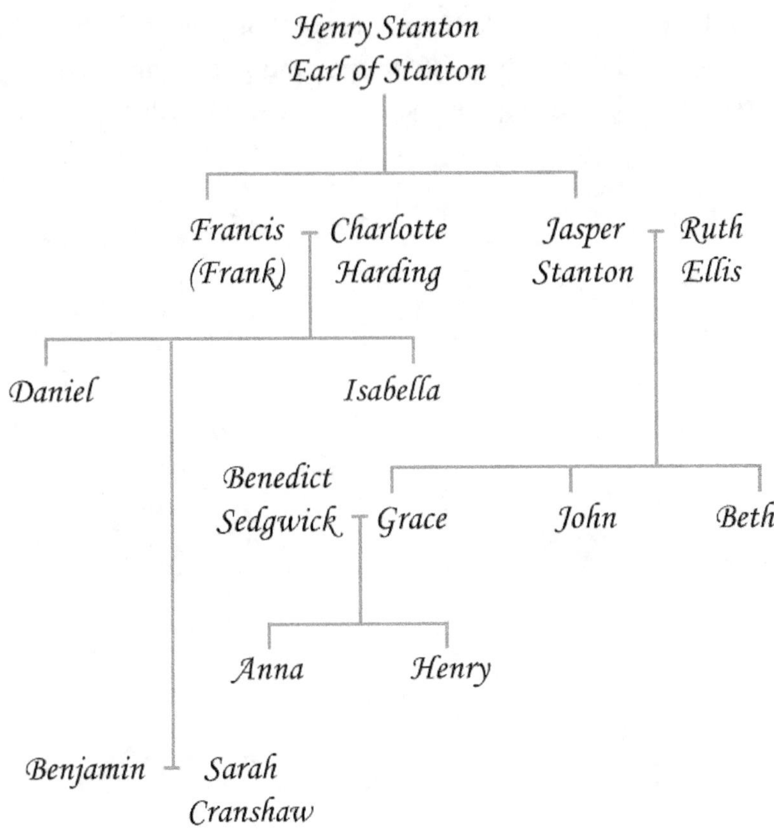

Preface

This is a historical novel written for a mature audience. There are sexual scenes that make this story unsuitable for anyone under the age of 18. Although it is part of a series, it can be read as a standalone, though for maximum enjoyment, I would recommend reading the books in sequential order.

Prologue

Ambrose

January 1866

Should he go to Ohio? There was one pressing reason to go, but he must not think of that. The question lay unresolved in his mind as he stared at a distant point on the horizon. Land had been sighted a short while ago and passengers had been informed that *The Scotia* would be reaching its destination—New York—within the next two hours.

Ambrose Cranshaw did not need to do much in preparation for this. His baggage was a meagre travel case with the few days' clothes that had been packed in a great hurry prior to leaving his home in Oxfordshire on this mad dash with his younger sister, Sarah, in pursuit of Benjamin Stanton. Ambrose had agreed to help Sarah on her quest to reunite with the man she loved before he sailed for America. They had travelled overnight on the mail train to Liverpool and reached *The Scotia* an hour before its departure, only to be told they could not get aboard without first purchasing a ticket.

So, at an expense that still made him shudder, they had bought a passage to America and boarded the ship. And now, Sarah was married to Benjamin, the ceremony having taken place a few days into their journey, presided over by Captain Fraser and blessed by Reverend Arnold, an elderly vicar who happened to have been a fellow traveller on the ship.

As the shoreline slowly grew from a minute point on the horizon to something more substantial, Ambrose assessed the situation he found himself in. Here he was, about to arrive in America, having never before set foot on this continent. He had only enough funds to cover the cost of his return journey to England plus a little more to spare. Once they disembarked, the newly married couple would be journeying onwards to their home in Ohio, where Benjamin's father and uncle had extensive landholdings.

And as for Ambrose… well, he should wish them a fond farewell and take the next ship bound back for England. His position as manager of the Stanton estate did not allow for him to absent himself for any great length of time. There were rents to collect, accounts to be done, works to be overseen. It was his duty to return as soon as possible and pick up the reins once more.

Yet there was another impulse tugging at his breast, and that was to accompany Sarah and Benjamin to Ohio. As her eldest brother and only sibling, he ought to ensure she was comfortably established in her new home before bidding her goodbye. He would not see her again for a very long time, and once back in England, they would be far apart from one another. His heart beat painfully in his chest at the thought. He would need to accustom himself to living alone at Ivy Cottage without his sister's cheerful companionship. It was not a heartening prospect.

The more he thought of it, the more he warmed to the idea of continuing on to Ohio. He had gone to the great expense of accompanying Sarah to America, therefore it would make sense to see the journey through to its end and to delay the final moment of farewell. He would ensure his sister was well settled and put his mind at rest as to her wellbeing before returning home. The Stanton estate would have to do without him for a few more weeks.

He refused to acknowledge the other reason why the idea of going to Ohio held appeal. It was nonsensical, not worthy of consideration. And yet, try as he might, he could not stop the thrill that coursed through him at the thought of seeing Daniel again. It had been over three months since he had last laid eyes on his friend, his employer and now also his brother-in-law. Three months since that forbidden kiss between them had spun his world on its axis. And much as he secretly longed for a repeat of that kiss, he understood very well that it must never, ever happen again.

Chapter 1

Ambrose

November 1860, some five years previously

He woke early, as usual, and partook of his breakfast alone. It was a simple meal, for he was a man of simple pleasures—a cup of coffee tempered with a dash of creamy milk, a thick slice of buttered bread and some slivers of ham. Breakfast complete, he went to put on his coat and hat. Then, whistling a cheerful tune, he let himself out of the house and began the short walk towards the stable at Stanton Hall.

It was a cold, crisp day with a hint of drizzle in the air. Today, he would be making calls on some farming tenants of the estate, and for this task, he would need a horse to travel on, for the Stanton lands were vast, spanning several thousand acres. Ambrose reached the stable in good time and smiled a greeting at John Saunders, one of the grooms that worked there.

"Good morning, Saunders," he said easily.

"Morning, sir," replied the groom. "Will you be needing Marigold?"

"Indeed I will," said Ambrose. "Can you have her saddled for me?"

"Yes, sir."

Ambrose followed Saunders to the stall where his mare stood chewing passively on some straw. She was not really his mare of course, but she had been assigned to his exclusive use as manager of the estate. She was a fine horse with a golden brown coat that had earned her the name of Marigold, and a sweet temper to go with it. She suited him very well. Ambrose patted her rump as she was led out of the stall. "Hello, my lovely," he crooned.

Once out into the yard, Saunders began to attach the saddle to her back. "Have you heard the news, sir?" he asked, throwing a curious glance at Ambrose.

"And what news would that be?"

"The master's family is here from America," replied the groom excitedly.

Ambrose's interest quickened at this. His employer, the rich and powerful Earl of Stanton, had taken sick recently and had been unable to leave his bed in the last few weeks except for brief periods of respite. Up until this illness, the earl had been a vigorous man who kept a sharp eye on all matters relating to his vast landholdings. Ambrose enjoyed working for him, even though he was kept on his toes much of the time, having to meet the earl's exacting standards.

Over the years, a strong mutual respect had developed between the older nobleman and his estate manager. But since his illness, the seventy-six year old earl had shown a worrying frailty. So worrying in fact that Ambrose had been tasked with sending a telegram to the earl's two sons, who had left for America decades ago, asking them to return.

Ambrose had often wondered about these two prodigal sons of the earl. He knew their departure for America had caused a rupture with their father and that it had taken years to mend the breach. In the meantime, Frank and Jasper Stanton had made a fortune for themselves from the land they had claimed, cleared and successfully farmed in the state of Ohio. And now, they were back, but for how long? And if the earl's illness proved to be fatal, would the estate then pass into the hands of the eldest son, Frank?

Ambrose did not want to think of the earl's demise, for he had developed a fondness for the old man as well as respect, but he could not help but wonder what would happen to the massive Stanton estate after the earl was gone, and how that would affect him. He felt sure that he would be ousted from his position. The family had no doubt their own way of doing things and would want to put a person of their choice in the trusted position of estate manager. Even were he to keep his job, he wondered if Frank Stanton would settle back in England with his family or if he would be an absentee landlord, running things all the way from America—and thereby placing ever more reliance on his estate manager. Would Ambrose be up to such a task? There were so many questions for which he as yet had no answers.

All would be revealed in due course, and whatever the case might be, he would make the best of things, as he had always strived to do. He told himself there was no point in worrying about his future and that of Sarah, but he did.

Only four years separated them, yet he felt the full weight of responsibility for his sister. Their parents on their death had left them with a very meagre inheritance, and Sarah had no income of her own or any means of earning any, apart from becoming a governess or some such thing. Ambrose refused to contemplate the possibility of this happening. As long as he was alive, of sound mind and able to earn his crust, Sarah would have a home with him—until she married. The position he held here at Stanton Hall was a fortunate one, and he enjoyed his job. He hoped that the coming of the earl's sons would not put it into jeopardy.

All these thoughts he could not, of course, reveal to the groom observing him curiously. "These are good tidings indeed," he said now in a measured voice.

"They arrived in two carriages late yesterday evening," went on Saunders confidingly. "I hear both the earl's sons are here with their families."

Ambrose put his foot on the block and easily mounted his horse. "Well, I shall have to pay my respects to them in due course," he said, ending the conversation. With a flick of his reins, he rode away.

The morning passed quickly, as Ambrose called on various tenants on the estate. News of the earl's family arriving from America had spread like wildfire, and everywhere he went, people were eager to discuss what this would mean for the estate. If only he knew. By the time he rode back to Stanton Hall, he was weary of all the conjecture and ready to find out for himself what manner of people were these new arrivals. The earl had often spoken proudly of his sons and their many achievements in America. It had left a positive impression of them in Ambrose's mind, but still, he was as curious about them as anyone else on the estate.

He reined in his horse and dismounted, leading the mare into the large stable. Seeing him, Saunders came over and began to untie the saddle. The groom raised his brow meaningfully then glanced quickly behind him. Ambrose followed that glance to see a tall, well-dressed gentleman stroking the mane of Midnight, a magnificent black stallion, and gazing at it in admiration. It did not take a genius to figure out that this must be a member of the Stanton clan, newly arrived from America.

Ambrose straightened his spine and stepped carefully in the man's direction. He was a few feet away when the man turned to observe his approach, his lips curving into a smile and his dark, almost black eyes twinkling with wicked humour. Ambrose stopped in his tracks, his pulse beating uncomfortably fast. He should say something, but he found himself tongue-tied. Instead, he stared and stared some more at this impossibly handsome vision before him.

The man's smile widened. "You must be Ambrose Cranshaw," he drawled in a deep, velvety voice.

Common sense returned like a splash of cold water, and Ambrose bowed stiffly. "At your service, sir," he managed to say, feeling his face flame. "Who do I have the pleasure of addressing?" he continued, trying to restore his dignity.

The gentleman held out his hand, and with some hesitation, Ambrose followed suit, feeling his own hand being clasped in a strong, confident grip. He was not much used to having his hand shaken by other gentlemen. Perhaps this free and easy manner had something to do with this man's upbringing in America. "Daniel Stanton, at your service," came the gently mocking reply. Then, there was a soft laugh. "Enough with the formality. Are you come to visit Grandfather?"

Daniel Stanton began striding out of the stable, and Ambrose was obliged to follow him, ignoring the curious stare from Saunders as they passed him by. "Ahem, yes, Mr Stanton," said Ambrose, clearing his throat. "I am come to ask after the earl and of course, to pay my respects to your family."

There was another laugh, the happy sound of which did something to Ambrose's insides. "Please, I beseech you, call me Daniel. Nobody I know addresses me as Mr Stanton. That is what people call my papa back home." He spoke in a cultured English accent, with only a slight elongation of his vowels hinting at his American background.

"I—I do not think it would be appropriate, Mr Stanton. I have no wish to be forward in my manner."

"Oh," exclaimed Daniel. "But I most particularly wish you to be so. Where I am from, nobody stands on ceremony, least of all me! Come, the matter is settled. You shall call me Daniel and I shall call you Ambrose, which by the way is a most delightful name." His gaze travelled the length of Ambrose, from the tip of his boots to the top of his hat. "And very fitting. Does it not derive from the Greek word for immortal and divine?" he added with a smile.

Ambrose did not know what to make of this. His cheeks still felt warm from that assessing gaze, and this bantering manner was well outside his customary experience. It was almost flirtatious, preposterous as that might seem. He tried to clear these disturbing thoughts with an inward shake of his head, then contented himself with a murmured, "As you wish, Daniel," though he promised himself that he would maintain the proper decorum in the presence of the earl and his sons.

By now, they had reached the main house, and Daniel flew up the front steps with athletic grace, forcing Ambrose to quicken his own steps in order to keep up. The door was opened for them by Siddons, Stanton Hall's butler. Daniel graced him with an easy smile. "We have a visitor, Siddons, come to pay his respects. Would you be so kind as to bring in a tray of tea and whatever cakes or biscuits cook has to hand?"

"Of course, sir," bowed Siddons.

"Splendid," beamed Daniel, then he turned to Ambrose. "Let us join the rest of the family. I believe they are all in the drawing room. Is that not so, Siddons?"

"Yes, sir," confirmed the butler.

"Well then, come along." Without a backward glance, Daniel strode confidently in the direction of the drawing room with Ambrose at his heels. As they entered the room, all eyes flew to them. Ambrose had but a moment to take in the assembled members of the Stanton clan before the earl, reclining in an armchair with a blanket tucked about him, spoke in a quavering but authoritative voice, "Ah, Cranshaw, good you are here. As you can see, my sons and their family are arrived from America."

Ambrose went to him with a smile. "I do see, my lord, and I can well imagine your joy at their arrival. I am glad also to see you look much improved in health."

A pleased expression came over the earl's lined face. "I am indeed feeling much more the thing. Cranshaw, let me make you known to my eldest son, Francis, Viscount Stanton." The earl indicated a distinguished looking gentleman beside him who looked to be around fifty.

Ambrose made a polite bow in his direction. "Viscount Stanton, a pleasure."

"Indeed, the pleasure is mine, Mr Cranshaw," responded the viscount amiably. "I have heard many good things about the work you do on this estate." He turned to a diminutive lady sitting beside him. "This is my wife, Lady Stanton."

Ambrose made his bows in her direction, and then proceeded to greet the rest of the family. As the introductions were made, he felt himself being scrutinised by Daniel, who stood by the window with his arms casually crossed on his broad chest. What was it about that young pup that was making Ambrose so hot under the collar? Despite his height and muscular frame, Daniel Stanton could not be more than four-and-twenty years old, which made him a good five years his junior. And yet he stood there, radiating authority and confidence like a man a dozen years older.

"I suppose that is the confidence born of being heir to a title and massive fortune," thought Ambrose wryly. *"Such people from early childhood have a different outlook on life than us ordinary mortals."* He could not say why such a thought irked him. It was not as if he aspired to befriend the man on an equal footing. Theirs was but a casual acquaintance. Soon enough, Daniel Stanton would be returning to his home in America and would be out of his way. In the meantime, Ambrose would be well advised to steer clear of him. There was something dangerous about the man

and the reaction he engendered in him. Daniel Stanton brought out those feelings in him that he had spent years keeping in check.

After what Ambrose deemed to be an appropriate passage of time, he stood to take his leave, but his plans for a quiet exit were scuppered by the earl, who looked at him with a frown and grunted, "Where are you going, Cranshaw? We are soon to have our luncheon and of course, you must join us."

"That is very kind, my lord," said Ambrose politely, "but I would not want to intrude any longer on this family reunion, and I really should be getting back to my duties."

"Nonsense!" barked the earl.

His eldest son came to the earl's aid, admonishing sternly, "We must insist, Mr Cranshaw. Besides, I would wish to discuss with you matters relating to the estate after our luncheon. In view of father's current indisposition, he has charged me with taking over all responsibilities from him."

The earl nodded. "That is right, Cranshaw. I wish you to deal with Francis in my stead until I am in better health."

Ambrose gave in with good grace. "In that case, I would be honoured to join you."

Soon, they all adjourned to the dining room. Ambrose found himself seated between Lady Stanton on one side and her daughter, Isabella, on the other. Whether it was due to poor luck or design, Daniel was seated immediately opposite him, which meant Ambrose had to endure more of that disconcerting scrutiny throughout the meal. As Ambrose conversed with the ladies at his side, he could not but feel that dark-eyed gaze on him. A few times, he intercepted Daniel's look, but was simply met with an amused smile upon the slight raise of his brow.

What could there possibly be about his person to inspire such interest in him? Was something amiss with his clothing?

He did not think so. Ambrose cast a surreptitious glance down at himself. His necktie was neatly tied and his jacket correctly buttoned. He might not be dressed in the height of fashion, but he was respectably turned out. Perhaps the young man was simply playing a childish game, trying to bait him into some kind of unseemly response. It was best to ignore him as best he could.

Throughout the remainder of the meal, Ambrose refused to look in Daniel's direction, keeping his attention entirely on the ladies at his side. Once luncheon was over, he stood and followed the viscount upstairs to the earl's study. It was with relief that he escaped Daniel Stanton's penetrating gaze and set to the more comfortable task of fielding enquiries about the estate. He spent the next several hours conferring with the viscount, going through the accounts and giving him a meticulous report of the state of affairs throughout the vast Stanton landholdings.

As they spoke, Ambrose discerned a striking resemblance between the viscount and his son, Daniel. Both had the same tall and powerful build. They had that distinctive Stanton jaw, the same dark brown eyes and almost black hair—though the viscount's was streaked with grey. But whereas Daniel displayed a playful demeanour, his father appeared to have a more serious and reserved disposition. By the time Ambrose rose to take his leave, he had concluded that the earl's eldest son was a well-bred man of considerable understanding. Should the estate pass into his hands after the earl's death, as it most probably would, then Ambrose would be fortunate to have such a man as his new employer.

It was with a great sense of relief that Ambrose took the stairs down to the main hallway and donned his coat. Despite himself he had worried about his future prospects as manager of the Stanton estate. While nothing was certain yet, he felt a trifle more sanguine about what lay ahead. Viscount Stanton was a man he could respect and see himself working for.

With a smile, Ambrose bid Siddons farewell as he stepped out of the house and bounded down the front steps. The sun had set on this early November evening, and he was eager to return home, where his old friend, Benedict Sedgwick, was to join him and Sarah for dinner. The smile fell from Ambrose's face an instant later as he saw who was leaning against the stair post, leisurely smoking a cheroot. Not Daniel Stanton again!

Chapter 2

Daniel

Daniel Stanton was a man who rarely hesitated. When he saw something he wanted, he went after it with vigour and with the confidence that the object of his desire would soon be his. In his youth, this had at times been a source of conflict between himself and his brother, Benjamin, who had a tendency to second guess himself, which meant, more often than not, that Daniel was the one to win whichever prize was coveted by the both of them in that moment.

This did not mean, of course, that Daniel was one to steal something that belonged to someone else. His mama had naturally ensured that he was inculcated with a proper Christian spirit towards his fellow man. It was just that his life experiences so far had taught him that very little was out of his reach. He had a natural academic aptitude and easily excelled in all his studies. He was blessed with wealth, good looks and charm, which made conquests of the opposite sex easy work. His kind nature and sense of humour meant that he was well liked in his society and had no shortage of friends. If anyone was born under a lucky star, it was Daniel Stanton.

At the age of four and twenty, Daniel had had his fair share of romantic adventures, though he would not go so far as to say he had ever truly fallen in love. Perhaps the closest he had ever gotten to that emotion was the six-week period in which he had been bedazzled by Agnes Lowe, the sister of Theobald, his closest friend at Yale. In his third year of college, Daniel had accepted an invitation to go stay with the Lowes at their summer home in Newport and there, he had met the lovely Agnes. He had spent the summer in thrall to her and had considered proposing marriage, for Agnes was not the type of lady to be seduced by any other means. He had left the Lowe home at the end of the summer determined to seek his papa's counsel on this matter.

A conversation had ensued with his parent, in which he had been advised to wait until he was older than his twenty-one years before entering the state of matrimony. "You are young and can afford to wait before settling down to marriage," had said his papa. "Let this be an opportunity to test your true sentiments. If in another two years you are of the same mind, by all means then do court this young lady."

Daniel had seen the sense of these words, and so, he had put aside his immediate inclinations. He and Agnes had pursued a correspondence all through the following year and met a few more times at social events. However, as the months went by, the fervour of his passion had waned, and when Agnes had accepted a marriage proposal from a rival suitor, Daniel had not been heartbroken or even mildly disappointed. The lesson he had learned from this experience was that "love" was an ephemeral emotion not to be trusted, for almost invariably this love was merely lustful infatuation.

He did, of course, have the example of his parents, whose enduring love for each other was undeniable. His father had given up immense wealth and privilege to make Charlotte Harding his wife. He had left England without a backward glance and forged a new life for himself and Charlotte in America, much to the anger and disappointment of the Earl of Stanton. To Daniel's mind, this was the true test of love. If he was willing to give up all his material riches and the home he knew to be with another person, then that was true love. Agnes had not managed to inspire such a degree of sacrifice from himself, nor any other young lady he had known since.

Daniel put aside thoughts of his disappointment in America. Here, in England, there were already many more intriguing possibilities. Earlier today, Daniel had met Ambrose Cranshaw. He had heard positive reports about the man from his grandfather before even coming to England. In letters to his grandson, the earl had written at length about the young man he had taken into his employ seven years ago and elevated to the position of estate manager some years later; a man on whom he had come to place a great reliance.

Daniel had long been curious to meet the person who had won the Earl of Stanton's confidence, for the earl was notoriously difficult to please. And now having met Ambrose, he understood why his grandfather thought so highly of him. Before and during luncheon, Daniel had observed him with avid interest. He had seen a soft-spoken gentleman of great intelligence and humility, who yet also displayed a subtle strength of character.

When he had first come across his grandfather's estate manager in the stable, he had thought him an angelic being, some immortal god sent to Earth—which made Ambrose a mightily fitting name for the man. From the windblown golden locks to the unblemished alabaster of his skin, long-lashed eyes the colour of a grey wintery sky and lushly formed mouth, everything about Ambrose's form was perfection. And in that instant, Daniel had wanted him.

Daniel knew enough of the world to be aware that there were some men that were attracted to each other and who engaged in sexual relations—sodomites they were called. He had never thought himself to be such a one, for he loved women well enough. However, an experience earlier in his youth had made him wonder if he was *partly* a sodomite, if one could be such a thing.

It was about a month after he had turned seventeen on a scorchingly hot day in July. He had gone down to the lake on the edge of his father's land, along with his brother, cousins and a small group of other young men, wanting to have a cooling dip in the water. All the men had stripped bare, as was usual, and jumped into the lake with glee. They had spent an hour splashing about like children and enjoying the refreshingly cool embrace of the water on their naked skin.

Daniel had been towelling himself dry when Ezra Matthews, a labourer on the neighbouring farm, belatedly joined them. Daniel had watched him remove his shirt and pants, and had inhaled sharply on seeing Ezra's naked form—acres of sleek, muscled skin of the most beautiful shade of bronze, and a thick cock swinging proudly from a nest of wiry dark hair. Daniel had been struck dumb at Ezra's beauty, and his own cock had thickened uncomfortably in response. Thankfully, he had a towel draped around him, hiding this particular evidence from view. He had looked up then into Ezra's knowing gaze, and the man had winked at him before running to the water's edge and jumping in.

Daniel had dressed and returned to his house, wondering at this strange reaction he had had to one man's nudity. The following week, it had happened again. He had taken one look at a naked Ezra and gotten hard. This time, his lower body had been submerged in the water, hiding his arousal. There had only been himself, Benjamin and Ezra swimming that day. And when his brother had decided he'd had enough of being in the water, he had left them alone and gone back to the house. That was when Ezra had swum towards Daniel and floated gently on his back beside him, his naked glory on full display.

Daniel had stared, and Ezra had smiled. "Do you like what you see?" he'd asked lazily.

"Yes, I do," Daniel had said impulsively.

Ezra had stood in the water then, which lapped at his waist, and looked him straight in the eye, saying nothing, waiting for Daniel to make the first move. And Daniel was nothing if not decisive. "I would like to kiss you," he had said, feeling a sudden desire to experience the feel of this man's lips.

"Then kiss me," Ezra had replied.

Slowly, Daniel had pulled Ezra's body to his and brought their lips together. The kiss had started softly, a gentle exploration, but quickly it became something more. Tongues tangled and teeth tugged sharply with a ferocity that was unlike any kiss Daniel had ever experienced with a female—and he'd had many. This was unrestrained, almost violent. And throughout it all, he had felt Ezra's hard cock nudging his own engorged shaft, rubbing against him until they had both simultaneously come in sticky spurts to their chests. Afterwards, they had washed themselves in the lake and dressed without a word, each going their separate ways.

The incident was never repeated, but the memory of that day had stayed with him. What did it all mean? Several nights in bed, he had stroked himself to the recollection of what had happened in the lake and come spectacularly hard. But then his wondering was put to one side when he had started a dalliance with Rachel Hewitt and had a lusty time with her in a deserted hayloft. The feel of her soft, abundant flesh and the feminine scent of her had driven him wild with desire. That attraction to Ezra Matthews, he concluded, had been an aberration. There was no doubting that he enjoyed the fleshly delights of women.

Daniel had turned eighteen and gone to college at Yale where he had indulged in more seductions of pretty women, and then had become infatuated with Agnes Lowe. The episode with Ezra became a distant memory. Beyond an occasional fleeting attraction, he had not again felt that level of desire for another man as he had felt for Ezra. So, he had put the whole incident away from his mind, until now.

He wanted Ambrose Cranshaw—that tall, slim man with the face of an angel and clever mind. Could he take him as a lover? His body quickened with excitement at the thought of it. He would like to give it a try and do those things he had done with Ezra, perhaps taking it a step further this time, taking the time to explore a man's body with his hands and mouth.

However, the matter was a delicate one. Much depended on how Ambrose would respond to sexual overtures from another man. Looking back, Ezra had left him in no doubt of his interest, and Daniel was hopeful that he would be able to find out quickly enough, and without crossing any lines of acceptable behaviour, whether or not Ambrose reciprocated his attraction. With this in mind, he perched himself by the front steps of Stanton Hall and waited for him. He knew what he wanted, and he was going to see if Ambrose wanted it too.

Chapter 3

Ambrose

Daniel blew out a puff of smoke from his cheroot and turned to face him with a mischievous grin. "Ambrose, just the person I wanted to see. May I walk with you to wherever you are going?"

Ambrose regarded Daniel with dismay. He could not refuse him without sounding churlish even though it would put pay to all his good intentions of steering clear of the man. With a faint tightening of his lips, he replied, "Of course, though it is getting dark, and I am only going a short way down the avenue to my home, Ivy Cottage."

"Is that the pretty cottage at the end of this road?"

Ambrose inclined his head. "Yes, it is."

"Perfect. Well, let us go."

Ambrose prevaricated a moment longer, then with a resigned sigh, he began to walk side by side with Daniel Stanton. Deciding it was best to take the bull by the horns, he queried, "Is there something you wish to discuss with me, Daniel?"

"Yes, there is," replied the other man unhesitatingly.

Ambrose glanced at him enquiringly when he did not immediately elucidate on the matter. Daniel met that glance with another of his quizzical smiles and took a pull on his cheroot. "First of all," he said, blowing out tendrils of smoke, "I would like to get to know you better. I have heard so much of you from Grandfather's letters that I have been quite agog with curiosity about the person that inspires such admiration in him."

"I hold the earl in high esteem, and I believe the sentiment is mutual, but I cannot believe that talk of me would excite such interest as you profess to have," demurred Ambrose.

"And that is where you are wrong," retorted Daniel. "Every letter from Grandfather these past few years has had mentions of 'Cranshaw did this' or 'Cranshaw did that'. I confess I have grown quite jealous at times."

Ambrose was quick to reply, "I should point out that the earl speaks of you and your father just as often. He is immensely proud of all your achievements."

A fond smile came over Daniel's face. "I am glad," he said simply. Then, directing his piercing gaze on Ambrose, he added, "With such talk of us from Grandfather, it almost feels as if we know one another already."

"In which case, there is no need to go to the effort of getting to know me," parried Ambrose with an ironic raise of his brow.

Daniel burst out laughing. "Oh, Ambrose, there is every need. All I have are the broad outlines of your character. Now, I wish to fill in the details."

Despite the chill of the evening, Ambrose felt his face warm once again. "I confess I still do not see why there is such a need to do so," he persisted. "I am merely an employee of this estate and not someone of import to you."

"You will let me be the judge of that, Ambrose." Daniel's tone sounded a little stern. They walked on in silence a moment more, their path faintly illuminated by the flaxen-coloured moon above and by the red flare on the tip of Daniel's cheroot as he smoked. The spicy scent of it wafted towards Ambrose, mingling with faint traces of a lemony cologne. The combination was dizzyingly seductive. Then Daniel spoke. "I would also beg a favour from you."

"What is it?"

"I would like, if I may, to accompany you on your work around the estate." On seeing Ambrose's doubtful look, Daniel went on, "I will not interfere in any way, merely be an observer. It will be useful in learning about this land which has belonged to my family for generations."

The request made sense, and with any other person, Ambrose would have been quick to assent. But it would mean spending time with a man he had decided to avoid as best he could, for it was clear that Daniel represented a danger to Ambrose's equanimity—he did not care to confess to himself why. However, he could not refuse his employer's grandson.

"Very well," he said, unable to hide the reluctance in his voice.

"You do not need to sound so enthusiastic about it. I assure you, I well know that my company is a rare delight indeed."

Ambrose forced a smile. "I am sure it is, and I look forward to showing you around the estate," he muttered, staring straight ahead.

He felt Daniel's scrutiny in the feeble light. The other man's voice had lost its levity as he said, "I feel, Ambrose, that we have got on the wrong foot. Let us start again." He stopped and faced him, bowing most correctly. "It is an honour to make your acquaintance, Mr Cranshaw," he said in a formal tone. "I have heard many good things of you from my grandfather. I hope we will have a chance to further this acquaintance over the coming weeks."

Daniel straightened and looked at him expectantly. Ambrose stared back, stubbornly resisting the olive branch. Undeterred, Daniel took a puff on his cheroot and waited him out. *An impasse.* Were they to wait here all night? This man was infuriating. With a sigh up to the heavens, Ambrose complied. He bowed, equally correctly, and replied in the same formal tone, "The honour is mine, Mr Stanton. I too look forward to furthering our acquaintance."

Daniel beamed in delight. "There now, that was not so difficult!"

Ambrose could not prevent the upward curve of his own lips. The man's charm was hard to ignore, especially with those dimples that appeared each time he smiled. They resumed their walk towards Ivy Cottage, and Daniel began in a conversational voice, "Tell me something about yourself, Mr Cranshaw. Do you hail from these parts?"

"No," responded Ambrose. "I grew up in Leicestershire, in a small village to the east of Melton Mowbray. My father was the vicar there."

"A clergyman's son! That would explain the moral virtues my grandfather likes to extol about you."

Ambrose's lips twitched. "I have met more than one debauched parson's son in my time, so my father's profession is, I feel, beside the point."

"I am going to have to disagree there," riposted Daniel, pointing the remaining stub of his cheroot at him. "You exude moral rectitude, Mr Cranshaw, which I am sure was instilled by your good parent."

"You make it sound like it is a disagreeable thing to have," remarked Ambrose.

Now it was Daniel's lips that twitched. "How can it ever be bad to be good, Mr Cranshaw?"

"Touché," said Ambrose, amused. The two men exchanged a smiling glance.

"And you pursued your studies at Oxford?" enquired Daniel, continuing his friendly inquisition.

"Yes, I studied classics and mathematics at Oxford. It was in my second year there that Father passed away after a short illness, leaving me to care for my younger sister. I was faced then with a difficult decision. I could not bring her back to live with me in my communal lodgings at the university, and for a time, it seemed as if I would have to abandon my studies to find some form of employment that would provide us both with a roof over our heads." Ambrose was not sure why he was spilling so many details of his life when a short answer would have sufficed.

"But in the end, you were able to complete your studies?" Daniel probed gently.

"Yes, and it was due to your grandfather's intercession. He is great friends with the proctor of my college and had come to visit. I suppose the story of my predicament must have been aired at some point during their dinner, for next day, the proctor came to me with a solution. The earl would provide my sister and I with room and board at his Oxford house for the remaining duration of my studies on two conditions. Firstly, that I was to complete my degree and distinguish myself with First Class honours. Secondly, I was to pledge a year in his employ, assisting his estate manager, Mr Finlay, in his work."

"Your proctor must have spoken of you in glowing terms to Grandfather for him to have taken such action," remarked Daniel. "It is another example of your stellar reputation preceding you, Mr Cranshaw."

"Or perhaps it is another example of your grandfather's generosity," countered Ambrose. "He is a good man."

"That he is," agreed Daniel, "but to single you out for such favour, having no previous acquaintance with you, makes me think that word of your excellence must have reached his ears."

"That may be so," hedged Ambrose. "It has long been clear to me that as a gentleman with no independent financial means, the only assets within my grasp are a good education and my good name. I have worked tirelessly to develop both."

Daniel cast a warm glance in his direction. "I find that admirable, Mr Cranshaw."

"I do not think it is admirable so much as an acknowledgement of reality. One must be rational about one's situation and make the best of what one is given. I do not have wealth, but I have been blessed with intellectual acumen. It made sense to nurture such a gift."

"Yes, I see," said Daniel throwing down the last remnant of his cheroot to the ground and crushing it under his boot. "So I take it, your university days were not spent carousing with the other young bucks."

"No indeed," laughed Ambrose. "Mine was a staid college experience, by necessity, for I am not naturally inclined to martyrdom. Sons of wealthy noblemen, much like yourself, could afford to spend their evenings frolicking to their heart's content, but not me. Alas the maintenance of my grades and scholarship took precedence, not to mention the need to uphold my reputation."

"Is that how you think I spent my time at Yale, Mr Cranshaw? Frolicking?" Daniel's eyes danced with mischief in the pale moonlight.

"I cannot say, Mr Stanton," replied Ambrose primly. "I have only my experience at Oxford to go on."

Ivy Cottage was now within view. They walked towards it in silence, Daniel nursing a mysterious smile which showed off those charming dimples again. Hell and damnation! Ambrose should not be paying attention to such things.

At length, Daniel spoke reminiscently, "You are right. There was certainly some frolicking. Those were happy and carefree days I will always remember fondly. Although I would have you know that I did not altogether neglect my studies. There is, I feel, a balance to be struck between duty and pleasure."

"I agree," smiled Ambrose. "Where one has the means to indulge in pleasurable activities, one should, though not to excess. As I said before, my sedate lifestyle was not due to any love of self-denial but to necessity." He paused at the small wooden gate that led to Ivy Cottage's front door.

Daniel eyed him searchingly. "And now that you are well-established here at Stanton Hall, do you indulge in pleasurable activities, Mr Cranshaw?"

"I cannot complain, Mr Stanton. I must confess to taking great pleasure in drinking some of the earl's fine sherry of an evening while reading a book from the Stanton Hall library."

Daniel continued to observe him closely. "And how about frolicking?" he asked softly.

No, he was not going to blush again from the heat of that gaze. Could Daniel be implying he wanted to frolic with him? Oh the danger of this man! It was imperative to bring this conversation to a swift end. With an effort, Ambrose met those dark, questing eyes with a hard stare of his own. In an even tone, he said, "I am partial to dining in the company of my friends, one of which, by the by, awaits me at home this evening. As for frolicking… I shall leave that sort of activity to you, Mr Stanton."

Was that a look of disappointment on Daniel's face? If so, it was quickly gone. With a mocking inclination of his head, he let the matter drop and said instead, "So tomorrow, I shall accompany you on your rounds around the estate."

"I start my work very early in the morning," warned Ambrose.

"All the better," smiled Daniel. "I am an early riser. I shall be ready whenever you call at Stanton Hall."

"Very well. Until tomorrow, Mr Stanton."

"Until tomorrow, Mr Cranshaw." With another inclination of his head, Daniel pivoted on his heels and strode away.

Ambrose watched him disappear in the dim light of the moon, wondering what the morrow had in store for him. Then, giving himself an internal shake of the head, he turned and walked to his front door.

Chapter 4

Daniel

In a thoughtful mood, Daniel walked back towards Stanton Hall. That had been an informative encounter. It seemed Ambrose was not amenable to any suggestion of frolicking with him. Staid and boring, that was Ambrose—at least on the surface. What lay beneath that eminently respectable exterior, Daniel longed to know.

He understood why Ambrose was so determined to maintain such a front. Not having the benefit of wealth or connections, Ambrose had made his way up in the world by dint of his intelligence, hard work and moral correctness. And having established himself here on the Stanton estate, he would do all to protect that position, not just for himself but also for his sister, who was dependent on him.

Beneath that proper exterior though, Daniel suspected there lurked a far more passionate, pleasure-loving man. He had seen hints of it tonight. They had enjoyed their verbal sparring. Ambrose himself had admitted that he had no love for self-denial; his actions were governed by necessity. But over and beyond those small clues, Daniel took encouragement from Ambrose's own reactions to him. He could swear he'd made him blush a time or two, and when he had suggested joining him on his work around the estate, Ambrose had poorly hidden his dismay. It had awakened every hunter's instincts Daniel possessed.

A lesser person might have given up the chase at this point, thinking it futile. Not Daniel. Their walk tonight had confirmed one salient fact. He wanted Ambrose. Daniel's nostrils flared with desire as he conjured a vision of him in his mind. By God, he wanted that man, and Daniel was in the habit of getting what he wanted. That delicious man was going to be his.

Back at the house, Daniel went to his room to change and prepare for dinner. He was in the process of knotting his necktie when there came a knock at his door.

"Come in," he called.

The knob turned and the door opened to reveal his younger brother, Benjamin, already dressed for dinner. Benjamin strode into his room, saying in a slightly accusatory voice, "Where were you just now? I looked for you earlier, but you were nowhere to be found."

Daniel gave his necktie one final tug then turned to his brother with a lazy smile. "I went out for a walk, that is all."

"You could have asked me to join you," reproached Benjamin. "It has been a damned dull day. I hope some diversion can be found soon to help pass the time or else I swear, I shall die of boredom."

"May I remind you, Ben, that we are here for Grandfather, not your enjoyment."

Benjamin shrugged his shoulders irritably. "Papa and Uncle Jasper perhaps, but in all honesty, Grandfather has no need of me—which is fine, for I have no great wish to spend time with the old martinet either."

Daniel ruffled his brother's hair, causing the latter to bat his hand away in annoyance. "Stop that, you rotter." Benjamin stalked to the mirror hanging above the fireplace and re-arranged his mussed hair to his satisfaction. "You know," he went on, "everyone acts now as if all is forgiven, but I cannot forget that if Grandfather had had his way, then Papa would have married some aristocratic lady instead of Ma, and we would never have come into existence. You know how Grandfather thought Ma was not good enough to be a Stanton, coming from 'Spanish trade'. Ha! If anything, it was Papa that was not good enough for her!"

Daniel sat on his bed to pull on his shoes and studied his brother in amusement. "What has you all in a bother about this now? What you speak of is well in the past, and Grandfather has learned the error of his ways. Why, there can be no greater champion of Mama than him these days, apart from Papa, that is."

With a sigh, Benjamin came to sit beside his brother on the bed. "I suppose it is being here that is making me chafe—all snooty with airs and graces, my lord this and my lord that. I want none of it."

"It is more formal here than we are used to," concurred Daniel. Cocking his head towards Benjamin, he added, "What you need is a distraction."

"Isn't that what I have been saying?" Benjamin narrowed his eyes at his brother. "You are looking mighty pleased with yourself. What have you been up to? Come on, spill the beans."

Daniel stood and pulled Benjamin towards the door. "That, dear brother, is none of your business, but I do suggest you take a walk to the village tomorrow and investigate possibilities."

"I am planning to," replied Benjamin thoughtfully. "Tell me. Is it that comely maid, Hetty?"

"No, it is not, and do not ask me more, for I will not disclose."

Benjamin huffed as they walked the corridor towards the staircase, "You are no fun at all. Will you at least come to the village with me tomorrow?"

"Alas I cannot, for I am to accompany Mr Cranshaw on his rounds so that I may become familiar with the estate."

Benjamin threw him a puzzled glance. "Why would you do that? We all know this place is going to Papa as the next in line. It won't be yours for a good many years."

"Hush, lower your voice." They had reached the bottom of the staircase and stood in the large entrance hall. Daniel looked to the left and right before responding in a whisper, "Papa will still need to go back to our home in America, even when he inherits this place. Someone will have to look after things here in his absence."

"And that someone would be you?" Benjamin looked disconcerted.

"Who else? I do not see you wanting to step up to the job."

"No," agreed Benjamin quickly. "That would be the last thing I would want to do. But this means you would stay on here and not come back home with us."

Daniel smiled. "It wouldn't be for ever, maybe just for a few months at a time. Unlike you, Ben, I have found much to like over here."

Now Benjamin stared in suspicion. "Out with it, Daniel. Who is it you are seeing?"

Daniel's lips curved of their own volition as he thought of Ambrose, but he would not be drawn. Strutting towards the drawing room door, he threw over his shoulder, "That is for me to know and you to keep wondering."

Chapter 5

Ambrose

Next morning, Ambrose woke early as usual and partook of his breakfast. As he ate, he reflected on dinner yesterday evening. He and Sarah had been joined by their childhood friend, Benedict Sedgwick, who had recently moved to Stanton Harcourt to take on the position of curate in the village. It was Ambrose that had put a good word in for him with the earl and helped him obtain this position.

Ambrose had recommended Benedict without hesitation, for he knew him as a good, conscientious person who would, he was certain, fulfil his pastoral duties admirably. Benedict was a few years younger than him, the same age as Sarah. In fact, he was more Sarah's friend than his. They shared the same passion for engineering and science, whereas Ambrose's interests lay more in literature and philosophy.

Not for the first time, Ambrose wondered if that friendship between Benedict and Sarah would ever blossom into something more. He could not help but worry about his sister's future. At the age of twenty-five, she gave all the indications of settling down into spinsterhood. He sincerely hoped that would not be the case and that some worthy man would one day propose marriage. Such a marriage would also put pay to her long-standing and hopeless infatuation with Mr Philip Templeton, a wealthy local landowner with a reputation for womanising.

Breakfast over, he fetched his hat and coat, then stepped out the door into the misty morning air. He started a brisk walk towards Stanton Hall. With each step forward, he could no longer put off thoughts of that man he had met yesterday. Last night, as he had lain in his bed, he had rationalised his interactions with Daniel Stanton.

This was a man born to privilege, and it was clear that he used his forceful charm to get everything he wanted. It was no wonder that he had raised Ambrose's hackles. No two people could be more different. On one side there was himself—deferent, working hard for every penny he earned, ever conscious of his precarious position in society. And then there was Daniel Stanton—powerful, authoritative and entitled, not to mention he was also too handsome for his own good. He and Ambrose were like oil and water, so it was unsurprising that they had not mixed well.

No matter, thought Ambrose now as he strode purposefully towards Stanton Hall. The young pup would be here a few weeks or months at most then return to his home in America. Ambrose would then be able to put aside the impossible feelings that Daniel had awoken in him. It was not him that would become his employer once the earl passed away, but his father, who was a sensible man. All Ambrose had to do was show Daniel around the estate, ignore his atrociously forward manner and maintain a courteous demeanour. That should not be too difficult a task. Persuading himself that there was no more to it than that, Ambrose hurried up the front steps and rang the bell.

The door was opened by Siddons a short time later. "Good morning, sir," the butler said, letting him into the entrance hall.

Ambrose smiled cheerfully. "Good morning, Siddons. I hope I find you well today."

"A touch of my usual rheumatism, sir, but I will not complain," replied Siddons.

"Perhaps this will help," said Ambrose, producing a small jar of ointment from the pocket of his coat. "Sarah made me swear not to forget to bring you this remedy for your joints. She says it worked wonders for Mr Phipps's painful knees."

Siddons took the jar, a pleased expression on his face. "That is very thoughtful of Miss Cranshaw," he said. "Please do thank her for me."

"I shall. Now, to business. I am here to see Mr Daniel Stanton. I believe he wishes to accompany me on my ride around the estate today."

Siddons inclined his head. "He has asked that I show you in the moment you arrive." With this, Siddons led Ambrose towards the dining room, opening the door ceremoniously. "Mr Cranshaw to see you," he said, stepping back to allow Ambrose inside.

Ambrose walked into the room, dominated by a large rectangular-shaped table, to find Daniel Stanton seated beside his mother, their breakfast finished. At his entrance, they both stood politely.

"Mr Cranshaw," smiled Lady Stanton. "How good to see you. Please do take a seat. May I offer you a coffee?"

Ambrose bowed in her direction then in Daniel's, before sliding into a seat across from them. "Good morning to you both," replied Ambrose good naturedly. "And yes please, I would be grateful for a cup of coffee."

As Lady Stanton went to pour him the coffee, Ambrose felt her son's fixed regard on him. He forced himself to look in his direction, which turned out to be not such a good idea. Dark eyes gleamed at him with an emotion he could not quite fathom. All at once, he felt flustered, stumbling on his words as he said, "Good morning, Mr Stanton. Erm, are you looking forward to riding around the estate today?"

"Very much so," said Daniel silkily. "Whereabouts will we be going?"

"I—erm, have calls to make to the tenants on the land that lies south east from here, towards Mulverley Grange, one of the manor houses on the estate. Erm—I shall need to make a stop there too, as it has recently been vacated by its tenants and there are a few repairs I need to look into."

"It is so very kind of you to let Daniel accompany you on your work, Mr Cranshaw," enthused Lady Stanton.

Ambrose took a sip of his coffee then set down his cup carefully. "Not at all," he said courteously. "It is my pleasure to do so." He would not look in his direction. He would not—but unwillingly, he found himself doing just that.

Daniel grinned at him, showing off those mesmerising dimples. "I cannot wait," he said smoothly. "If you are done with your coffee, let us be on our way."

"Of course." Ambrose gulped the rest of his drink and stood.

"Have a good day, Mr Cranshaw," said Lady Stanton kindly. She turned to her son. "And you too, Daniel. I shall see you when we get back from our trip to Witney."

As Ambrose watched, all trace of wicked mischief left Daniel's face. He bent down to kiss his mother's cheek, love radiating from his eyes as he teased, "Enjoy your shopping trip, Ma. Do try not to buy half the contents of the bookshop there."

She chuckled. "I shall try, but you know how I am once I enter a shop with books."

"I do," he laughed. "Do remember though, there is only so much baggage we can take back with us to America."

She touched his cheek fondly. "I shall endeavour to do so. Now off with you."

Something about this exchange did strange things to Ambrose's heart. Maybe it was the poignant reminder of the much loved parents he had lost. Be that as it may, he felt himself soften towards Daniel. No person who looked at his mother that way could be so terrible.

A few minutes later, he revised that opinion. Walking side by side on their way to the stable, Daniel let his glance slide over him from head to toe, then stated softly, "You are looking very handsome today, Ambrose. I almost feel I am walking in the presence of an angel."

Ambrose was at a loss for words. "I—err…"

"It's quite alright, beautiful one. You do not need to say anything."

"Will you please stop calling me such names!" spluttered Ambrose, speech finally having returned. "It is not at all the thing."

"And why not? I am only stating the truth. You do look divine."

Ambrose stopped in his tracks and turned to face him, face heated. Was the young pup mocking him? Drawing himself up to his full height, he said stiffly, "I do not know, sir, what it is you are trying to do by saying such things to me, but I would ask you to please stop."

"Does it discomfort you that I think you are beautiful?" There was an urgency in Daniel's tone, almost as if it was important that Ambrose believe him.

"It does," gritted Ambrose. "I am a man, not a young miss to be wooed with compliments."

"Why is beauty only the preserve of women?" challenged Daniel, arguing his case with unwarranted fervour. "And why is it only females that can be wooed? I will have you know that I would be happy indeed to have someone compliment my looks." Daniel struck a pose with hands on his hips. "In fact, now would be your chance to do so. Does not this new riding suit fit me admirably well?"

"Mr Stanton!"

"Well, Ambrose, what do you think? Does it not flatter my muscular physique?"

Unwillingly, Ambrose let his gaze travel up Daniel's extremely fine form. Yes, he did look exceedingly good, but he was not about to tell him so. "That is beside the point," he said quellingly. "I do not engage in flattery with other males."

"Why do you say it is beside the point?" demanded Daniel. "Do you think I look good, Ambrose, or not? I would think that was very much the point."

Ambrose cast his eyes down as he ground out, "Sir, I will ask you again to desist from making such remarks. I—I do not look upon fellow men in that way. I hope you get my meaning."

He felt Daniel's stare burrow into him. He heard the man's ragged breaths. Then in a rough voice, Daniel spoke, unutterable words gushing forth from his mouth. "Are you telling me, Ambrose, that you are not attracted to me? I am an adult, you know, and capable of bearing the rejection. Just tell me the truth. But before you do, let me give you my own truth. I too am not in the habit of looking at my fellow men that way, but it is different with you. From the moment I first met you, I have felt an inexplicable attraction. I want you, Ambrose, and I am unashamed to say it. Now speak."

By the latter parts of this speech, Ambrose's eyes had flown up to stare at Daniel. No man had ever spoken to him that way, nor had he ever dreamed that one could. His mind was awash with a maelstrom of emotions—confusion, horror and unbidden elation. The words of outright rejection were on his lips, but they would not come out. Instead, he stood as if struck dumb.

Daniel's severe expression softened. "It's alright, Ambrose," he murmured. "I can see you are not ready yet to say the words. I have been too hasty in speaking out." He gave an unamused bark of laughter. "If I have one fault, it is impatience. Let us leave the matter here. We will come back to it another time. Come now, let us be on our way." With that, he strode towards the stable, and Ambrose let his feet follow him, still in a disbelieving trance.

Was he dreaming? Had his employer's grandson propositioned him just now? Called him beautiful and divine? It was beyond belief. He must have imagined it. His heart pounded in his chest in fear and delight, but mostly fear.

He had known from the moment he met Daniel Stanton that this man was dangerous to his wellbeing, that it would be best to keep well away from him. And he had been proved right. That man was brazenly opening the Pandora's box of feelings Ambrose had strived all his adult life to keep shut. It needed to stay shut. It was imperative those forbidden sentiments were stamped out. Lips tight with furious determination, Ambrose made his way to the stable and without a word, mounted his horse.

Chapter 6

Daniel

Well, that had gone downhill fast, thought Daniel as he rode beside a tight-lipped Ambrose. Damn his loose tongue. What streak of impetuousness had made him spew all those words of seduction to a man he had only met the previous day? Of course, he knew. He had taken one look at Ambrose this morning and nearly burst with the force of his desire. Whatever feelings had been stoked yesterday were ten times stronger today.

Now his cards were on the table, and Ambrose had retreated into a shell of frigid formality. Damn and blast! He would have his work cut out to undo the damage that had been done. Patience—something he had in short supply—would need to be exercised to regain lost ground. His mind replayed Ambrose's words. *I do not look upon fellow men in that way. I hope you get my meaning.* He got the meaning alright. He was barking up the wrong tree.

For the first time, it occurred to Daniel that this particular chase was one he might not win. It was a novel sensation, not coming out on top. He could charm, he could persuade, but could he change a person's God-given nature? If a man did not inherently have sexual desire for other men, then that was not something that could be changed. He could have sworn though, that Ambrose was not indifferent to him—his blushes, the way he had avoided his eyes, his stumbling speech earlier in the dining room—all these clues had given him hope. But it seemed he was mistaken.

He entertained one other possibility. This one was even harder to contemplate. It was that Ambrose was lying about not looking upon fellow men in that way, and doing so out of fear. Society did not look kindly upon men who engaged in "bestial" acts with one another. Although sodomy itself was no longer punishable by death, there were laws against it which could result in prison sentences for the unfortunate men caught in the act.

Consumed by his own overwhelming desire, Daniel had never stopped to consider what danger he was putting Ambrose in by openly propositioning him. Not only was he putting the man's livelihood at risk, but also potentially risking his liberty. If that was the case, it was little wonder that Ambrose was running scared. A wave of mortification rolled over him as he glanced once more at Ambrose's rigid countenance. How crassly he had behaved!

As for himself, he had no fear—for who would ever dare say a word against the Earl of Stanton's grandson? Neither did he have shame for the feelings he was experiencing for Ambrose. Society may have viewed them as impermissible, but wanting another man seemed as natural to him as breathing. The desire he had felt for Ezra, and now more strongly for Ambrose, had risen spontaneously from within him, without any corrupting outside influence. Those feelings were a true part of his nature. It would seem strange indeed if God Almighty had made him so, only to condemn him for following the dictates of the nature with which he was formed.

On that last thought, they arrived at their first destination, one of the tenanted farms on the estate. Ambrose swung down from his horse and led it to a small outhouse, tethering it to a post. Daniel followed suit. For the first time since they had left

Stanton Hall, Ambrose addressed Daniel directly. His tone was matter-of-fact, reciting information as if by rote. "This is the Summerford farm, one of our largest tenanted farms. It is held by Hugh Stanley and has been tenanted by his family for generations. It comprises four hundred acres of land rented at eighteen shillings an acre per annum."

"How often do you raise the rents?" wondered Daniel.

"I prepare a report for the earl each year in April with the latest information on land rents across the county," replied Ambrose. "The earl uses this to decide whether rents need to be raised or not and by how much. When doing so, he of course takes into consideration the individual circumstances of each tenant and their ability to take on additional debt. Then, I am tasked with discussing the new rent with the tenant and reaching an agreement as to when it is to come into effect, which is usually three to six months further down the line."

"I see," said Daniel thoughtfully. "That sounds eminently fair."

"I can vouch for the earl's fairness in all such matters," affirmed Ambrose. "Many other landlords hereabouts are far less considerate of their tenants' needs and demand higher rents than we do here."

Daniel said with a smile, "Grandfather may be a testy old goat, but he has never been greedy." He nodded towards the farmhouse ahead of them. "And what is the order of business today?"

"Two things," replied Ambrose, not quite looking him in the eye. "Firstly, as it is the time for ploughing and seeding, I will enquire as to how the acreage is to be planted for the year ahead. Most farms hereabouts operate on a four-year crop rotation system. I will note down how many acres have been laid to wheat, turnips or barley, and which fields are to be planted with ryegrass and clover for grazing. Secondly, I will inspect the farm building to ensure that it is being maintained to an acceptable standard."

This differed to what Daniel was used to back home, as the vast acreage of their land in Ohio was not tenanted out. Instead, his father and uncle farmed the land directly, employing labourers and a foreman to oversee their work. This system of landlord and tenants seemed positively feudal to him, but he kept his own counsel. "Lead on," he said with a small smile.

For the rest of the morning, Daniel followed Ambrose and observed him at work as they stopped at one farm after another. The people they encountered were curious about him but too polite to address more than a greeting in his direction. Ambrose too said very little to him apart from the bare facts about each farm they visited. In that time, Daniel was at leisure to study him. He noted the way he spoke in a quietly gentle yet firm tone, his impeccable memory and meticulous attention to detail, and the way he inspired a grudging respect from each tenant they saw.

Daniel noted other things too, such as how Ambrose had a tendency to press his plush lips together when he was deep in thought and to rub a long-fingered hand along his smooth jaw. He yearned to brush his fingers through the shock of golden hair that fell across his forehead. It looked soft, silky and inviting. Damn it but he wanted that man! His seduction of Ambrose may have suffered a severe setback today, but Daniel was determined to discover finally if Ambrose felt a corresponding attraction or if it was a lost cause. He would not give up just yet. How could he when every fibre of his being thrummed with desire for him?

At last, they reached their final destination of the day, drawing up outside the front steps of Mulverley Grange. It was a large stone house which brought to mind the gothic novels that his mother liked to read. Ambrose took out the leather bag he used to carry his notebook, pencil and various other items of equipment he required to perform his duties. After rummaging in it for a minute, he withdrew a large set of keys, and walking up the steps, he used one of the keys to unlock the door. With exaggerated courtesy, he stood back to allow Daniel inside.

On first glimpse, Daniel saw a dimly lit entrance hall from which rose a grand oak staircase that bifurcated into two separate sets of stairs on either side. Ambrose went quickly to light a candlestick that sat on a side table. With the additional illumination, Daniel was able to further examine his surroundings. The house on the inside was far more appealing than its exterior suggested. To their right was a large stone fireplace, above which hung an oil painting of a leafy landscape. The surrounding walls were panelled with ornately carved wood, and the floors were covered with large, polished flagstones.

"This is quite the place," remarked Daniel.

"Yes," agreed Ambrose. "Of all the manor houses on the Stanton estate, this is my favourite, though by no means the grandest. Netherwick Hall, which lies some ten miles from here, is much more substantial."

"How long has it been vacant? It seems a waste to have no one living here."

"It was leased by an older gentleman, a retired solicitor who lived here with his wife until three weeks ago," replied Ambrose. "However, they decided to travel to the Continent, hoping warmer climes would help with the gentleman's health. I have since placed an advert in the London newspapers and hope to find a new tenant soon, for as you say, it is a waste for such a house to lie empty."

Daniel took a turn around the hall, looking about him curiously. He voiced the questions at the top of his mind. "Why on earth would Grandfather need to own several other large houses such as this one? Is not Stanton Hall sufficient for his needs?"

Ambrose gave a short laugh. "More than sufficient, I would think. This house and the lands that came with it was part of your great-grandmother's dowry when she married the earl's father. I believe your grandfather planned to grant it to your uncle upon his maturity, and Netherwick Hall to your father." He paused uncomfortably. "Then of course, they both left for America, and these plans had to be set aside."

"Ah, yes, that makes sense. Papa and Uncle Jasper caused quite the upset with their exodus across the ocean." Daniel huffed in sympathetic amusement. "Poor Grandfather. Still, I cannot say I regret their decision. My life—had I even come into existence—would have been far different had they stayed here."

Ambrose gazed at him in interest, finally overcoming the reserve he had shown the past few hours. In a mellifluous voice that soothed Daniel's soul, he asked, "What is it about your life in America that you prefer?"

"Oh, a great many things," responded Daniel turning his attention back to Ambrose. "For one, I like the less formal way of life we have in Ohio. Papa's title holds very little meaning there—nobody addresses him as Viscount Stanton. To most people, he is simply Frank Stanton. I like that it is a place where a man can make something of himself by dint of his own hard work. Take our neighbour, Robert Ellis. Back in England, he had been a small farming tenant, much like the people we visited today. Now, he is the owner of a prosperous estate, and on an equal footing with Papa and Uncle Jasper."

Ambrose's eyes were fixed on his. Daniel thought he would drown in that smoky grey gaze. His pulse quickened; his chest tightened uncomfortably within the confines of his jacket.

"When I was a small child," murmured Ambrose, "my father considered emigrating to America as part of an Anglican mission. In the end, he decided against it because Mother did not want to leave the familiarity of home."

"Well, I for one am glad he did not go, for otherwise I would not have had the privilege of meeting you, Ambrose," said Daniel huskily. He regretted it immediately as a shutter came down over those heavenly grey eyes. Damnation! Was he forever going to say the wrong things to this man?

Ambrose took hold of the candlestick which he had placed on the table while they talked. "Let me inspect the east wing of the house," he said briskly. "There was some damage to the walls following a heavy thunderstorm a few weeks ago, and I sent some workmen from the village to make the repairs. I would like to see the results of their work." With that, he turned and began to walk nimbly up the staircase.

Daniel followed in silence. They walked along the main corridor and inspected each of the rooms on the east side of the house. In the last room, Daniel paused, looking at the beamed ceiling which sloped down to just a foot above his head towards one end. Was that rot on the beam? He ran a finger along it to check and gave a startled cry.

"What is it?" fired Ambrose sharply.

Daniel bit back a curse, examining his hand in annoyance. "A splinter," he muttered. "It has embedded itself under my skin."

"Let me see." With surprising firmness, Ambrose took hold of his wrist and brought it up close to the light of the candlestick. After a moment's examination, he looked up at Daniel. "If I do not take this out now, it may cause infection," he said. He glanced across the room and pointed to a dressing table and stool. "Please sit there," he instructed.

Daniel thought of arguing, but Ambrose's words made sense. The splinter needed to be removed, and he had no intention of getting back on a horse to ride home with a hand that caused him such discomfort. Without a word, he went to sit at the table. Ambrose placed the candlestick on it, then opened the flap of the leather bag which he carried crossways across his chest. He took out from it a small bottle, a clean cloth and what looked like a set of tweezers. He smiled down at Daniel. "I keep these with me for such emergencies, having learned to the hard way."

He went to kneel at Daniel's side, taking his injured hand carefully between his. "I will clean it first with a little alcohol," he said. "It may sting briefly."

"Do what you must," Daniel ground out hoarsely. The sight of Ambrose on his knees before him was having a powerful effect. Dear God, what would it be like if Ambrose were to lean his head forward just a few more inches? A vision of those lush lips wrapped around his throbbing cock flew unbidden into his mind. He took a steadying breath, trying in vain to prevent the thickening of his shaft.

Fortunately, Ambrose's attention appeared to be on Daniel's hand, not his groin. Daniel thought he saw him glance quickly at his lap, too quickly surely to have noticed his arousal, and now Ambrose's gaze was fixed on his finger—although did he perceive a certain breathlessness? Daniel watched him as he unstoppered the bottle and wet the cloth with alcohol. Using that cloth, he wiped gently at the injured finger, then also cleaned the tips of the tweezing implement.

Ambrose glanced up, seeing Daniel's intense look but seemingly misinterpreting it. "This is what my sister, Sarah, tells me always to do with any wounds," he explained. "She is of a scientific disposition and informs me that there are invisible micro-organisms all around us which are the cause of disease. Cleaning with alcohol ensures they are destroyed."

"Yes, I have heard of Pasteur's germ theory," replied Daniel, his voice still sounding gravelly.

Ambrose brought his attention back to the task at hand. He inspected the splinter again. "I believe I can pull it out with this implement," he said. "I will need you to stay absolutely still."

"I will not move an inch," promised Daniel. He observed closely as Ambrose brought the tweezers to his finger, finding the end of the splinter and capturing it with the tips pressed tightly together. Slowly, he pulled the offending item out from under his skin. A pinprick of blood oozed from the wound, which Ambrose deftly wiped clean.

"There," he said with a smile. "All done." He let go of Daniel's hand and made to stand, but Daniel stopped him with a firm hand on his arm.

"A minute please, Ambrose." He blew out a soft breath as Ambrose paused, a troubled expression coming over his face. "First of all, thank you," Daniel said.

Ambrose inclined his head. "No thanks are required." He made to move again, but Daniel continued to grip his arm.

"Ambrose," he began again in a throaty voice. "I owe you an apology for this morning." Under his hand, he felt Ambrose's arm stiffen, so he continued quickly, "It was careless of me to say such words, especially after having known you for so short a time. All I can say in my defence is that from the moment we met, I have been struck by a powerful attraction to you. It is as if I have been bewitched. But I should not have acted on those feelings with so little care for yours, and for that, I apologise."

Ambrose replied in a taut voice, staring down at Daniel's hand on his arm, "Your apology is accepted, Mr Stanton. Let us not speak of this again." He tried to pull away again, but Daniel held on tight.

"Call me Daniel, please."

Ambrose shook his head. "It is better if I do not."

Daniel sighed. "Very well. But before we become formal with each other again, Ambrose, may I say one last thing?" On seeing Ambrose's faint nod, he went on bravely. "I understand this is a difficult subject to broach, but I would like you to know, Ambrose, that if we were ever to act on our desires—that is, if you too felt an attraction for me—then we could be discreet. No one but us would ever know. I would make sure of it."

He huffed uncomfortably. "That is to say, if you ever were to feel for me what I feel for you, but feared the consequences of such feelings, then I would keep this thing between us private—it would be our business and ours alone. Your safety and good name would be my highest consideration, I promise." He took another deep breath. "With this said, do you think you might ever come to feel such things for me?" he asked, his pulse thudding at his temple.

Time stood still in the frozen silence that ensued. Daniel stared into Ambrose's downturned face. Finally, Ambrose looked up, wearing a closed expression. "I am sorry, Mr Stanton," he said in a clear, composed voice. "I do not hold such desires and would prefer if we never speak of this again."

Disappointment, mingled with sadness, flooded through Daniel's being. "I see," he said softly. "May we at least become friends?"

"Friendship has to be earned."

"Then let me earn it," cajoled Daniel.

"We shall see." Ambrose looked pointedly at Daniel's hand still gripping his arm. "Now, it is time for us to go."

Reluctantly, Daniel released him. He watched Ambrose get to his feet and pack away everything into his bag. Then, in silence, he followed him out of the room and down the stairs back to the hall. There, Ambrose extinguished the candles and let Daniel out of the door, locking it securely behind them. Quietly, they returned to their horses, mounted them and rode back to Stanton Hall. The day, which had started out so promising, had turned so very badly wrong.

Chapter 7

Ambrose

If yesterday had been a strange, unsettling day, then today had been even more so. It was as if the universe were playing some sort of trick on him. First, he had met the most handsome and infuriating man on this earth. Then that same man had tried to seduce him. It was unheard of. Preposterous. Terrifying. And a tiny bit thrilling.

As they rode back towards Stanton Hall, Ambrose found himself still in a state of profound shock. This was so outside the scope of his usual staid life, he could barely believe it. Had Daniel Stanton really declared his attraction and proposed they conduct an illicit relationship? Why would he do such a thing? A troubling thought occurred to him. Was there something in his appearance or manner that hinted he would welcome the advances of another man? Ambrose recoiled inwardly in horror. No! That could not be so.

Though perhaps he should consider growing whiskers and a moustache as was becoming increasingly fashionable. He had always preferred the look and feel of being clean shaven, but now, surely it was time to change this. Maybe then Daniel Stanton would stop looking at him in that unnerving way.

They reached Stanton Hall and dismounted from their horses, handing them over to the care of the grooms in the stable. As they walked out, Ambrose finally turned to address Daniel. "I shall bid you good day, Mr Stanton," he said punctiliously.

"Will you not join us for luncheon?" asked Daniel, his dark eyes solemn. "It is the least we can do to feed you after you have so kindly allowed me to accompany you today."

"I thank you, Mr Stanton, but I have work to do still and my sister expects me for our meal." Ambrose made a determined effort to meet Daniel's gaze as he spoke, schooling his features to look politely indifferent.

In contrast, Daniel made no effort to hide his consternation. "Ambrose—Mr Cranshaw," he corrected, "please forgive me. I do not want to bid you farewell today under a cloud of enmity."

"There is none, I assure you. Whatever happened is over and done with now. I would that we could forget all about it."

Daniel took a step closer and stood facing him, his face set along stern lines, his earlier mischievousness gone. "I cannot easily forget, Mr Cranshaw," he said in a mournfully low voice. "Please know that I have never before spoken so to any other gentleman. It is only you that has sparked this reaction in me." He sighed heavily. "I cannot promise to eliminate my desire, for that may prove to be beyond my human capacity, but I will endeavour not to speak of it again or cause you any further discomfort. I—I was in earnest when I spoke of my wish for us to be friends. I hope one day, you will honour me with your trust and friendship."

He looked so disheartened that Ambrose could not help but soften his stance. "It is my hope too," he murmured. "Good day, Mr Stanton."

"Good day, Mr Cranshaw." Daniel bowed, and with one final smile, turned to walk towards the main house. Ambrose cast one last look in his direction, then he too began to walk, heading towards Ivy Cottage.

His journey home was sombre, a pall having been cast on his mood. He had done the right thing to rebuff Daniel's advances. There could not have been any other reaction to that most startling of propositions. After all, he was not going to consort with another man. How absurd! While it was true that in the past, he had had occasion to admire other men, he had always kept a tight rein on such feelings, never letting them overcome the rational and sensible way he chose to comport himself.

Today, however, he was finding it more difficult than ever to maintain this discipline, and it was all that handsome man's fault. Daniel Stanton was like a whirlwind, capable of wrecking all the carefully erected structures of his life. That was why it was imperative he stand on his guard and never let his defences down when it came to that man. His earlier assessment had been correct. Daniel Stanton was dangerous, though not in a vindictive way.

Oh, he was willing to accept that Daniel had been sincere in assuring him he could be discreet, that he would let no harm befall him should Ambrose be foolish enough to enter into a sordid liaison with him. How naïve! Daniel was young and had grown up coddled in the heart of his wealthy family. He knew nothing of the realities of the world. If he did, then he would know that nothing could be kept secret for long in villages populated by busybodies. Ambrose would not be risking his reputation, his livelihood and the entire fabric of his existence for a few moments of stolen pleasure. That would be madness. He had his life neatly ordered, and that was the way it would stay.

It was not long before he arrived at Ivy Cottage, letting himself in through the front door. He took off his coat, hanging it on a nearby peg, and placed his hat on the side table. As he did so, Elsie, his housemaid, came out of the kitchen. Ambrose gave her a friendly smile. "Good afternoon, Elsie."

"Afternoon, sir," she replied with a curtsy.

"What is it we are having for luncheon and is it nearly ready? I am famished."

"There's turnip soup, sir, followed by steak pudding," said Elsie. "It be ready to serve now."

"Excellent! Then we shall sit for luncheon shortly."

Some minutes later, brother and sister sat down to their meal in Ivy Cottage's snug dining parlour. As Elsie brought in the turnip soup, Sarah asked Ambrose, "How was your day with the earl's grandson? Tell me all about it."

He kept his eyes on the soup being ladled into the bowl in front of him. As close to his sister as Ambrose was, there were some things he could not reveal to her. She was a vicar's daughter after all, with a firm understanding of right and wrong as dictated by the Church. Like other people in the village, and in wider society in general, she would not condone—even worse, she would condemn in the strongest of terms—the feelings he kept hidden in his breast. He dipped his spoon in the soup and tasted it. "Mmm, this is good," he said, stalling for time.

Sarah regarded him impatiently. "Oh, do tell," she urged.

"There is nothing to tell," he replied blandly. "He accompanied me on my rounds but did not say much, merely observed." He took another spoonful of soup.

Sarah though, was not to be pacified. "You are being very sparse with your information. There must be more you can tell me about him. Is he crass, full of himself, intelligent or stupid? What about his looks. Is he handsome? Come on, Ambrose, tell me more!"

Putting on an air of nonchalance he did not quite feel, Ambrose replied, "He is a well-turned out gentleman with an easy manner, a little on the informal side, but that is to be expected, I suppose. He seemed well informed—in fact, he was familiar with Pasteur's germ theory."

"Oh really!" Sarah's interest sharpened. "I think I like him already, which is more than can be said for that cousin of his. Did you know we met the Stanton ladies in town?"

"I was not aware, but it makes sense. Lady Stanton did say she was going to Witney today."

"We met them at the Angel Inn," explained Sarah, "and Mr Templeton was there too."

"And that is when you developed a dislike for one of the Miss Stantons?" enquired Ambrose. "Which one was it? The pretty blonde one?"

"Do not tell me you too have fallen under her spell," muttered Sarah in disgust.

He chuckled. "Nothing of the sort. However, it is an objective truth that Grace Stanton is a very good looking woman. I would have to be blind not to have noticed. But surely you are not going to hold her looks against her." As an afterthought, he added, "You need not worry about being outshined, you know, for you can look very fetching indeed when you put the effort into it."

Sarah made an inelegant snort. "As if I care about such things!" she protested. "All I meant to say is that she seemed a little flighty and shallow. Mr Templeton was very taken with her though."

Ah, thought Ambrose. There was the crux of the matter — nothing more than good old fashioned jealousy. He forbore to comment, choosing instead to pose the question, "And how about Benedict? Was he as charmed by the delightful but flighty Miss Stanton?"

Sarah scrunched her nose in thought. "Do you know, I cannot say. He sat next to Grace, but I did not notice him conversing with her." She smiled in satisfaction. "In fact, I did not see him look her way at all."

To Ambrose's mind, that raised all manner of interesting questions. He knew only too well that to avoid looking at a person was not in itself evidence of disinterest. It could be an act of self-preservation. He wondered if poor Benedict had fallen for beautiful and vivacious Grace. He hoped not, as Ambrose still dreamed of a match between Sarah and Benedict.

They finished their meal in companiable conversation, then Ambrose adjourned to his study to write out some reports for the earl—or rather, for the viscount, now that the earl was incapacitated. His progress was slow, for he stopped every so often as a memory of today's events flashed into his mind. The fifth time it happened, he tossed his pen down in disgust and sat back in his chair. Closing his eyes, he relived the moment he had knelt down beside Daniel and taken his hand in his.

Up close, he had breathed in the scent of him, the masculine musk of his sweat underpinning the light lemony fragrance of his cologne. Daniel's hand had felt warm, the skin smooth with a little roughness on the pads of his fingers denoting manual work, which was unusual in a gentleman. Ambrose had focused his attention on the effort of pulling out that splinter, but when the task had been completed, he had glanced back fleetingly at Daniel's lap and seen a thickening in his groin. Ambrose's proximity had made him hard.

Now, it was Ambrose's turn to become hard. Without volition, his hand slipped down to grasp his thickening shaft. He stroked himself through the fabric of his trousers as his mind conjured up a forbidden fantasy. What if he had leaned his head a few inches further and brought his face to that hard length that had strained beneath Daniel's trousers? His cock jerked under his hand. Quickly, he fumbled with the fastenings and pulled it out. His hand wrapped around the throbbing length, squeezing it tight, then moved to the tip, collecting the sticky emission that had gathered there and spreading it over his length.

With his eyes closed, he imagined Daniel pulling his own cock free while Ambrose knelt at his feet. He imagined his lips descending on the velvety tip and licking it clean. What would it taste like? If it was anything as good as Daniel's musky scent, it would taste heavenly. His strokes quickened on his aching shaft as his mind continued weaving the fantasy. He would lick the tip, circling his tongue over and over it. Then, inch by glorious inch, he would slip that smooth hard penis into his mouth. He would take as much of it as he could until it hit the back of his throat. He would bury his nose in the hair of Daniel's groin and inhale. His cock pulsed under his hand at the thought.

His hand stroked frantically, chasing his release. He would suck that velvety shaft in his mouth and make Daniel cry out in ecstasy. On and on he would suck until Daniel gushed his sweet release into his welcoming mouth. On that tantalising vision, his own cock shot a stream of his seed into his hand. He gasped in the throes of a powerful climax.

When finally it was over, he let out a long breath. And that was when the guilt came. He should not have let his mind wander to such a dangerous place. He could not afford to. He needed to clamp down and suppress all illicit thoughts of Daniel. No good would ever come from giving in to such desires. Had he not witnessed for himself what happened to men that were in thrall to such unnatural impulses?

It had been during his first year at Oxford. His friend, John Driscoll, a gifted mathematician, had developed strong feelings for Henry Staines, another student who was in the final year of his studies. Ambrose had observed John's growing infatuation for Henry and understood it, nay shared it, for Henry was dangerously handsome and wickedly charming. In the event, it was John that had captured Henry's fancy, not Ambrose. The two had engaged in a passionate and indiscreet love affair which had culminated in their inevitable discovery.

There had followed quite the scandal. Henry's powerful family had acted quickly to hush it up, placing all the blame for the affair on poor John, who was expelled from the college in disgrace. Henry's marriage to a young lady of his connection was hastily brought forward. He had graduated shortly afterwards and left with his bride. Over the ensuing weeks, Ambrose had tried to console his heartbroken friend but to no avail. Distraught over his lover's departure, ostracised by society over the affair and facing penury, John had elected to end his life.

The whole episode had had a profound effect on Ambrose. Not only had he lost a dear friend, but he had learned an enduring lesson about the high cost of giving in to those deep, dark desires that lurked within his breast. It was why Ambrose was clear in his mind that he should and would resist all amorous overtures from Daniel Stanton.

With a sigh now, he used his handkerchief to clean the mess he had made. He tucked himself back into his trousers and refastened them. Already, his mind was rationalising his actions and making excuses. It had been too long since he had achieved sexual release. His body had been in need of it, and the recent memories of Daniel's attempted seduction had put ideas of him into his head. That was all it was. Still, it was a good thing he would be travelling to Oxford next week and paying Lexie a visit.

Chapter 8

Daniel

Over the following week, Daniel was as good as his word. Twice more, he accompanied Ambrose on his work around the estate, listening and observing carefully to learn about the vast patrimony that would one day pass down to his father and then to him. The size of it took him aback. He had known that his grandfather was a rich man; he had not known quite how much.

Not once during that time did Daniel say or do anything to offend or embarrass Ambrose. He could not help but look and admire, though he tried not to stare too much, and he maintained the formal manner that Ambrose seemed to be more comfortable with. By the end of that week, Ambrose's tension around him had eased. They were a far cry from becoming friends, but at least they were civil with each other.

On this particular afternoon, Daniel was sitting with his grandfather, reading aloud to him. The earl, who had insisted on rising from his bed despite his frailty, was ensconced in an armchair and wrapped in a warm blanket. His eyes were closed, but he was awake, listening intently to his grandson's voice. There came a knock on the door, and Daniel paused. The door opened gently to reveal Ambrose. As ever on seeing him, Daniel was overwhelmed by the strength of his attraction. The man was unfairly delicious.

Ambrose glanced inside, saw the earl reposing and whispered, "I do not mean to disturb. I was told the earl was awake, but I can see I have come at an inopportune time."

The earl's eyes fluttered open. "I am awake, Cranshaw," he rasped. "Do come in and stop hovering by the door."

"Yes, sir." Ambrose stepped into the room and shut the door quietly behind him. He went over to the earl and bowed. "I came to see you how you are, my lord," he said, "and to bid you farewell before I travel to Oxford tomorrow."

"Is it that time of the month already?" the earl asked, sounding perplexed.

"It is, my lord," replied Ambrose, taking a seat on the other side of him. "I shall go to the bank as usual. Do you wish me to also make a stop for you at Thornton's bookshop?"

"Yes," said the earl thoughtfully, "I should like that." He turned his gaze towards his grandson. "Daniel," he croaked, "I think you should go with Cranshaw tomorrow."

With an effort, Daniel pulled himself out of the stupor induced by the sight of Ambrose. "Grandfather?"

"It will be good for you to make yourself known to Mr Thomson at Parsons, Thomson & Parsons, the bank patronised by our family," said the earl, adding, "And you should acquaint yourself with the house in Oxford which may one day become yours."

Daniel quirked an amused brow at this. He knew, as the rest of the household did, that the earl had been closeted with his solicitor the previous day, updating his last will and testament. "Are you leaving the Oxford house to me in your will?" he asked, thinking the earl would appreciate a direct question.

The earl pursed his lips. "Never you mind what is in the will, my boy. Just do as I say and go with Cranshaw to Oxford."

Now Daniel transferred his gaze once more to Ambrose. Was that dismay, quickly concealed, that he saw on the man's face?

Well, well, well, it seemed Mr Cranshaw was still intent on avoiding his company. Daniel's first instinct was to keep on with the chase and go to Oxford with Ambrose regardless. The opportunity of being in close proximity with him for an extended period of time was too good to miss. Then, he remembered he had made a vow to himself not to cause Ambrose any discomfort, however much he suspected that the man was repressing his feelings for him. If Ambrose was uncomfortable in his presence, then Daniel was the one to blame for it, having caused the rupture between them by being too impatient. It would be unfair of him to seek to mend it by forcing his presence on Ambrose for this trip.

Decision made, he swallowed the feeling of disappointment that arose and smiled at the earl. "I think I have imposed on Mr Cranshaw's time far too much already this past week. There will be plenty of other opportunities for me to go to Oxford, but for now, I would much rather keep you company, Grandfather."

The earl huffed, but he looked too pleased to remonstrate. "Very well, my boy," he wheezed, "but see that you do go sometime soon."

Daniel's eyes, though, were on Ambrose, who let out a shaky breath. The relief emanating from him told Daniel he had made the right decision, much as it pained him. He wasn't sure how long Ambrose would absent himself, but he knew he would miss him. Already, he had grown addicted to the daily sight of him.

For the next few minutes, Daniel listened as the earl instructed Ambrose on what items he wished purchased. Then, as Ambrose stood to take his leave, Daniel got to his feet. "I will see you out, Mr Cranshaw," he said with a stubborn tilt to his mouth that told Ambrose not to protest. Out they went, then down the stairs to the entrance hall, where Siddons brought out

Ambrose's coat and hat for him. Once he had slipped them on, Ambrose inclined his head and murmured, "Good day, Mr Stanton."

Deciding to brave the cold, Daniel said quickly, "I will come outside with you." Not waiting for an answer, he stepped out the door Siddons was holding open and made his way hurriedly down the front steps. He turned and watched Ambrose make a more sedate journey down to where he stood.

"You will catch cold," scolded Ambrose.

Daniel shrugged, unconcerned. "I am used to it," he said. His dark eyes ran over Ambrose's tall, lithe form, coming to stop at his handsome face which sported a light stubble. "You are growing a beard," he remarked, apropos of nothing.

Ambrose ran a hand over the golden bristles on his jaw. "Not a full beard," he said. "I thought I would grow whiskers and a moustache, as seems to be fashionable in this day and age."

"It suits you," rumbled Daniel, with a warm smile. His pleasure quickly disappeared at Ambrose's obvious discomfiture. Damnation! Even the mildest of compliments flustered him, it seemed.

Ambrose looked pointedly away, muttering, "I should go."

"Will you be away long?" asked Daniel, hearing a note of urgency in his voice.

"No, I will be gone only one night and should return Friday."

Daniel shivered in the cool December air, but still he had more to say. "You did not want me to come with you, did you?" he demanded.

Ambrose did not answer immediately. After a lengthy pause, he said, "It is best this way."

"I have kept to my promise, have I not?" Daniel did not like the note of plaintiveness in his voice. Good Lord, when had he turned into this needy, pitiful creature? He cleared his throat and stated, "I have been everything that is right and proper with you this last week."

Ambrose gave a faint smile. "I can have no complaints."

"But still you did not wish to have my company on this trip. You know, I would not say or do anything untoward with you. I merely want to spend time with you."

Now Ambrose lifted a sceptical brow. "Nothing untoward? You will pardon me, Mr Stanton, for having my doubts on the matter."

Daniel narrowed his gaze at him. "Do I frighten you, Ambrose?"

"Of course not!"

"Then what is it to you whether I accompany you on this trip or not?" remonstrated Daniel.

"If you wish to accompany me," said Ambrose stiffly, "then of course I can have no objections."

"You did not answer my question," accused Daniel. "Why the reluctance to have me come with you, if you have no fear of me?"

Ambrose sighed. Then softly, he said, "Perhaps it is not fear but concern for you. I do not wish to… to lead you on in any way."

"You have made your position very clear, Mr Cranshaw. However, I thought that we were to become friends."

Ambrose inclined his head. "My apologies then. Please, feel free to accompany me to Oxford. I leave early in the morning, just after eight o'clock, if you could be ready by then."

Daniel stared at him, torn. He desperately wanted to go, if only to prove his point—and also to have the pleasure of Ambrose's company. But something held him back. Despite the words he had just spoken, reluctance radiated from every fibre of Ambrose's being. And some honourable part of Daniel refused to put this man he admired on the spot.

"No," he murmured. "I will leave you in peace this time, but perhaps next month when you go, you will let me accompany you then."

"Of course," said Ambrose, letting out a breath.

"Relieved are we?" queried Daniel, an ironic gleam in his eyes.

"Not at all," huffed Ambrose.

"Liar," said Daniel very softly. Then, in a louder voice, he went on, "I bid you safe travels, Mr Cranshaw. Good day." He nodded his dismissal and turned to make his way back up the steps to the house.

Chapter 9

Ambrose

Ambrose arrived in Oxford late morning the following day. His first stop was the Old Bank on the High Street, where he made quick work of depositing the funds he had brought with him and collecting a written receipt. Once that important task was done, he headed to the earl's townhouse on St Michael's Street. Upon his knock, the door was opened by the aged butler, Briggs, whose wife was also the housekeeper.

"Good day, Briggs," smiled Ambrose, depositing his small travel case on the floor while he divested himself of his coat and hat.

"Good day, sir," replied Briggs, taking his hat and coat from him. "It is good to see you."

"Likewise, Briggs. I hope you and Mrs Briggs have been keeping well."

"Must not complain, sir," said the old retainer.

Ambrose picked up his travel case before Briggs, whose elderly joints could ill support such a task, could take it upstairs for him. He headed towards the staircase, saying, "I shall go to wash and come right down, but could you please ask Mrs Briggs to prepare a light luncheon for me?"

"As to that, sir," said the butler ponderously, "I have been informed by Mrs Forbes that she expects you for luncheon. I will send word to her now that you have arrived."

Ambrose beamed. "Even better! Please tell her to expect me in the next fifteen minutes."

"Very well, sir."

Ambrose climbed nimbly up the stairs to the room that had been his ever since the earl provided him and Sarah with lodgings here, all of eight years ago, while he attended the university. He made quick work of washing his face and hands, then neatly re-arranging his hair. He abhorred the unkempt, windswept look and took pride in his tidy appearance. On his dressing table was an old bottle of cologne, scented with bergamot, orange and a touch of cinnamon. Ambrose dabbed a few drops of it to his throat. Then, with one last glance at his appearance, he exited the room and made his way back down the stairs.

He did not bother with a coat and hat, for Lexie lived right next door. With a nod of acknowledgement towards Briggs, he opened the front door and walked the few steps to the next house, then rang the doorbell. No sooner had the footman let him in than Lexie came flying down the stairs toward him. As always upon seeing her, he felt a warmth soothe his soul. Alexandra Forbes, estranged wife of William Forbes, a fellow student with him from his Oxford days, was one of his favourite people on this earth, apart from Sarah.

"Finally, you're here," she said breathlessly, holding out her hands.

He took both her outstretched hands in his and smiled down at her. "Finally, here I am," he repeated. Mindful of the servants, he led her to the drawing room and shut the door behind them. Next moment, Lexie was in his arms and he was kissing her sweet lips. It was a loving kiss, more affectionate than passionate. Truthfully, no woman had ever excited passion in him, nothing like the eruption of desire he had felt on seeing Daniel that first time—but no, he would not let his mind wander there. He brought himself back to the present, breathing in Lexie's familiar floral scent and raining kisses along the soft skin of her throat.

She shivered in his arms, and he held her closer. It had been too long, one whole month, since he had last held her. This was how it was between them—how it had been for seven years now—a shared night or two of loving once every month, to coincide with his business trips to Oxford. And though theirs might not have been a passionate union, it was one that sustained him in many ways, giving him the affection he craved, true friendship and the opportunity to, at least partially, slake his lustful urges.

Eventually, he pulled back and gazed into Lexie's soft brown eyes. "You look beautiful, darling," he said, and meant his words. Lexie might not have been a conventional beauty, but her rosy face was graced by an intelligence in her regard coupled with abundant kindness, and it had gained in beauty the more he knew her. Hers was a dear face indeed.

She huffed. "Flatterer!" Inspecting his face closely, she brought a hand to the golden stubble along his jaw. "You are growing whiskers," she stated.

"Do you like it?"

She cocked her head to one side. "Yes, I do. You look all golden and god-like," she teased.

"Now who's the flatterer?" he laughed. They drew apart and went to sit next to each other on the settee, her small hand clasped in his.

"How long can you stay?" she asked.

"Just for this night, I'm afraid," he replied apologetically. "The earl is getting increasingly frail, and I do not like to be away for long. I believe it is only a matter of time now until the end."

She rested her chin on his shoulder and sighed, "Poor man. Under the arrogance and imperiousness, there beats in him a good heart."

"Yes. I shall miss him when he is gone."

"But at least he now has his family gathered around him," Lexie pointed out. "What are they like?"

Ambrose's thoughts jumped to Daniel. Damn that man! He contented himself with saying, "Let us talk of it over our luncheon. I still have errands to complete and must get to the shops before they close for the day."

A short while later, they reconvened to the dining room and began their meal. "So, now will you tell me about the Stantons?" urged Lexie.

Having had time to compose his thoughts, Ambrose regaled her with descriptions of the viscount, his brother and their wives. He glossed over their offspring, with a quick mention of the younger Stantons' names and ages, but nothing more. She listened attentively, asking the occasional question. Finally, she rested her cheek on her hand thoughtfully and said, "It augurs well for you, I think. The viscount sounds like a sensible man of principle. However, I do wonder at how he will manage once he inherits from the earl, with having two large estates, one in England and the other in America."

"I have wondered about it too," mused Ambrose. "From what I have seen of him, I do not believe he would turn his back on the estate he built from scratch in America to come live permanently in England again." He put down his cutlery and dabbed his lips with the napkin. "I can only conclude," he went on, "that he will correspond with me on the regular and make it his business to visit England once a year or so to look in on his estates. It will entail greater responsibility, if he is willing to entrust me with it."

"I do not see why he would not," reassured Lexie. She pondered the matter further. "Although he could delegate one of his sons to oversee the English estates on his behalf. Are they not grown men?"

Ambrose was suddenly troubled. No, the viscount would not do that! Or would he? Ambrose feared that if he spent much more time with Daniel, he might succumb to his unwelcome desires, but he was banking on him leaving soon to return to America. How on earth was he to cope with having the man so near him? And on what basis? As his de facto employer? That could not be borne.

Lexie sensed his unease. "Darling, what is it?"

He shook his head. "It is nothing really, but I would infinitely prefer to deal with the viscount than his sons."

"Spoiled and entitled are they?" guessed Lexie. "I know the type well. I am married to one after all." It would be fair to say that Lexie and William Forbes's marriage was not a happy one. William had spent his adult life seducing anything in a skirt, but the chicken had come home to roost when one of his seductions resulted in an unwanted pregnancy and then a hurried marriage to Lexie. No sooner had she given birth to their son, Edwin, than William had considered his duty done and decamped to London to live the bachelor life, rarely if ever returning to visit his wife or son.

It was during her first lonely year as an abandoned wife that Lexie had struck up a friendship with her neighbours, Ambrose and his sister, Sarah. Then, in the final months of that year, one tipsy night, she had kissed Ambrose in a fit of desolation, and he had cautiously kissed her back. She had taken him to her bed then, and he had gone along with it, never having made love to a woman before and wanting to prove that he was man enough to do so, despite the worrying desire he experienced for other men.

It had gone well enough. Lexie had been a thoughtful and considerate lover, tending to his needs as well as hers. It had been pleasant to be touched and to touch naked flesh, to commune with a person he cared deeply about, and he had achieved a pleasurable release as he buried his cock in her tight, wet heat.

Over the years of their affair, their emotions had blossomed into a gently tender and enduring love. Ambrose's prowess in the bedroom had improved, and they had both found comfort and relief in the physical act of love. They had found a way to be together a few nights every month, the proximity of their houses making it easy to conduct their affair with discretion. At night, Ambrose would slip out through the back door of the earl's house into the gardens beyond and enter Lexie's house, the door conveniently left unlocked for him. Once their bodies had been sated, they often talked late into the night, their heads close together on the pillow, before Ambrose roused himself to return to his house.

In that time, Ambrose never had thoughts of courting any other woman. His relationship with Lexie suited him very well. He lived comfortably with his sister, had a job he enjoyed and that paid well enough, and when the itch for physical release came upon him, he could find comfort in Lexie's arms. They wrote to each other often, sharing thoughts, worries and moments of joy. More importantly, Lexie helped to keep the troublesome feelings he had for males at bay. When he was with her, he could convince himself that he was not one of those men society decried, not one of those sodomites—the memory of what had happened to John still fresh in his mind. Ambrose had carefully constructed this life, was contented with it, and now a young pup by the name of Daniel Stanton was putting it all at risk.

Lexie regarded him curiously, seeing him lost in thought. "Ambrose, where did you go?" she wanted to know.

With an effort, Ambrose shook off the vision of Daniel that kept intruding on his mind. He was accustomed to honesty with Lexie, so he told her some of what concerned him. "The viscount's eldest son, Daniel, accompanied me on my visits to the tenant farms last week and is very interested in learning about the workings of the estate."

Lexie nodded her head encouragingly. "That is good, surely."

"I found him very forward in his manner. It was... most disconcerting."

There was a pause as Lexie digested this information. "Perhaps it is to do with different customs he is used to," she ventured. "I am sure he does not mean to offend by it."

"No, I am sure he does not," admitted Ambrose, "yet I find myself ill at ease around him."

"You have been used to the earl's stiff formality all these years," suggested Lexie, "so it is natural that you are finding this change of approach discomfiting. Give it time and perhaps you will become accustomed to the forwardness of this American."

Ambrose leaned forward and pressed Lexie's hand. "Thank you, darling," he said fondly. "You always abound with good sense. Now, I must excuse myself and go do my errands."

"Come over once you are done. I know Edwin is very excited to see you," said Lexie.

"I have brought a Christmas gift for him—and one for you too," smiled Ambrose. "I will bring them round later." He stood and kissed the top of her head. "Now I must go. Goodbye, darling."

Much later that night, Ambrose gently disengaged himself from Lexie's sleeping form. They had made quick, urgent love upon first getting into bed, as was usual after a long absence, then they had talked and made leisurely love again. Shortly after, Lexie had drifted off to sleep, and feeling slumber begin to take hold of him, Ambrose forced himself to rise. It would not do to be discovered by the servants or by Edwin when morning came.

He reached over for his discarded nightshirt and robe, quickly putting them on. Then, he bent down and kissed Lexie gently on her brow before retreating silently from her room. He tiptoed in the dark, well acquainted with the layout of the house, then let himself out through the back door and made his way to his own bed in the house next door. Next morning, he completed his remaining errands then set off for Stanton Hall, arriving back in the early afternoon in a contented mood. Surely his time with Lexie would remove any feelings of attraction he might have felt for Daniel.

Chapter 10

Daniel

Late December 1860, two weeks later

The carriage rattled along the cobbled road as it headed towards Stanton Hall. Inside were Daniel, his cousin, Grace, and Benedict Sedgwick. All three sat in silence, deep in sombre thought. Earlier that day, Daniel, accompanied by his cousin, had gone to fetch Benedict, the curate of the village. It was on the behest of the earl, who lay sick and frail in his bed, knowing the end was near.

The carriage now drew up outside the front steps and without delay, all three descended and made their way inside the house to the earl's bedchamber. Daniel, along with the rest of his family, sat outside the room while Mr Sedgwick administered the final rites. A heavy weight was on everyone's heart. Even his brother, Benjamin, who had no great affection for the earl, seemed deeply affected. None of them had truly experienced the passing of a life from this world to the next.

"Do you think a person is aware of what is happening to them the moment of their death, or is it like falling asleep?" wondered Benjamin out of the blue.

"What sort of inappropriate question is that?" snapped Isabella, his younger sister.

"I would think it is entirely relevant, given the circumstances we are in now," riposted Benjamin.

"You do not need to be upsetting Papa or Uncle Jasper at a time like this with such a question," admonished Isabella.

"It may have escaped your attention, Bella, but they're upset enough already," fired back Benjamin.

Daniel sighed inwardly. Those two were always bickering. Before he could step in, a sharp voice belonging to Auntie Ruth, Uncle Jasper's wife, interrupted them. "That's enough, both of you!"

Isabella was about to speak again in her defence, but Daniel sent her a quelling look. With a huff, she sat back in her chair, silenced. Beside Daniel, his mother's gentle voice soothed their ruffled feathers. "To answer your question, Benjamin, I would think it is a bit of both. A person may be aware that the end is near and then feel themselves slipping away from consciousness as we do before sleep. I would like to think that when the time comes, I shall meet my death from the comfort of sleep rather than from full consciousness of what is happening to me." At these words, his father squeezed her hand tight in silent communication.

Poor Papa, thought Daniel. He was taking this badly. Uncle Jasper too. He wondered if this moment would have been any easier had there not been an estrangement between the earl and his children all these years. As if on cue, the door opened then and Benedict Sedgwick stepped out of the sickroom and invited them inside.

Addressing the two older Stantons, he said, "I hope you do not think me forward in saying this, but I do believe it would ease the earl's mind to hear some words of forgiveness. I sense a deep regret in him about things he may have done in his life, perhaps thing to do with the both of you. It would comfort him in his last moments to be forgiven."

Uncle Jasper sighed, "I forgave him long ago."

"And I too," murmured Papa.

"Let him hear the words," said Mr Sedgwick gently.

Daniel watched as his father and uncle entered the room, each taking it in turn to approach his grandfather and speak words of forgiveness into his ear. Yes, he thought, the long estrangement had created a gulf between father and sons which had not been fully bridged, despite their return from America. If there was one lesson to be learned from this, it was that rifts between loved ones caused pain to all involved, and no matter the rights or wrongs of each side, were not in the end worth the pain of the rupture.

For the first time, Daniel considered the viewpoint that in turning their back on their father and leaving for America, both his papa and uncle had done wrong. Yes, his papa should have gone after the woman he loved and married her, but then it would have been better if he had come back to England and tried to mend fences with the earl. Instead, year upon year had been spent with the family torn asunder.

And now, with estates on both sides of the ocean, Daniel envisioned that the Stantons would continue to be split between England and America. Those vast lands, tenant farms and manor houses he had visited over the last few weeks could not simply be abandoned when the family returned to America. Someone would have to stay on and care for this land that the earl loved so much, this land that had been part of his family's heritage for generations. Daniel knew already, with a deep sense of conviction, that he would stay on in England after his grandfather's death, regardless of the terms of the will.

He felt a tightness in his chest at the knowledge this would entail a separation from his family and the home he had known all his life. So be it, he thought. This was the result of the chain of events that had been set in motion twenty-five years ago when two headstrong young men had boarded a ship and headed to America. All this time later, the family was reaping the rewards, good and bad, of this decision. The only difference this time, he hoped, was that the separation would not be built on bitterness and disappointment.

Daniel vowed to himself also that he would heed the lesson clear to him today. Never, by word or deed, would he do anything to sever the precious connection between himself and his loved ones. He gazed at his brother and sister, sitting in sulky silence after their little tiff, and smiled inwardly. They could be annoying and drive him to distraction, but he loved them all the same. He would not let anything drive a wedge between them.

The same went for his mother and father. He observed them now with love in his heart. He was close to them and always had been, their relationship loving and strong. He would keep it this way, he vowed, no matter the circumstances. When the time came for any of them to depart this earth, he hoped it would not be with the sort of regrets the earl was facing now.

The vigil continued. Daniel lost track of the time as the family gathered around the dying earl, listening to the prayers intoned by Benedict Sedgwick and reciting prayers of their own in their hearts. Evening turned to night. The fire in the hearth crackled bright while the pungent scent of the incense candles that had been lit wafted all around them. Daniel realised he would forever associate this smell with death.

Late in the night, he sat by the bed, holding his grandfather's hand. It was cool to the touch, the skin fragile and covered in thin veins. Daniel bent forward and kissed it. As he raised his head, the earl's eyes fluttered, opening briefly and looking straight at him. Daniel leaned closer and whispered close to his ear. "I love you, Grandfather. May God ease your soul." Something made him add, "And Grandfather, I love this place. I promise to stay and take care of it. There will be Stantons here for generations to come." The earl gave a barely audible sigh.

When next Daniel raised his eyes, he saw Ambrose standing beside him. How long he had been there, he did not know. Their gazes met in silent communication. Without a word, Daniel stood, letting Ambrose take his place beside the earl. He stepped back, watching as Ambrose took the earl's hand and spoke softly to him. He did not catch the words, though it did not take a genius to know they were words of gratitude and love. Finally, Ambrose stood to go. Their gazes met again, both sets of eyes sparkling with unshed tears. Ambrose gave a slight nod of acknowledgement then turned to leave.

More hours passed. Just before the appearance of the first streaks of dawn, Daniel heard Benedict Sedgwick say quietly, "He is gone." The curate stepped away from the bed and began to recite words of prayer while around the room, soft cries and sobs were heard. Daniel sat down in a chair by the window, numb with weariness and grief. Then, seeing Isabella's distraught face, he sprang into action, taking her into his arms and soothing her as best he could.

"It's alright. It's alright," he repeated over and over, stroking her hair and letting her cry into the soft folds of his jacket.

Over the next hour, Daniel stood by his family dutifully, helping, soothing, standing strong. There was no time for his own grief when others needed him. There would be time enough for that later. Eventually, everyone dispersed, most to get some sleep in their rooms. Daniel too went to his own bedchamber and washed, but though he was tired, he could not think of settling down to sleep. After so many hours closeted in the earl's room, he felt the need for fresh air. He looked out the window. It was a dry and bright December morning, the sun shining for the first time in days, as if in some macabre celebration of the earl's passing. He would go out for a walk, he decided.

He pulled on his coat and hat, then went down the stairs to the main hall. It was deathly quiet, the servants nowhere in sight. Without a sound, he opened the front door and stepped outside. As he did so, he spied a figure seated on the front steps below, his face buried in his arms. He knew immediately it was Ambrose.

Quietly, not wanting to disturb him, Daniel made his way down the steps and went to sit beside him. From the hitch in Ambrose's breaths, it was apparent he was aware of Daniel's presence, yet for long minutes, they sat in silence, each lost in their own thoughts. At long last, Ambrose sat up and turned to face Daniel. "I am sorry for your loss, my lord," he said in a voice roughened by emotion.

"Don't you dare my lord me right now, Ambrose," growled Daniel. Then, more softly, he added, "I am sorry for your loss too."

Ambrose nodded in acknowledgement. "I shall miss him," he said simply.

"Me too."

Ambrose went on, "The earl came into my life at a time like this one, when I was feeling the grief of a sad bereavement. We had lost Mother only the year before, and then it was Father. To add to that, not two days after the funeral I learned that we had been left with nothing but debts, and that we would have to vacate the vicarage before the week was out. In days, we sold whatever furniture we could not keep and packed our belongings, readying ourselves to leave the only home we had ever known. Then I took Sarah with me back to Oxford where I used my meagre savings to put her up in an inn while I tried to arrange our affairs. I went to the proctor at the university and informed him of the change in my circumstances, asking for a letter of reference and any recommendation regarding finding employment."

He paused his tale for a few breaths, deep in recollection. Daniel waited patiently for him to continue. Finally, Ambrose resumed the thread of his story. "The proctor told me to come back the following day, when he would have the letter ready for me and some suggestions as to what I could do next. The following morning, when I went to see him, there was someone with him—a tall, imperious looking gentleman with greying hair and turbulent dark eyes just like yours. I was introduced to the Earl of Stanton. He asked me question after question, and I answered them as best I could, unsure where the conversation going. It seemed the earl was satisfied, for in the end, he stood and addressed the proctor, saying, 'Proceed with what we agreed,' then left without another word."

This was the longest speech Daniel had heard from Ambrose since he had met him. He listened, mesmerised by the sound of his voice and by the emotion imbuing every word. When Ambrose spoke no more, Daniel prompted, "And that was when Grandfather offered you and your sister lodgings at his Oxford house?"

"Yes," replied Ambrose. "Overnight we went from a hand-to-mouth existence to living in luxuriously appointed accommodation, waited on by servants like we had never been before. I could never in this lifetime repay the kindness of that gesture. And then we came here, and I began my apprenticeship under Mr Finlay, who was estate manager then at Stanton Hall. Throughout those years, the earl showed an interest in my progress and in our welfare, never stinting in generosity despite the gruff demeanour he showed to the world."

"Yes indeed, miserliness was never one of Grandfather's sins," concurred Daniel.

"Three years ago, after Mr Finlay's passing, the earl sent for me. I thought perhaps he would ask me to assist whatever new estate manager he had decided to appoint. I was barely twenty-six years old, and this estate is so vast that only a seasoned professional could be entrusted with its management. You may imagine my shock when he offered the position to me."

"I am not at all surprised he chose you," smiled Daniel. "Even on this short acquaintance, I have seen what calibre of a person you are, Ambrose. Grandfather was lucky to have found you."

"I was the lucky one," said Ambrose quietly.

He shivered then, and Daniel said quickly, "You will catch cold, sitting on these front steps. Come inside and have something warming to drink."

Ambrose got to his feet, shaking off the dust on his trousers. "Thank you but no," he said. "It is past time I went home." He faced Daniel who had stood up with him. "What will you do now?" he asked.

Daniel let out a sigh and murmured, "I am restless and thought to take a walk."

He could have been knocked down with a feather when he heard Ambrose's response. "Perhaps then you could walk with me back to Ivy Cottage."

"I should like that, thank you," replied Daniel hoarsely. He had no thought of his attraction to Ambrose at this moment nor of seduction. What he wanted now was a friend who could share in his grief and help assuage it.

Together, they began the short walk along the avenue towards Ambrose's cottage. After a few moments, Ambrose spoke. "I heard what you said to your grandfather, about staying here and taking care of this place. Did you mean it?"

"I meant every word," stated Daniel firmly.

"I saw the earl's reaction to your words. He sighed as if in relief. I think it comforted him to hear them."

"I hope so," said Daniel. Then he felt the need to explain himself. "I had been feeling… I suppose you could call it a sense of disquiet all evening, ever since Mr Sedgwick came over and told my father and uncle that Grandfather was feeling troubled and in need of hearing words of forgiveness. It brought home to me the enormity of the consequences to that decision, twenty-five years ago, to leave everything behind in search of a new life in America. In addition to that I have seen, over the last few weeks, just how well regarded Grandfather is hereabouts and what level of responsibility he took on his shoulders, looking out for the welfare of countless people on this estate. All this, he did without the help of his sons who should have been by his side."

Daniel bit his lip in consternation. He did not like to think badly of his father. It pained him to realise that the man he had looked up to all his life could also be capable of making very human mistakes.

As if sensing this, Ambrose said, very gently, "Do not be too hard on your father, Daniel. From what I gather, your grandfather was a very difficult man when it came to his eldest son, very exacting in his standards and very controlling. Plus, he had decided that only a prestigious political career would do for the viscount. Even had your father stayed, he would not have been tasked with assisting your grandfather here on the estate but with finding public high office. I think it was only later in life, after his sons had left for America, that your grandfather became so involved with the welfare of people on this estate. He also came to understand what kind of a noose he had put around his son's neck and to live with regret for his actions. It is easy for us to judge now, but at the time, I am sure there were reasons aplenty for your father and your uncle to do what they did."

Daniel sniffed, his eyes and nose suddenly running. In an irritated gesture, he wiped at his face and tried not to succumb to the tears he so desperately wanted to shed. In a throaty voice, he said, "That might be so, but the consequences were many. These great houses that were destined for my father and uncle and their offspring—these tenants, these farms—are all now left without anyone to care. I know, you see, that as soon as he possibly can, Papa will return to America, my uncle too. That is where they have made their home now. And I cannot bear to think of all of this—" Daniel pointed all around him, "—without the presence of a member of the family that bears its name."

He breathed heavily, emotion clogging his chest.

"If you stay," stated Ambrose, quickly getting to the heart of the matter, "then your family will be torn apart once more. And you will be exiled from the place you have called home your entire life."

"I know it," said Daniel bitterly. He wondered for a brief moment if Ambrose were trying to persuade him to go. Resolutely, he went on, "Yet I am compelled by a sense of duty towards the old man. Perhaps in some way, I wish to atone for the abandonment of my grandfather twenty-five years ago."

"Then stay," urged Ambrose.

Daniel flashed a glance his way. Perhaps he had been wrong in his earlier thoughts. They had by now arrived at Ivy Cottage and paused before the front gate. Ambrose seemed to hesitate before making the invitation. "Will you come in? I have a bottle of your grandfather's finest sherry which we can share."

Daniel's heart began to pound in his chest. "I would like that very much," he said. "Thank you." He followed Ambrose to the front door, then stepped inside. As soon as he entered the cottage, Daniel was gripped by a sense of welcoming warmth. The cottage was small by Stanton Hall's standards, but it was perfectly formed and well proportioned. He saw Ambrose hanging his coat and hat on a peg, and followed suit. A moment later, there was the sound of footsteps, and Sarah came rushing towards them. "You're back!" she cried. Then, noticing his presence, she came to an abrupt halt. "Pardon me, my lord," she said more sedately. "I have heard the sad news. Please accept my most sincere condolences for your loss."

This was the second time today someone had addressed him as "my lord". He understood of course that it was now his due as Viscount Stanton, but he despised the formality all the same. "Please, do not call me 'my lord', I beg you. I am easier with just being called Daniel. And thank you for your condolences."

She nodded doubtfully as Ambrose spoke, "Sarah, we are going to be in my study. We are both in need of some fortification from the late earl's fine sherry."

"Of course," she said. "Do you wish me to send in any food? You have missed your breakfast today."

Ambrose looked at him enquiringly, but Daniel shook his head. Addressing his sister, Ambrose said, "No, thank you. I do not think either of us could eat now." With a nod towards a side door, he invited Daniel in. "Shall we?"

Daniel inclined his head politely towards Sarah. On first catching sight of her a moment ago, he had instantly noticed the resemblance she bore to Ambrose. She was of similar stature to him, tall and slim, but in female form. And of course, she had the same grey eyes. He was minded to like her already. "I will bid you good day, Miss Cranshaw," he said to her now with a smile.

"Good day," she said. "Do call for me or Elsie should you need anything." With that, she turned and went back to the room at the back of the house from which she had recently emerged. Daniel followed Ambrose into his study and looked around curiously.

"This place feels just like you," he remarked.

Ambrose raised a brow at Daniel "How so?" he asked, then went over to the fireplace and proceeded to efficiently light a fire using a tinder box.

"Very scholarly and respectable," Daniel mused. "I like it."

"Thank you. I do spend a lot of my time here doing very scholarly and respectable things," said Ambrose mildly.

An image, unbidden, flew into Daniel's mind of doing some most unrespectable things with Ambrose in this room. He batted it away in annoyance. This was not the time or place for such unruly thoughts.

"Do take a seat," said Ambrose pointing him to an armchair by the fireplace. A vigorous fire was now burning in the hearth. As Daniel settled himself in the armchair, Ambrose went to a sideboard and removed from it a bottle of sherry and two glasses, bringing them over to him. Daniel wondered why Ambrose was being so hospitable. Was it merely to condole with him about the earl's death? Or had they reached a greater intimacy by sharing their thoughts? He hoped it was the latter.

Ambrose took a seat across from him and held up his glass. "To the late earl—a generous, kind and ornery man."

Daniel smiled, holding up his own glass for the toast. "I will drink to that," he said, and proceeded to take a long sip of his sherry. "Mmm, this is good," he murmured appreciatively. A few more sips and he had downed his glass.

"Have some more," offered Ambrose, leaning across with the bottle to pour him another shot. Once done, he sat back in his seat and gazed speculatively at him. "Your turn, Daniel. I have told you my story with regards to your grandfather. Tell me something of how you first met him."

Daniel lounged back in his chair, legs outstretched before him and thought back to that first meeting. "I would have been around five years old," he said. "We had just come back from church one day when we saw a strange carriage stopped outside our house. From it stepped out this impeccably dressed older man. Papa took one look at him and blurted, 'Father?' That's when I knew this was my grandfather from England. My papa talked of him a lot, you see. We then went in the house and this I remember. He looked about him with a regal air and said, 'I understand you turned your back on Stanton Hall for *this.*' It was quite awkward at first. It had been six years by then since Pa and Uncle Jasper had left for America. I remember Ben and I thought it very funny that Grandfather had brought his valet with him and always insisted on being properly dressed for each meal. We were used to a much more informal way of life." Daniel smiled reminiscently and took another drink of his sherry.

"It must have been a very emotional reunion after so many years," speculated Ambrose.

"That it was. Oh, and it was also then that Uncle Jasper proposed to Auntie Ruth. Grandfather stayed long enough to attend the wedding before starting his journey back to England. Before he left, he made me promise to write to him. So I did — some very childish epistle no doubt — but we have maintained a regular correspondence since then." Daniel thought wistfully to all the letters that would never be sent now. He gulped down the remnants of his glass and went to pour himself some more, asking, "You do not mind if I get gloriously drunk, do you?"

Ambrose smiled gently. "Not if you will allow me to get gloriously drunk along with you."

Daniel held up his glass. "The more the merrier!"

Time passed as they reminisced about the late Earl of Stanton, then strayed into recollections of their childhood misdeeds and mishaps. As their stomachs were both empty, it did not take long for them to become quite merry, though this was quickly followed by fatigue. Daniel yawned languorously and mumbled, "I should be getting back home."

"In a while, Daniel," came the response from Ambrose. "Why don't you rest for a time on the settee over there?"

Daniel glanced at it longingly. He was too tipsy and tired to attempt the walk back to Stanton Hall. "Good idea," he agreed. Pausing only to clumsily take off his boots, he stumbled to the settee and laid his head to rest on a plump pillow that miraculously appeared there. Distantly, he was aware of a blanket being tucked around him, but already he was slipping away into unconsciousness.

He did not know what time it was when he finally stirred awake. His muscles felt cramped, curled up as he was on the settee that could ill accommodate his tall length. His head too, was not in a happy condition. Slowly, he lifted himself to a sitting position and felt the full brunt of a pounding headache in his temple. He cast a bleary eye about him. Memories flooded back. He was in Ambrose's study, and Grandfather was dead. They had drunk their sorrows away, and Ambrose had finally shed that reserve he had had about him. They had talked without restraint, long and intimately. And then he had slept.

Daniel's gaze landed on Ambrose's sleeping form. He sat up straighter and studied him. Even dishevelled and asleep, his lips slightly parted as he breathed heavily in and out, Ambrose was a sight to behold. He was the most beautiful being Daniel had ever had the privilege of seeing. He stared at him now, long and longingly, and as he did, it was his heart more so than his loins that reacted to the sight of a sleeping Ambrose. So help me God, he thought. *I think I may be falling in love with him.*

He huffed quietly. Love! Had he not already learned from his experience with Agnes how deceitful and fleeting this emotion was? This was just another case of infatuation, and one he would recover from quickly enough. And then... then he hoped what would come out of the ashes of his desire was a deep and lasting friendship with this man. His overtures had been rebuffed, and he had few expectations of his feelings being reciprocated. All he could hope for was friendship. This knowledge did not stop Daniel from drinking in the sight of Ambrose for long, fervent minutes. With each minute his heart ached a little more. If this was not love, then it was the strongest case of infatuation ever.

He heaved a sigh and looked about for his discarded boots. As he did so, he noticed a sheet of paper with scrawled writing which lay on the side table, held in place by a paper weight. He reached over for it and read:

Dear gentlemen,

If you have awoken from your drunken stupor and are feeling the ill effects of intoxication, please come through to the dining room where I have left a pot of ginger tea brewing by the hearth which will help chase away the headache. There is also bread, ham and cheese to eat.

Sarah

Daniel smiled and put the note down. Ambrose's sister was quite the character. Spying his boots, he pulled them on and then stood. Casting one last longing glance at Ambrose, who was still sleeping soundly, he tiptoed to the door and quietly let himself out. It did not take too much guessing to find the dining room. There, he helped himself to the vile concoction of ginger tea and forced it down his throat. It burned a little, but he could admit he felt marginally better as a result. His rumbling stomach reminded him he had not eaten anything since yesterday morning. Quickly, he buttered two thick slices of bread and helped himself to some ham and cheese. He ate hungrily, blessing the absent Sarah with each delicious bite.

When he was finished, he returned to the study and examined Ambrose, who still slept on. He gazed at him some more, feeling that same ache in the region of his heart. Then, he forced himself to look away. Going to the desk, he found some paper, a pot of ink and a pen. He wrote two notes.

Dear Ambrose,

Thank you for the sherry, the fine company and the dubious comforts of your settee. Already, my pain at losing Grandfather feels a little less sharp, and that is due in part to you.

Yours,

Daniel

To Sarah, he wrote:

Dear Sarah,

The food was delicious and the tea, though vile, did the trick. I am nearly restored to my normal self. Thank you!

Daniel

He placed Ambrose's note on the table beside Sarah's original missive, then with a last yearning glance at Ambrose, he made his way out, leaving Sarah's note on the dining table. He found his coat and hat, slipped them on, then quietly let himself out of the house and walked back to Stanton Hall.

Chapter 11

Ambrose

They were all assembled in the library for the reading of the late Earl of Stanton's will. Just yesterday, the earl had been laid to rest. Now the family and faithful servants waited for Mr Ridley, the earl's solicitor, to begin. Ambrose sat to one side next to his friend, Benedict Sedgwick. From across the room, he watched Daniel as discreetly as he could.

They had spoken little since that day they had got drunk on sherry in his study. The family had been kept busy with visitors wanting to pay their respects and with the arrangements for a suitable funeral for a man of such stature as the late earl. It seemed to have taken its toll on Daniel. He looked weary. There were shadows under his eyes and a pallid tinge to his skin. His mouth was set in a straight line, a stern expression on his handsome countenance. Long lost was the mischievous and playful Daniel of their first meeting a month ago. That playfulness had preyed on Ambrose's nerves but now conversely, Ambrose missed it. What he would give to see those eyes light up with wicked humour again and for those mesmerising dimples to grace Daniel's face.

His attention was brought back to Mr Ridley as the solicitor cleared his throat and began to read the will. It began with legal preambles then a list of the earl's bequests to his servants. Ambrose should not have been surprised to be included in that list given the late earl's generosity and their close relationship. Still, it was with a curious jolt that he heard the solicitor intone,

"To my estate manager, Ambrose Cranshaw, I bequeath a sum of £250, in appreciation of his loyal and excellent service. I also take this opportunity to express my desire that Mr Cranshaw be kept on as estate manager following my demise."

Ambrose felt his face heat with pleased surprise, not only at the words of the will but at the reappearance, finally, of Daniel's dimples as the latter looked across at him and smiled with his first show of genuine warmth that day. Ambrose could not help but smile back. The two of them exchanged a long look, their gazes fixed on the other. Ambrose lost track of what Mr Ridley was saying as he got caught in Daniel's riveting regard.

"Finally, to Daniel, the new Viscount Stanton, I bequeath Stanton Hall..." The import of Mr Ridley's words broke into Ambrose's reverie. Along with everyone else in the room, he listened in astonishment as the solicitor explained how the late earl had decided to leave nothing to his two sons. Instead, his vast estate would be split between four of his grandchildren, with the lion's share going to Daniel.

The solicitor went on to read the late earl's words, explaining that this decision was not taken out of anger at his sons but in acknowledgement of the reality of their vast landholdings in America. Ambrose listened, much moved, as Mr Ridley read the final section of the will, in which the earl addressed his sons with words of apology for the past and assured them of his love.

There was hardly a dry eye left in the room as Mr Ridley concluded the reading, Ambrose included. He blinked repeatedly, trying to keep his tears at bay. As he had long known, his former employer had hidden a generous and proud heart beneath his cantankerous exterior. And now, if Ambrose was to understand the terms of this will, he was to have four new employers—chief of them being Daniel Stanton.

Ambrose had known that Daniel planned to stay on in England, the only difference was that now, he would be representing himself, not his father. For the foreseeable future, Ambrose would be working closely with the man. This knowledge caused a mixture of pleasure and fear to arise in his heart. He would see that devilishly handsome face nearly each day, feel the force of that man's charm, enjoy verbal sparring with him. Ambrose could not suppress a thrill of pleasure at the thought even if at the same time, he reminded himself to stay on guard. Never, by a word or even the smallest gesture, could he betray his true feelings. It would be his end.

He stood, readying himself to leave. Across the room, Daniel caught his gaze once more. They nodded to each other in acknowledgement. Soon, they would need to discuss the business of the estate, but not right now in this moment of grief. With one final glance at his new employer, Ambrose departed and headed back to Ivy Cottage.

Chapter 12

Daniel

Christmas Eve, 1860

So, all this belonged to him now. He stood in the ornamental gardens of Stanton Hall and let his gaze roam over the grand house and lands that were now his own. There had been Stantons on this land for over three hundred years. Now, the legacy had passed on to him. He would be keeper of this place for however many years God granted him, after which it would pass on to the next generation.

Pride filled his breast, together with a heavy sense of expectation. His responsibility it was now to maintain this grand home, to ensure the sound management of the land and proper care of all who lived on it, from servant to tenant. He remembered how he had once thought this system of landlord and tenants as feudal. He still thought it so, but he was also reminded of a salient fact: feudalism had been a two-way contract between a liege lord and his vassals.

While it was true a vassal was granted land from his lord in return for loyalty and service—just as his tenants were granted land in return for paying rent—the lord had a duty in return to protect all those who pledged allegiance to him. And by the same token, Daniel now had a great duty to protect the welfare of those who worked on his estate. His mama, God bless her, had a quote from classical philosophers for all aspects of life. And he was sure in this instance, she would remind him of

Cicero's famous maxim: "The higher we are placed, the more humbly we should walk."

He huffed out a laugh. Yes indeed, he felt humbled, not just by the responsibility that now weighed on his young shoulders but also by the trust his grandfather had placed in him. Staring at the magnificence that was Stanton Hall, he whispered a vow: "I shan't let you down, Grandfather. I promise."

"Admiring your new kingdom?" came a sarcastic voice from behind him. He swivelled around to see Benjamin strutting casually in his direction.

"As a matter of fact, I was," replied Daniel evenly. "It's quite a view, isn't it?"

Benjamin came to stand beside him and perused the massive stone building before them. Cocking his head to one side, he gave a knowing grin. "I have discovered an even better view," he boasted.

Daniel studied him quietly a second or two. Then he relented. "Very well. What is this view you talk of?"

"If you would follow me, I will show you." Benjamin pointed with his chin towards the house. "Let us go inside and you will see."

"This had better be good," muttered Daniel.

"It is," came Benjamin's airy reply. "Come along, brother mine."

Intrigued, Daniel followed his brother up the path that led back to Stanton Hall. They let each other into the house by the side door that was for the servants, and Benjamin proceeded to take him up the stairs. Mystified, Daniel followed his brother along the galleried corridor, past the library, until they reached a large sash window. He raised a sceptical brow as Benjamin lifted the sash up high to open the window.

"Dear brother, do you trust me?" enquired Benjamin mockingly.

"Absolutely," replied Daniel promptly, amused at the taken-aback expression on Benjamin's face.

"Well," mumbled his brother. "I am glad to hear it." He nodded towards the window. "If you climb over the sill, you will be able to stand on a wide ledge. From there, we will take two steps to the right, from where we can access a flat part of the roof. Just follow me. I assure you it is quite safe."

Daniel did not think twice. "Lead on," he said.

With a grin, Benjamin climbed over the window sill and perched on the ledge, then moved to the side. "Come on, your turn," he called out. Without hesitation, Daniel lifted a leg across the sill and came to stand on the ledge beside his brother, then followed Benjamin two steps to the right until they reached a part of the roof that was L-shaped, creating an unorthodox type of seat. Benjamin dropped down onto the cold slate tiles, and Daniel followed suit. Only then did he take in the view on display.

From where they sat, they could see the gardens and parkland, and beyond that, acres and acres of cultivated fields. Mulverley Grange could also be seen, a distant dot on the horizon. From this elevated perch, Daniel had a clear view of the vastness of the lands that were now his. As if reading his mind, Benjamin murmured beside him, "That is quite a kingdom you have inherited."

"Yes," replied Daniel laconically.

"Told you there was a better view."

Daniel laughed. "I will admit you were right."

They spent some minutes in quiet contemplation of the sight before them. Eventually, Benjamin broke the silence with a question. "So, how does it feel to be a viscount and master of all of this?"

Daniel sat back on his elbows, considering his answer. "It feels very strange to be called 'my lord' by everyone," he said musingly. "Whenever they do, I am tempted to look behind me and see who they are really addressing."

"You can go sit in the House of Lords now, you know, and make frightfully boring speeches," observed Benjamin. "Fancy a trip to London?"

Daniel chuckled. "In time perhaps. Not just yet."

"You haven't answered my question fully," reminded Benjamin. "Are you excited about your new situation?"

"Excited? No, not really," replied Daniel. "It is more a feeling of pride, of gratitude to Grandfather, and also a sense of duty."

"Oh come on, Daniel, pull the other one!" expostulated Benjamin. "You are now your own man and rich to boot. Do not tell me you do not feel just a tad pleased at your new circumstances."

"Very well, I won't," retorted Daniel. "I was trying not to sound like I am gloating, but of course it pleases me to now be a man of independent means and rich to boot as you say."

"That's better," approved Benjamin. "Honesty is good."

"If we are talking honesty, then tell me, Benjamin, and tell me truly, how do you feel about the terms of Grandfather's will—specifically as they pertain to you?"

"I... I cannot complain about it," mumbled Benjamin. "The terms were fair. You get the land in England whereas I will in due course inherit the land in Ohio. I understand Grandfather's thinking. What he decided makes sense."

"You do not mind that I got all of this instead of you?" Daniel studied his brother carefully.

Benjamin met Daniel's stare head on. "When I think about it, this place could not have gone to anyone but you. I would not have wanted it for myself. To be honest, I cannot even imagine being in your position right now."

Daniel let out a relieved breath. "Good. I am glad." He placed a hand on his brother's shoulder. "I would not want anything to come between us," he said quietly.

His relief, however, was short-lived when Benjamin added, "I do, however, envy the freedom you now have to do what you want."

"It is not as much freedom as you think. Along with all this great wealth comes great responsibility that I am not free to walk away from." Daniel looked again at the miles of parkland before him and was conscious of the great obligation that now weighed on his young shoulders.

Benjamin was not convinced. He listed each point on his fingers. "You have the freedom to decide how you wish to spend your great wealth, to decide who you wish to befriend or marry, to decide what you wish to do with your time. You have a say in nearly every matter that involves this village, such as who gets appointed to be the next vicar of the parish, and you also have a say in what laws get passed in parliament. You are now in a position of great power, Daniel."

Daniel's mind was stuck on the second point. Did he have the freedom to befriend and marry whoever he wanted? His thoughts went to Ambrose, as they constantly did these days. No, he did not believe he had that freedom. If he could, he would proclaim his feelings for the man to all and sundry, and claim him as his chosen partner in life. No, he was not as free as Benjamin supposed. But all he said, in a flat tone, was, "I take your point."

Benjamin raked his hand through his hair in irritation. "I am sorry, Daniel. I do not want to sound mean and envious. I suppose, going back to your original question about the will, that my main feeling is one of loss. We are going to be parted, as before too long we shall return to America while you will stay on here. And I fear that next time we meet, you will be much changed, for great power and wealth will inevitably change a person. I will have lost the brother of my childhood."

Daniel threw an arm around Benjamin's shoulder and drew his stiff, unyielding body towards him. "I may have money now, Benjamin, but I am still me. That will never change. You cannot rid yourself of me, you know. I will always be your brother."

"Lucky me!" snorted Benjamin.

"Indeed, lucky you," echoed Daniel with a smile.

He decided it was time to change the subject. Dropping his arm from around his brother, he turned to face him, narrowing his eyes. "So tell me," he drawled. "Where were you earlier today? I saw you walking down towards the village. Is it that draper's daughter you went to see? What was her name?"

"Daphne Phipps," said Benjamin, "and no, that affair ended the night of the Christmas ball when she failed to come to our assignation in the library."

"How very remiss of her."

"It was, but also a blessing, for instead of meeting with Daphne I had the pleasure of making Sarah Cranshaw's acquaintance," explained Benjamin.

At the name Cranshaw, Daniel began to scowl, overcome by a protective instinct for Ambrose's sister. "Do not tell me, Benjamin, that you are messing around with that lady."

His brother had the decency to look affronted. "Messing around? I am doing nothing of the sort. We are friends; that is all. She shares my interest in engineering. In fact, I am helping her to build a miniature railway in her house. That is where I was earlier."

Daniel's stern gaze did not waiver. "You will promise me now, Benjamin, not to overstep the boundaries of acceptable behaviour with Sarah Cranshaw."

"What has got you in a bother all of a sudden? And you need not worry. I have been a perfect gentleman without any need for a lecture from you."

"What has me in a bother," grated Daniel, "is that Sarah is the sister of Ambrose Cranshaw, a dear friend and someone who I shall be working closely with to manage my estate. I do not want him taking offence because my foolish brother has forgotten the proprieties when it comes to his sister."

"Have I not said I am being the perfect gentleman? Do cease with the tiresome lecturing. It ill becomes you," snapped Benjamin. Then he too narrowed his eyes. "And what do you mean he is your dear friend? Since when?"

"Since he took the time to show me around the estate," stated Daniel.

"Hmm. He seems very prim and buttoned up. I would not have thought him the type of person you would befriend."

Daniel's mouth curved into a smile as he thought of Ambrose—yet again. Benjamin had it right. Ambrose was prim and buttoned up, at least on the surface. Daniel was sure there was a lot more to the man than he allowed the world to see. There had been glimpses of that man when they had gotten drunk on sherry the day of his grandfather's death. As the alcohol had loosened inhibitions, Ambrose had told sparkly tales of childhood pranks. His eyes, those beautiful smoky eyes, had gleamed with mischievousness. It tickled Daniel that he had been privy to this private side of Ambrose's character. He wanted to see more of it.

However, he did not reveal this to Benjamin, contenting himself with saying, "Well, that goes to show how little you know of my likes and dislikes." He stood. "I think we have seen enough of this view for now," he said, and began to edge towards the window. Benjamin followed close behind. Once inside the house, and the window secured shut, Daniel headed towards the staircase, calling behind him, "Now I shall bid you goodbye."

"Where is it you are going?" wondered Benjamin.

Daniel paused his step and looked back at his brother with a grin. "I am going to pay a visit to my prim and buttoned up friend, of course."

Chapter 13

Ambrose

Christmas Eve, 1860

The pace of the day had been relentless. From early morning until about a half-hour ago, Ambrose had been closeted in meetings with Mr Ridley, the solicitor, and both Frank and Jasper Stanton, who were the trustees of the late earl's will. Daniel too, had been present in most of these meetings, as the new viscount and primary heir to the estate.

Now, back in his cottage, over a relaxing drink of sherry, Ambrose thought about what was to happen next. There would be plenty of work for Daniel and him to do setting out the new estates and dividing all the earl's properties amongst his heirs — particularly since Daniel's father and uncle would be returning to America soon.

There were other matters to be resolved by the trustees too. The earl had not thought to mention several of his other lesser properties in the will—the Oxford house, for instance, and several tenanted cottages dotted around the village. There was also a hunting lodge in Norfolk that was rarely, if ever used, and thus must have escaped the earl's attention when he sat to write his will. All these properties would need to be equitably portioned out between the four heirs of the late earl, and the deeds transferred into their names.

With a deep sigh, Mr Ridley had bemoaned to all, "I did try to explain to the lately departed earl the complexities of carving up the estate into separate entities, and that the matter required a great deal of time and effort to untangle, but he would have none of it. He insisted that Francis and Jasper would manage the thing for him." He had gazed apologetically at the late earl's two sons.

Frank Stanton, now the new Earl of Stanton, had not been amused. "I do not know how we shall manage in the time we have," he had muttered. "In another two weeks at most, we must depart for America. We cannot be absent from our estates there for much longer."

Sensing his father's distress, Daniel had placed a hand on his shoulder and said soothingly, "Do not worry overmuch, Papa. You can only do what you can, and the rest we shall deal with afterwards, Mr Ridley, Mr Cranshaw and I. Once all matters are in order, we will write to you in America with the details set out and await your signed affidavit before proceeding in the courts. It will take longer to do that way, of course, but there is no great rush in any case."

Frank Stanton had clasped his son's hand on his shoulder in gratitude. Observing this, Ambrose's opinion of Daniel had gone up a notch. He was beginning to realise that his original assessment of the man—a charming, careless flirt—had not been quite correct. Of course, Daniel was all those things, but with the responsibility thrust upon him, he had become a lot more. From what Ambrose had seen these last few days, Daniel Stanton was a man of great loyalty to his family, coupled with a great sense of duty.

Damnation! He should not like him more than he already did. It would be dangerous to his peace of mind. He had to remember to stay on guard lest his true feelings be discovered. Ambrose wondered how he would be able to work with the new viscount over the coming days, weeks—even years—all the time hiding the way he felt about him. In the quiet privacy of his study though, he could admit to himself what it was that he felt—an intense desire and liking for his handsome new employer.

Ambrose downed the last of the sherry he had poured and set his glass down. Rubbing his eyes tiredly, he stretched his legs before him and rested his head on the back of the armchair. Yes, it had been a long and taxing day. He had come home and gone straight to his study, reaching for the tried and trusted bottle of sherry to help ease his frazzled nerves. He glanced up at the clock across the room. A quarter past five o'clock. Soon, it would be time for dinner and after that, he would retire early to bed with a book to read.

In the quietness of the early evening, there came a loud and distinct knock on the door. Ambrose frowned. Who could be calling at this time? He heard Elsie go open the front door and the sound of an unmistakable male voice. He sat up abruptly. What the dickens could Daniel Stanton want with him now? He got to his feet and whipped open his study door. At once his gaze met the striking, almost black eyes that haunted his fevered dreams. "Viscount," he said. "This is a surprise."

"May I come in?" asked Daniel.

"Of course."

Ambrose stepped aside and let him enter his study. Daniel stopped in the middle of the room and focused his intense stare on him. "Do forgive this unannounced call," he said in his deep, baritone voice.

"Not at all, please, my lord, take a seat." Ambrose's voice was not as steady as he would have wished. He wondered what purpose Daniel had in coming to see him in his home.

The viscount frowned, unbuttoning his coat and placing it on the settee, together with his hat. "We have spoken of this, Ambrose," he said sternly, taking the offered seat. "You are not to call me 'my lord'. We are to work closely together and we are also well on the way to becoming friends. There is no longer any need for excessive formality between us."

"So you keep saying, my lord," replied Ambrose stubbornly, "but I cannot feel comfortable addressing you informally when you are my employer."

Daniel directed a mocking look at him. "You had no trouble doing so the last time I was here, getting drunk on Grandfather's fine sherry."

Ambrose shrugged uncomfortably. "That was different. We were both… in need of solace that day." The real truth of the matter was that Ambrose used Daniel's formal title to help create a protective barrier around himself where this man was concerned.

Daniel sighed but did not pursue the point. "Ambrose," he said firmly, "we have not had an opportunity for a private word since the reading of the will. I had hoped we could talk."

Ambrose stiffened his spine. "What were you hoping to talk about, sir?"

Daniel scowled, probably at the use of the word "sir", but Ambrose could not help it. He had to maintain a formal distance between them. It was the only shield he had. Silence reigned as Daniel continued to look at him in disapprobation. Finally, he spoke. "When I first met and flirted with you, Ambrose, I had in mind that I would be in England for a short time, and I thought to engage in some enjoyable dalliance. I had no idea then that this estate would become mine and that consequently, I would become your employer. Then of course, you made it categorically clear that you had not an ounce of interest in me, much to my chagrin."

Ambrose gazed at the fire crackling in the hearth. If Daniel only knew—but no, he must never know. In a low voice, he said, "We agreed not to talk of this anymore. I would wish to put the whole episode behind us."

"Yes, I know, but I think we are both finding it hard to do so," responded Daniel. "Your stiff manner with me is evidence of it. And as for me? Ambrose, my logical mind tells me that there is nothing here but the possibility of friendship with you. Unfortunately, I am not made up simply of my rational mind. There is also that part of me that cannot stop wanting you, even when logically, all hope is lost." Ambrose felt the fixed regard of those fervent dark eyes, but he refused to let himself see, staring stubbornly at the fireplace. His pulse pounded in his temple. Daniel's words were lighting a fire of exultation in his breast, a fire which he had to extinguish at all costs.

"So, what is to be done?" asked Ambrose hoarsely. "Should I resign my position here and seek employment elsewhere?"

"No!" Daniel snapped the word. "Do not even think of leaving. This whole situation is my fault. If anyone is to leave, it is me. Only I am not able to do so just yet, not until our estate affairs are all in order. After that, if you wish me to—if it will make life easier for you—then I will base myself in London or at the Oxford house, and only come here when estate business dictates it necessary."

Now Ambrose's eyes flew to stare at Daniel aghast. "You cannot possibly do that!" he cried. "It would be wrong. This is your home, your ancestral right. You cannot seriously think of deserting it because of me."

Daniel held his gaze, his expression sad. "It is not what I would want. But Ambrose, I do not think I am capable of pretending that I feel nothing for you when…" He took a deep, steadying breath before continuing, "when each day my feelings for you grow. Ambrose, I desire you like I have nobody else. It is like a physical burn in my body. But that is not all. I also respect and admire you and think you are the best of men. What I feel for you is no careless passing fancy. It is deep and strong."

Ambrose could not look away. Each word Daniel spoke received a resounding echo in his own heart. He felt the same. By God, he felt the same. He reminded himself, desperately, to stay on guard. With a calmness he did not feel, he said, "I am sorry you feel this way, my lord. It is… most unfortunate."

Daniel sighed and looked down at his trembling hands. Then it was as if he took courage again, and he fixed his gaze on him once more. "Ambrose, what I would like to say to you is this. I desire and admire you greatly, and I would like nothing more than for you to reciprocate what I feel. If ever, if ever, you begin to develop any semblance of those feelings for me, then I beseech you please to tell me and I shall be yours. Yours, do you hear?"

Ambrose heard. By God he heard, and his heart rejoiced. But he could not, would not, show any emotion. "My lord," he began carefully. "I am sorry for you, but it is not to be. I cannot be any clearer on the matter."

Daniel nodded. "You are being very clear, and I am sorry too, both for myself and the situation I am putting you into. Know this, Ambrose. Whatever my feelings may be, and though I shall try to put a veil over them, I may not always succeed in doing so, but no matter my feelings, I will always have the utmost respect for you and your livelihood as the estate manager. Never would I do anything to jeopardise your position here or that of your sister's. Please believe that."

Ambrose inclined his head. "I do, sir."

"So we come to this," declared Daniel. "Could you work with me, knowing how it is I feel, even though you do not have such feelings for me? Again, I tell you. If ever my presence becomes too cumbersome for you, then I will make myself scarce and spend more time elsewhere. I do not wish ever to importune you, Ambrose." Daniel's voice broke on this last word.

Ambrose was not able to withstand it. In a voice thick with emotion, he replied, "I shall be well, sir. Do not worry over me on this matter. We shall strive to find a way to work together."

Daniel stood and held out his hand. "Can we shake on it?"

Ambrose got to his feet too. Slowly, he lifted his hand and let it be gripped in Daniel's strong grasp. A jolt of electricity went through him at the contact. "To working together," said Daniel, "and to becoming friends."

"To working together and becoming friends," agreed Ambrose.

Daniel let go of his hand, picked up his coat and hat, and walked towards the door. "I shall leave you in peace now, Ambrose. Good evening to you."

In peace? That was not at all likely. Ambrose forced a smile on his lips. "Good evening, my lord."

With one final frowning glance at him, Daniel turned and left.

Chapter 14

Daniel

Two weeks later

The day had arrived to say goodbye. Daniel clasped his tearful mama in his arms one last time. She touched his cheek with a trembling hand. "Take care of yourself, my love, and please write as often as you can," she pleaded brokenly.

"I will," he promised.

He felt his father's hand on his shoulder. "It is time. We must go now, Charlotte," Frank Stanton told his wife in a grave voice. His mama nodded and wiped at her wet cheeks. Then, with a last regretful look at her son, she let her husband guide her to the carriage.

The Stantons staying behind in England watched as the rest of their family prepared to leave for America. There were three of them staying—himself, his sister, Isabella, and Grace, who had recently married the curate, Benedict Sedgwick, in rather unseemly haste. As the carriage pulled away, Daniel tucked Isabella into his comforting embrace. She was only nineteen, and now his responsibility, one that he intended to take seriously.

A few weeks ago, soon after the reading of the will, the family had met to decide who was to stay on in England and who was to return to Ohio. Of the four heirs to the Stanton estate, only the youngest, his cousin, Beth Stanton, had elected to return to America. Her new estate of Gorston Manor would be managed on her behalf by himself and Ambrose. The matter of Grace's staying was settled upon her marriage to Benedict, and she had gone to live at her new home, Mulverley Grange. As for Isabella, she had had this to say when asked on the matter, "I wish to stay here and take charge of my estate, with Mr Cranshaw's guidance."

Papa had frowned at this, stating, "You are young and cannot be living alone at Netherwick Hall."

"I am aware of that," had replied Isabella. "However, I can live at Stanton Hall with Daniel until such time as I am old enough to live independently or until I marry. My estate is not ten miles from here, and it should be easy enough to make regular journeys there to visit tenants and ensure the property is well maintained. I mean to take an active role in its management, and I have no wish for anyone to remind me that I am a female. My brain is as good as that of any male in this family."

So, his headstrong sister was now living under his roof at Stanton Hall and taking an active part in the management of her estate. Earlier this week, Ambrose and Daniel had taken her to visit Netherwick Hall, a manor house only a fraction less grand than Stanton Hall. It seemed a shame that it too was lying vacant, its numerous rooms gathering dust. All three had been in agreement that a tenant would need to be found for it soon, with Isabella declaring that she would personally interview prospective candidates—adding, at Daniel's narrowed look, that she would of course do so with Mr Cranshaw's guidance.

And now, with the senior Stantons gone, Daniel was at last in sole charge of his new estate. As he held a weeping Isabella to him, he chanced to look sideways at where Ambrose was standing in respectful silence. Since that humbling interview with him at Ivy Cottage two weeks ago, they had worked together amicably enough. Ambrose had maintained a professional and distant manner with him, never dropping the formality of addressing him as "my lord".

Daniel, for his part, had also strived to act as professionally as possible. Whenever in meetings with Ambrose, he had tried to stay focused on estate business, though of course, his hungry eyes had taken in and catalogued all aspects of Ambrose's fine form—the soft gold of his newly grown whiskers which Daniel longed to stroke, the dark sweep of his eyelashes, the enticing fullness of his lips. With each day, Daniel's feelings grew stronger, not weaker. He was beginning to suspect that this was no passing infatuation, as had been his feelings for Agnes Lowe, but something deeper and far longer lasting. He hoped he was wrong, for he had no wish to condemn himself to years of heartbreak.

There had been times when Daniel caught a look on Ambrose's face that betrayed more emotion than was apparent from his formal manner—a warmth in his gaze and something that could only be described as longing. But on a second glance, that look was quickly gone, and Daniel berated himself for wishful thinking. He had better get over it. Ambrose was not interested sexually or romantically in him, nor, it seemed, in anyone else.

Daniel had made surreptitious enquiries about Ambrose, but there was no gossip hinting at any connection between his estate manager and any female in the village nor in nearby Witney. The man lived the life of a saint, if rumour was to be believed. Could it be that Ambrose was one of those aesthetic beings that felt little need for sexual companionship? Daniel could not be sure. He doubted it somehow. He had seen hints of a passionate nature that one time they had got drunk on sherry together. Maybe it was that Ambrose, for reasons best known to himself, simply repressed those passionate instincts. Daniel's curiosity though, once aroused could not be eradicated. Every chance he got, he studied the man and tried to learn as much as he could about him. He was sure that much of Ambrose's character remained a mystery, skilfully hidden behind a studiously bland façade.

Over the course of the next month, Daniel settled into his new life as master of Stanton Hall. It was a busy time as he worked to acquaint himself with all aspects of his new domain. There was not much socialising to be had either, as the family was still in mourning for his grandfather. For company, he had Isabella, as well as his newly married cousin and her husband, Benedict Sedgwick. They met often for luncheon or dinner, either at Mulverley Grange or Stanton Hall. Often when he and Isabella visited at Mulverley Grange, there too would be Ambrose and his sister, by dint of their close friendship with Benedict.

In the presence of his sister and friend, Ambrose relaxed his formal manner somewhat, teasing and even once going as far as telling a risqué joke. These were convivial gatherings in which Daniel spent much of his time studying Ambrose as discreetly as he could. He had decided that if the village could tell him nothing about him, he would discover more about Ambrose by observing him closely. He learned that Ambrose loved carrots but hated peas with a passion. He gleaned that he had a love for poetry, particularly Tennyson and Keats, that he read modern fiction and classical philosophy, but that he did not much share his sister's passion for science and engineering.

Despite this, Daniel noticed that Ambrose seemed very close to Sarah, much more so than he himself was to Isabella, though of course he loved his sister dearly. The pair were openly affectionate with one another, rather endearingly so. Perhaps, being the other's sole surviving family member had made them cleave to each other more than was usual. Sarah herself, Daniel found refreshingly different in her eccentricity and plain speaking. She was much more of an open book than was her brother.

It made Daniel wish that he could foster a closer relationship with Isabella. Five years her senior, he was accustomed to treating her with the disdain of an older brother, but he resolved to do better, recalling the vow he had made on Grandfather's deathbed that he would never let anything drive a wedge between himself and his family. He would make an effort to talk more with Isabella as an equal rather than as a domineering older brother.

Since Ambrose and Sarah were often present when he visited Mulverley Grange, it became obvious to Daniel that they should be included in the family group whenever they gathered for luncheon or dinner at Stanton Hall. One morning in early February, he broached the subject with Ambrose as they sat going over the latest set of accounts. "Ambrose," he said, "you and Sarah will join us for luncheon here this Sunday."

"Is that an invitation or a request, my lord?" asked Ambrose in a mild voice.

"Both," declared Daniel. "I am inviting you to luncheon with us, but I am also making it clear that I expect you to accept."

"Well in that case, sir, I thank you kindly for the invitation, and in line with your expectations, I accept on behalf of myself and Sarah."

Daniel stretched his long legs out, crossing them at the ankle. "Careful there, Ambrose," he drawled. "I am detecting a trace of insubordination in your tone."

Ambrose raised a brow. "Insubordination? From me? No, my lord, I know too well which side my bread is buttered ever to act insubordinately with you."

"Is that so?" Daniel eyed him speculatively. He had detected a hint of self-mockery in that last remark.

"It is indeed."

"So, if I were to ask you to get on your knees and bow to me as your liege lord, you would do it?" Daniel waited on Ambrose's response with baited breath.

His estate manager gazed at him expressionlessly. "I am not one for speculation, sir," he said evenly.

Daniel straightened up in his chair, his body tensing with anticipation. "Then let us move from the realm of speculation to an actual order," he said softly. "Ambrose, kneel down before me now and bow your head."

He watched in fascination as Ambrose hesitated. His alabaster complexion turned a shade of pink, and there was a fiery burn to the smoky grey of his eyes. Then, with a stubborn tilt to his mouth, Ambrose stood, took two steps towards where he sat, and in one fluid movement, sank to his knees, head bowed. Daniel caught his breath. In the heavy silence that ensued, he felt the pounding of his heart in his chest and the thickening of his groin. Ambrose looked regal, even in this subordinate position. Daniel wanted him then, with a visceral intensity that had his body trembling.

He stood abruptly and approached Ambrose. His breaths heaved in his chest as he stared down at the bowed head that was level with his thickly engorged groin. For a few tantalising instants, he fantasised about freeing his cock from his trousers and ordering Ambrose to put his mouth to it.

His hand crept down to his groin and squeezed his aching shaft through the material of his trousers. It was at such an angle as to be nearly visible to Ambrose's downturned eyes. All it would take was one pull of the drawstring of his trousers and his cock would be free. He breathed heavily, trying to recollect himself. In a voice thick with desire, he grunted, "I shall see you and Sarah here for luncheon on Sunday." And with that, he left the room hurriedly, striding past a startled footman and rushing up the stairs.

Once in his room, he shut the door behind him and turned the lock. Leaning against the door, he finally freed his throbbing cock from his trousers. Then, spitting onto his hand for lubrication, he began to rub himself with wild abandon. He came not long afterwards with a deep groan, streams of his pearly ejaculate dripping onto the polished wooden floor. When he was done, he closed his eyes in relief and guilt. What had he been thinking? Never again should he play such dangerous games with Ambrose. He would lose each and every time.

Chapter 15

Ambrose

Ambrose heard the door close and let out the breath he had been holding. Dear God, that had been intense. He stayed a moment longer in his bowed position remembering the sight of Daniel's big, strong hand clutching at his very obviously erect penis through his trousers. For a moment, Ambrose had been convinced that Daniel was about to free it from the confines of his clothes and offer it to him. And if he had, dear Lord but he did not think he would have been capable of saying no.

His hand slid to his own straining erection. He gripped it tight and then forced himself to let go. Slowly, he came to his feet and walked to the door, leaning his forehead against it while he tried to bring that unruly part of his body under control. It was no good. His mind could not stop replaying the scene that had just taken place. In a frenzy of need, he unbuttoned his trousers and released his shaft from its confines. Spitting quickly into his palm, he began to stroke himself violently, emitting a soft groan when shortly after, he showered the wood floor with his seed.

He stood, leaned against the door, for what seemed an eternity, eyes unfocused as he slowly returned to his senses. Then, gazing in horror at the mess he had made, he set about cleaning himself up and the floor using a large handkerchief from his pocket. Once he was done, he returned to the desk and tidied up the papers, putting everything away neatly. Then, very quietly, he let himself out of Daniel's study and made his way down the stairs. He smiled at Siddons with a calmness he did not feel, put on his coat and hat, then left Stanton Hall to return to his home.

Next morning, Ambrose woke from a troubled sleep feeling tired and fractious. His throat ached and his head throbbed. It was a Saturday, thankfully, which meant he did not have to go out to work. He dressed and came down to the breakfast table, where his sister sat, drinking a cup of tea. "Good morning," Sarah said cheerfully. Then she took a good look at him. "Ambrose, did you not sleep well? You are looking rather haggard," she said with concern knotting her brow.

"I am afraid not," he said in a raspy voice. "Do pour me some of that hot tea, Sarah. My throat is parched."

She did so quickly, and he took it from her with a grateful smile. "I am sure it is nothing," he said after taking a refreshing sip. "However, I think I will spend a quiet day in today. Do you mind very much if I do not join you on your trip to Witney?"

"No, I think you had better stay home," replied his sister with a frown. "I will stop by at the apothecary and buy you a throat remedy."

"Do make my apologies to Mr and Mrs Phipps," he told her. The village draper and his wife were always kind enough to make space in their carriage for them on their expeditions to nearby Witney. Ambrose remembered to ask Sarah if she could also shop for a birthday gift for Edwin to take with him when next he went to Oxford. "Oh and before I forget," he added, "we are invited to luncheon at Stanton Hall tomorrow."

"How lovely!" smiled Sarah, her enthusiasm for the invitation far greater than his. He did not quite know how he was to face Daniel again after yesterday's antics.

A half-hour later, the Phipps carriage stopped by to pick up Sarah, on its way to town. Ambrose spent a quiet day alone, resting, reading and thinking about what had happened the previous day. On further reflection, he decided he had been at fault. He should not have risen to Daniel's bait and dropped to his knees at his command. It would have been quite possible to have responded in a reasonable manner that such a command was beneath both of their dignities and left it at that. But instead of doing that, he had let the devil ride his back and provoked Daniel by brazenly following his improper order. When would he learn the lesson when it came to Daniel Stanton? It seemed he never could disobey the man when he was near him. But it was more imperative than ever that he remain on his guard.

Later that afternoon, Sarah returned, laden with her purchases. For Edwin, she had found a delightful zoetrope, which he hoped the boy would enjoy. No sooner did she arrive than she had Elsie prepare the remedy she had got for Ambrose from the apothecary, a distasteful herbal infusion which he drank obediently. It did help a little to soothe his throat which by now was on fire. He hoped the night would bring about a recovery in his health. It did not.

The following morning, a Sunday, he woke feeling even worse than the previous day. With an effort he dragged himself out of bed and dressed for church. He ignored Sarah's protests that he should stay abed, drinking another fortifying if unpleasant brew of the herbal remedy. "I shall be very well," he declared. "Stop fussing, Sarah." Wrapping himself in a thick scarf, coat and hat, he managed the short walk to the church, and then also managed to endure the duration of the service—though he probably did not listen with his usual attention to his friend Benedict's sermon.

Once the service was over, they were joined by Daniel and Isabella Stanton, who offered them a ride in the carriage, given that they were all going to Stanton Hall for their luncheon. Throughout the ride, Ambrose felt the weight of Daniel's eyes on him, but he could not bring himself to meet that dark gaze. At Stanton Hall, they were ushered into the drawing room, where shortly after their arrival, Benedict and Grace Sedgwick were shown inside.

Ambrose tried to follow the conversation, smiling when appropriate, responding to simple enquiries, but otherwise not joining much in the conversation. Still, he felt those dark eyes on him. They adjourned to the dining table and were served an elaborate meal, though Ambrose ate little of it. Sweat gathered at his brow. Conversely, he felt a bone deep chill. Fever, he realised. The influenza. He took a fortifying breath as a sponge pudding was placed before him. He need only endure another half-hour of this at most, and then he could make his excuses and leave. With a hand that shook, he picked up the spoon and cut through the pudding on his plate. However, he could not bring himself to lift the spoon and bring it to his lips. He simply stared at it in dizzy confusion.

"That is enough!" said an angry voice across from him. "Ambrose, I am taking you home now. Siddons, fetch the carriage please."

"Yes, my lord."

He felt a hand at his shoulder. The same voice spoke, more gently this time. "Can you stand, Ambrose, if I help you?"

It was Daniel. And Sarah was there too, at his other side. "Mmm," mumbled Ambrose. With an effort he tried to get to his feet. He felt Daniel and Sarah supporting his weight, assisting him to stand. He swayed, but a hand held him firm.

"I have you," said Daniel's voice. "Lean on me. It is but a short walk to the front door."

Ambrose felt he should say something, apologise for the spectacle he was making of himself. "S-sorry," he managed to say indistinctly.

"Do not apologise," rasped Daniel. "You are sick, Ambrose, and we need to take you home."

"Yes," was all Ambrose could say. They made their painfully slow way to the door. With Sarah's help, he was bundled into his coat, and then once more, he felt those strong hands supporting him as they negotiated the steps down. Each step felt like agony to his pounding head, but somehow, they made it to the waiting carriage below. Strong hands helped him inside. He supposed he should say some words of farewell. "Bye," he slurred.

That voice again, this time with a hint of amusement. "No point saying goodbye, Ambrose, as I am coming with you. Here, lean on me." It was with relief that Ambrose let his head loll sideways onto a wide shoulder. He breathed in the faint scent of tobacco and lemony cologne.

"Mmm," he mumbled close to Daniel's ear. "Smell nice."

He felt Daniel's shoulder shake briefly with laughter. "I am glad," he whispered back.

Then the carriage was moving at a swift pace. The journey was not long, no more than two or three minutes at most. They came to a halt, and the carriage door sprung open. Ambrose heard Sarah's familiar voice saying, "I shall go ahead and open the door."

Then Daniel was once again helping him to stand and descend from the carriage. "That's it, Ambrose. Lean on me. I have enough strength for the both of us," he grunted reassuringly. Somehow, they made it into the house, then up the short flight of stairs. Daniel walked him to his bedchamber. Sarah was already there, turning down the bed covers.

"Thank you, Sarah," he heard Daniel say. "I can take it from here. Is there a hot broth that you can prepare for him?"

"I shall go down now and have it made."

"Thank you." The door closed behind her, and he felt Daniel lead him towards the bed. With relief he collapsed onto it. "Woah, wait up, Ambrose," came Daniel's voice. "We need to get you out of these clothes first. Let us start with your shoes." Hands tugged at his shoes, then pulled at his stockings. Once these were gone, he felt those hands untie the drawstrings of his trousers. "Can you lift yourself up a bit while I pull these off?"

Ambrose grunted a reply and lifted his hips a fraction. The trousers were quickly snatched away. "I will need you to sit up now, Ambrose, so that we may take off your coat," said Daniel. Strong hands once again hauled him upright. He swayed but managed to stay sitting. The most beautiful dark eyes in the world crinkled up at him. "Good man," Daniel said approvingly. "Let me take off your coat and jacket." Swiftly, the coat was removed, then the jacket was unbuttoned and pulled off each arm. Hands came back to undo his necktie and the buttons of his shirt.

"I have dreamed of undressing you countless times, Ambrose, but I must confess it was never in such circumstances," came Daniel's amused voice.

Somehow, Ambrose mustered the power of speech. "Enjoy it while you can. Won't happen again."

The tinkle of Daniel's laughter warmed his shivery body. The shirt was off. Now all he had on were his underthings. He hoped Daniel would have enough decency to stop there. It seemed he did, for his next question was, "Where is your night shirt?"

"Over there." Ambrose pointed to a chest at the end of his bed. Daniel went to it and withdrew the night shirt, bringing it back to him.

As he pulled it over his head, Daniel murmured, "It is a shame to cover up such a lovely body."

"Do not call me lovely," Ambrose grumbled then added the thought that flitted through his woozy mind. "Do you think I have a handsome body?"

"You, my dear, are quite beautiful," affirmed Daniel in a gruff voice. Ambrose's arms were tucked into the shirt and then it was pulled down to his waist. He felt Daniel's smile. "I will turn around now and give you privacy while you pull your underpants off. Then you can get under the covers." With that, he turned and presented his back to him.

As quickly as he could, Ambrose removed his undergarments and tucked the nightshirt down to his knees. He swung his legs onto the bed and brought his weary head down to his pillow. Gentle hands tucked the covers around him. His eyes drooped closed, and he did not have the strength to open them again. Something cold and damp touched his brow. "You are hot to the touch," spoke Daniel quietly. "We need to cool you down."

Ambrose grunted an indistinct reply. There came a knock on the door, and he heard Sarah's low voice. "Here is some broth for you, my love. Can you sit up just for a short while?"

Once more, Daniel's strong hands helped him up. He leaned tiredly against the headboard of his bed but then began to sway again. "I will hold him up," said Daniel. An arm came around his shoulder, helping him remain upright.

He heard the clatter of crockery as Sarah came to sit beside him, a small tray propped on the bed. "Open up, my love," she instructed. With an effort, he opened his eyes and let her feed him the broth. When he had taken half of it, he bade her stop.

"No more," he croaked.

She sighed. "Very well. Get some sleep now, my love."

Daniel's comforting arm moved from around him, and he felt its loss. He was helped back to a supine position on the bed and the covers tucked around him. He shivered. Daniel's voice came again from somewhere on his left. "He needs to be sponged down regularly to keep his body from overheating."

"Yes," said Sarah. "Let me take this tray back down and I shall come straight back to do it."

"No, Sarah," said Daniel firmly. "I will stay with him for now. We can take it in turns until his fever breaks."

Sarah hesitated. "Viscount Stanton, you have done enough already. We cannot impose."

"Enough with the formality, Sarah," growled Daniel irritably. "He is my friend, and I will help you care for him. Now you go rest and come back in a few hours."

"Very well." Ambrose felt Sarah kiss his clammy cheek. "I will go now, my love, but Daniel will stay and look out for you. I will be back soon. Get some sleep."

Ambrose grunted, "Hmm."

The door shut behind Sarah, and the cool cloth returned to his brow, his cheek, his neck. Ambrose forced his eyes open. "Thank you," he mumbled.

"Shh, do not talk," chided Daniel.

Ambrose ignored the instruction. "So, I am your friend now?" he enquired.

"Of course." Then, he caught the whisper he was probably not meant to hear, "Much more than a friend."

"Yes," breathed Ambrose dazedly. With the comforting presence of someone who had come to be much more than a friend, he felt himself drift off to sleep.

Chapter 16

Daniel

He came awake slowly, his body stiff from being in an armchair that did little to accommodate his tall form. The fire in the hearth had died down, and he shivered in the chill of the February morning. Daniel stretched his arms above his head and opened his sleepy eyes. Tendrils of light came through the gaps in the curtain, signalling the beginning of day. He had come to relieve Sarah from her vigil by her brother's bedside some time just after midnight, which meant he had been here, in this damned uncomfortable armchair, for close on six hours.

With consciousness returning, his eyes sought out Ambrose. He was asleep, breathing regularly in and out. Daniel reached a tender hand to feel his brow. It was still warm with fever, but not quite as hot as the previous day. After bringing Ambrose home from yesterday's luncheon, Daniel had sat with him for hours, trying to cool his heated body down with a cold compress.

Ambrose had been restless in his fevered delirium, tossing in his sleep, batting away the hands tending to him. His nightshirt had gotten sodden with sweat until finally, Daniel had taken it off him. Then, he had set about sponging down his upper body with a cool cloth. It seemed to have brought Ambrose relief, for by the time Sarah came back some hours later, he had fallen into a more restful sleep.

She had bade Daniel to eat a light supper laid out on the dining table for him, then sent him to rest in the guest bedchamber. He had done so only on the promise that she would come wake him when it was his turn to take over the vigil by Ambrose's bedside. She had been as good as her word, waking him shortly after midnight. Since then, Daniel had been here, in this lumpy armchair, watching over Ambrose.

The fever had continued to rage throughout the night. Daniel had tried his best to ease it with a cool wet cloth, occasionally feeding Ambrose a little of the broth. It seemed to help. At one time, Ambrose had woken, needing the chamber pot. Daniel had brought it to him, helping Ambrose to a sitting position so he could do his business. There had been no thought of modesty in that moment of need, not that Daniel had seen much in the dim light of the fire in the hearth. Ambrose had settled down to sleep after this, and so had Daniel, until he woke just now. Tired and stiff as he was, there was no other place he had wanted to be last night than at Ambrose's side.

There came a light knock on the door and the maid, Elsie, came in. With a shy smile, she brought in some fresh broth and laid it on the bedside table, then took the soiled chamber pot away. She returned a few minutes later and placed a clean pot under the bed. She paused at the door on her way out and whispered, "Will you be needing anything else, sir?"

Daniel shook his head with a smile. "No, thank you," he said as quietly as he could. She left then, closing the door with a gentle click. However, the light noise was enough to wake Ambrose from his sleep. His eyelids fluttered open, and he stared at Daniel for a long moment, his gaze confused at first until understanding of his predicament came to him.

"H-how…" He cleared his throat and tried again. "How long have you been here?"

"Never you mind. Do you think you can sit up and drink some broth?"

Ambrose nodded. With an effort, he brought himself to a sitting position and took the broth Daniel handed to him, indicating quite clearly that he wished to drink it without help. Daniel watched him take the drink with trembling hands, at the ready in case he needed to catch the small bowl, but Ambrose managed to drink the whole thing without spilling a drop. Once he was done, Daniel took the empty bowl from him and assisted Ambrose back into a lying position on the bed.

"You do not need to stay, my lord," he protested feebly. "I shall be fine."

"Yes, you shall," agreed Daniel, "but I will stay until Sarah comes in."

Ambrose did not argue further, exhaustion catching up with him once more. From his armchair beside the bed, Daniel watched him take each breath in and out. There were dark shadows under Ambrose's eyes, and the usually soft skin of his lips was dry and cracked. And still, he was the most beautiful man he had ever seen. Daniel's mouth curved in a sad smile. There was no doubting his affections now. He was well and truly in love with this man. How he was to conduct the rest of his life, knowing he loved Ambrose but was not loved back, he could not fathom yet, and he was too weary to ponder the matter. He yawned sleepily. Time would tell.

Shortly after, Sarah came in, looking fresh and rested. She took one look at his tired, dishevelled appearance and ordered him to go home. Daniel did not argue. He had learned by now that Ambrose's sister could be quite fiery when she got the bit between her teeth. He needed to go home in any case, to wash and change. Furthermore, he knew that to stay on would begin to invite unwanted attention and the sort of gossip that Ambrose shied away from.

Daniel stood and threw one last glance at the man he loved. Ambrose was over the worst, he thought, although there was still a long road to recovery. He would go home now and return later in the day to look in on him. Giving what was probably a weak smile at Sarah, he took his leave.

Over the next three days, Daniel was a regular caller at Ivy Cottage. He did not stay longer than propriety required, merely long enough to check on the patient's progress. On the third day, he was told in no uncertain terms by Ambrose that there was no longer any need for him to visit. "While I appreciate the kindness of your concern," he stated, "I do not think, my lord, that my condition warrants any further imposition on your time. In fact, I believe I shall be well enough to return to my duties tomorrow."

"You will do no such thing!" said Daniel sharply.

Ambrose relented. "Very well," he said, his voice still hoarse. "I shall work from my home the rest of the week and return to my duties on Monday."

"As you wish." Daniel stood to go, adding, "I shall see you at church on Sunday, if you are well enough to go. There is luncheon too at Stanton Hall if you feel up to it."

Ambrose inclined his head. "Thank you, my lord. I shall see you then."

Daniel grimaced at the continued use of "my lord" to address him. It felt out of place, given he had spent a whole night with this man in this very bedchamber, tending to him like a babe. But he let it pass. He knew by now that it was Ambrose's way of trying to keep the appropriate employer to employee distance between them—or, more likely, to keep his amorous advances at bay. If only Ambrose knew the truth. Daniel was not the hunter here, but the prey. For it was Ambrose that had pierced his heart, irrevocably marking him, not the other way around.

Chapter 17

Daniel

On Sunday morning, Daniel waited impatiently in the hallway of his house. "What can be taking her so long?" he asked Siddons irritably. The butler made a noncommittal response. It was another few minutes before Isabella finally made her appearance, making her way down the stairs to where her brother stood scowling at her.

"What is it?" she asked in surprise.

"You are going to make us late for church," he ground out. If he was not careful, Ambrose would decide to walk there instead of going in the carriage as he had suggested.

"No I am not," Isabella protested. "And in any case, since when do you care? It is not as if we will lose our pew seats if we are a few minutes late."

"Come along now," he chivvied. "There is no time to argue the matter." He escorted her to the waiting carriage, calling out to the coachman, "Please make a stop first at Ivy Cottage."

They set off and halted by the front gate of his estate manager's cottage not a few minutes later. Daniel quickly descended and knocked at the door. When no response came, he bit back a curse. Ambrose and Sarah must have already left for church and gone on foot. Rage and hurt burned in his breast at the stubbornness of the man. With an irritated huff, he returned to the carriage, resuming their journey to church.

On arrival, he cast his glance around the hall and located Ambrose, sitting straight as a rod in his pew a few rows back from where the Stanton family sat. He looked pale and wan. Damn him, he should have kept to his bed.

Throughout the service, Daniel paid little heed to Benedict's sermon, fine though he was sure it must be. Finally, when it was over, he stood, intent on reaching his wayward estate manager. However, he was accosted by this person and that, all vying for his attention now that he was Viscount Stanton and master of Stanton Hall. Lord, how tiresome people could be. It was all he could do to respond civilly to the enquiries and good wishes. By the time he had finally extricated himself, Ambrose and Sarah were nowhere in sight. "They must have gone on foot," said Isabella, stating the obvious.

"Come on, Bella," he said hurriedly. "Let us see if we can catch them up." There were some worrying dark clouds overhead. The last thing Ambrose needed was to get caught in a rain shower.

In haste, they climbed into the waiting carriage and proceeded on their way to Stanton Hall, Daniel keeping a sharp lookout through the window for two lone figures walking along the road. A minute later, he spotted them. "Stop the carriage," he called out to the coachman. As soon as it ground to a halt, he jumped out and strode towards the Cranshaws, his worry turning to righteous fury.

"What do you mean by this, Ambrose?" he demanded.

"If you could elucidate what 'this' is alluding to, my lord, I would be happy to explain myself," responded Ambrose mildly.

"Do not 'my lord' me, and you know perfectly well what this is about," thundered Daniel.

"Perhaps you mean me to explain why my sister and I are walking towards Stanton Hall. I believe it is because you have invited us to dine there," said Ambrose smoothly.

Daniel narrowed his eyes in annoyance. "What I wish you to explain, Ambrose, is why you are traipsing around in what is soon to be a rain storm, when there is a perfectly good carriage to take us all to Stanton Hall."

As Ambrose went to answer him, he held up a hand. "Later, Ambrose. Let us not tarry in the middle of the road." Remembering his manners, he bowed to Sarah, then hurriedly ushered the both of them into the carriage. For the remainder of the journey, Daniel battled to keep his anger in check, especially when Ambrose broke into a continued fit of coughing. Damn the man for being so stubborn. He should have stayed in bed.

As soon as they reached their destination, Daniel was once more out of the carriage like a shot, going to confer with Siddons, asking him to have a warm fire going in the main parlour, which was less draughty than the drawing room, and requesting a ginger and honey infusion from the kitchen for Ambrose to drink. Only then did he return and escort his guests into the house.

When they reached the main parlour, he made sure Ambrose sat in the armchair closest to the fireplace. Soon after, a servant came bearing the ginger infusion. Ambrose took it and for the first time that day, cast his eyes towards him. He held the drink up in his hand and inclined his head with a shy, grateful smile. Daniel felt the fury finally ebb from him at that smile. My God, he loved this man. There could be no doubting it anymore. On the back of that thought, came another, much less salubrious in nature. He was bloody well done for. He could not think of a less coarse way to describe his predicament.

What on earth was he to do with these unwanted feelings? Live with them, he supposed, and keep busy. "*I must lose myself in action, lest I wither in despair,*" thought Daniel, remembering a line from a Tennyson poem. He had taken to reading Tennyson, and Keats too, now that he knew they were a favourite with Ambrose. Was there no end to what he would do for the man?

Luncheon was served. They were joined by Grace and Benedict Sedgwick together with an unexpected further guest, Walter Sedgwick, Benedict's father. Ambrose and Sarah greeted him warmly, like some long lost family member. Over the course of the meal, conversation was cheerful and lively, but Daniel kept mostly to himself, busy as he was watching over Ambrose like a hawk. The only time he contributed to the discussion was when he heard Ambrose say, "I was supposed to go to Oxford last Thursday, but I was unfortunately taken sick. I shall have to go this coming week instead."

"I will go with you," stated Daniel firmly.

Ambrose hesitated a fraction, no doubt seeking some sort of excuse. Then, he gave a faint smile. "Of course, my lord."

Quite clearly, his estate manager was still reluctant to have his company on the journey. Well, damn it, Daniel was tired of tiptoeing around the man. He wanted to go and acquaint himself with this house in Oxford that he now owned and to make himself known to his bankers. He had every justification for going on this trip.

Later that afternoon, after the Sedgwicks had taken their leave, the remaining members of the group sat in the main parlour again, drinking tea and conversing desultorily. From where he sat, Daniel noticed Ambrose's eyes droop shut. A minute or two later, his even breathing was proof that Ambrose had fallen fast asleep in his snug armchair by the fire. Sarah had noticed too. She went as if to wake him, but Daniel stopped her and said softly, "Let him be for now. There is no rush for you to get back, surely."

"Well, if we are to walk back, then we should be going before it begins to get dark."

"You will be taking the carriage," said Daniel in a voice that brooked no disagreement.

"In that case," murmured Sarah, "we can stay a short time longer. Perhaps I can peruse the books in the library while Ambrose rests."

So it was that Sarah went up to the library while he and Isabella sat quietly in the parlour, each with a book to read. Though Daniel did not manage to make much progress with the worthy tome in his hands. His eyes strayed far too often towards the sleeping man at his side. In sleep, Ambrose looked so much younger than his twenty-nine years, and more vulnerable. It tugged at something in Daniel's heart. He was truly in the grip of this ailment called love, he thought sardonically, but he must repress the emotion.

Finally, some minutes later, Ambrose stirred and woke with a start. A flush came over his face as he realised he had fallen asleep in the midst of company. He sat up, saying quickly, "Apologies, my lord, but I think we had best be on our way home." He looked around for his sister. "Where is Sarah?" he asked.

"In the library, choosing a book," replied Isabella helpfully.

Ambrose made to stand, but Daniel stayed him. "Do not trouble yourself. I will go fetch her," he said. He had an ulterior motive for finding Sarah and speaking in private with her, for he had just remembered something. A letter had arrived from America addressed in Benjamin's unmistakable scrawl, addressed to Sarah Cranshaw. He was still not sure what was going on between his brother and Sarah, but his protective instincts were out in force.

With quickness of step, he made his way up to the library. He found Sarah reading in an armchair by the window and informed her that Ambrose wished to return home. "Before we go down, Sarah, I have something for you," he said, fishing

Benjamin's letter out of his pocket. She took it with evident pleasure. Giving in to his curiosity, he could not help but wonder out loud about the nature of her relationship with his brother.

"We are friends. That is all. Is that so very unusual?" Sarah raised a brow in response.

Ah, friends. Just as he and Ambrose were "friends". Or maybe he was being too much of a cynic, and it truly was a platonic relationship.

Together, they made their way down to where Ambrose waited patiently in the hallway, coat and hat already on. Daniel directed a stern glance towards him. "You are still not back to full health, Ambrose, and do not argue with me on this. Until we leave for Oxford on Thursday, you are to stay in your house and do your work from there. I will ensure whatever documents you need are sent to you."

"My lord—" began Ambrose, but Daniel would hear none of it.

"I said do not argue with me. Now go. I shall pick you up in the carriage bright and early on Thursday morning."

"Of course, sir." Ambrose inclined his head, then with Sarah on his arm, took his leave.

Chapter 18

Daniel

February 1861

On an overcast and drizzly morning the following Thursday, as promised, Daniel arrived at Ivy Cottage in the Stanton carriage. Ambrose was ready and waiting for him. He climbed aboard and slipped his travelling case in the space under the seat. Daniel observed him closely for any sign of illness, but he looked back to his usual health. To be sure, he enquired, "Are you well, Ambrose?"

"Never better," smiled his estate manager.

Daniel's relief was palpable. He had been more worried about Ambrose than he realised. The carriage began its rattling journey towards Oxford, a journey which would take around two hours to complete. They accomplished the first half-hour in companiable silence, each deep in thought. Finally, Daniel spoke. "So tell me, Ambrose, what is the plan for our visit to Oxford?"

"First, we shall stop by at the Old Bank on the High Street," said Ambrose. "It is the nickname given to the bank of Parsons, Thomson & Parsons. I have already written to Mr Thomson, informing him that we shall be paying him a visit today, so he should be expecting us. He is the grandson of the founder of the bank, and a man of integrity. Last I met him, he expressed his great wish to make your acquaintance."

"I see," responded Daniel. "But correct me if I am wrong, our family does not bank our funds solely with this establishment."

"You are quite right, my lord," concurred Ambrose. "The Stantons also have many investments held with Barings Bank and other business ventures in London. However, Mr Thomson's bank plays an important role, since the rents from your land are paid there directly each month upon my visits. Then, twice a year, usually in April and October, the late earl travelled to London and took some of these funds from the bank, in the form of letters of credit, and made new investments with them there. Mr Ridley's firm advised him as to the best manner of investing those funds." Observing Daniel enquiringly, he added, "The late earl also used such visits to take his seat in the House of Lords. Perhaps you may wish to follow suit, my lord?"

Daniel sighed. "I suppose so, though I am not acquainted with anyone in London, nor do I know much of the proceedings of the House of Lords. I suppose I shall have to learn." It was a sign of how at ease he was with Ambrose that he could confide something of the vulnerability he felt at having been thrust into this elevated social position. So great were the recent changes to his situation in life that even someone as naturally confident as Daniel felt at times overwhelmed.

"Your father and your grandfather were members of White's, and I believe the membership has passed on to you, my lord," said Ambrose with a sympathetic smile. "I do not know much about these things either, not being part of their rarefied circles, but I believe you may make the required social connections at this renowned club."

Daniel scratched the stubble on his jaw, grunting in irritation, "And now, Ambrose, you have successfully put me off wanting to go to London at all." At length, he added, "I shall be the curiosity, the outsider from America trying to fit into the ways and rituals of the upper crust of society."

"I am sorry for it," replied Ambrose, not sounding much chastened. If there was one thing Daniel had learned about Ambrose, it was that he gave short shrift to the trivial concerns of people placed much higher than him in society. "Do not forget that you are a member of that upper crust by right," Ambrose went on. "If I may hazard a suggestion, Mr Templeton, whom you have met, is also a member of White's and travels to London on regular occasions. Perhaps, he may assist you in the way of introductions."

Daniel sat up and smiled. "Mr Templeton! Such a charming, amiable fellow. Good thinking, Ambrose. That is just the thing. I shall go pay him a visit on our return." He paused suddenly and fixed his narrowed gaze on Ambrose. Was that a displeased frown he had detected just now on his estate manager's face? "That is," he added slowly, "if you do not mind."

All expression was ironed out of Ambrose's face. He returned his gaze with limpid grey eyes. "Why should I mind, my lord? Did I not suggest it to you?"

"Yes, of course," murmured Daniel, lounging back in his seat with an unexpected thrill of delight. That sour look had crossed Ambrose's face just as he had said that Mr Templeton was a charming, amiable fellow. Could Ambrose be jealous? Surely not! Besides, Mr Templeton was a handsome, charming man, but he could not hold a candle to Ambrose. Though if he were feeling jealous, then this would indicate that there was hope after all.

Daniel spent the rest of the journey in a cheerful mood, his thoughts much uplifted by the possibility, a slim one to be sure, that Ambrose was beginning to reciprocate his feelings. They reached Oxford shortly after eleven o'clock and made their way directly to the bank, where much fuss was made of Daniel's visit. He was introduced to the partners at Parsons, Thomson &

Parsons and plied with refreshments while Ambrose completed the business of paying in the Stanton land rents.

Once this business was done, they returned to their carriage, but Ambrose did not join him. "If you will excuse me, my lord," he said, "I will walk down the High Street to complete various errands which are of no interest to you—ordering paper and ink and some other such things. Please do go on to the townhouse without me. I shall join you there within the hour."

Daniel was not pleased. He did not yet want to end this companiable time he was having with Ambrose. "I can accompany you on these errands," he remonstrated.

"No, no, there is no need to trouble yourself, my lord." Ambrose was already striding away as he said these words.

Daniel stared after him in annoyance. He considered following him, then decided against it. He was travel weary and wanted an opportunity to refresh himself. He would see Ambrose again soon enough. With a grumpy sigh, he bade the coachman begin the short journey to St Michael's Street, where his house was located. He was curious to see it.

It did not take long to get there. Soon, the carriage stopped in front of an elegant brick house in the Georgian style. Daniel jumped down eagerly and went to ring the doorbell while the coachman brought out the cases. The door was opened by an elderly looking butler who stared at him enquiringly for a few seconds before breaking into a beaming smile. "My lord," he said. "You have such a look of your father that I would have recognised you anywhere. I am Briggs. Please do come in, sir, we have been expecting you."

He ushered Daniel into a surprisingly large hallway adorned with a large portrait of his grandfather on one side and a gilded mirror on the other, above a feature marble fireplace. "Good day, Briggs. It is good to be here," replied Daniel jovially, handing over his coat and hat.

Briggs looked expectantly behind him. "Mr Cranshaw does not accompany you, my lord?" he enquired.

"Yes, he does. He has some errands to complete and shall join us shortly," answered Daniel. "In the meantime, I would be grateful if you could show me to my room and send some water up."

"Of course, my lord. Do follow me."

Briggs guided Daniel up the polished mahogany staircase to a room on the first floor. It was a pleasant bedchamber decorated in shades of blue, the curtains pulled back and a slight breeze from the window showing it had recently been aired. Briggs preceded him into the room and shut the window, saying, "There is water already in the jug, my lord. Please do come down to the drawing room whenever you are ready, and I shall have Mrs Briggs, who is the housekeeper here, prepare some light refreshment for you."

"Thank you, Briggs," said Daniel.

Once the door had shut behind the butler, Daniel availed himself of the commode in the dressing room, then poured water from the jug into a nearby basin, bathing his hands and face. Feeling much more refreshed, he went downstairs some minutes later and found his way to the drawing room. There, a tray of tea and finely cut sandwiches awaited him. He poured himself a cup, blessing the invisible Mrs Briggs, and placed a sandwich on his plate. He had barely taken his first sip when the door burst open and a female voice called out, "Ambrose, you are finally here! I have been waiting an age for you."

The owner of the voice stopped short upon seeing not Ambrose, but himself sitting in the drawing room. "Oh," she said, blushing furiously. "I beg your pardon. I—I believe you must be Viscount Stanton."

Good manners had brought Daniel to his feet though he was not best pleased with this interruption. Who was this female who claimed she had been waiting an age for Ambrose? It was his turn today to feel the pinpricks of jealousy. He stared down at her from his impressive height, wearing a look of hauteur he had perfected from observing his own father. "I am indeed Viscount Stanton. And who do I have the privilege of addressing?"

The lady curtsied awkwardly then replied, "I am Mrs Forbes, my lord. Mrs William Forbes."

The name meant nothing to him. Again, he wondered who this woman was who swanned into his house as if she had a right to be here and made free with Ambrose's name. He had to ask. "Mrs Forbes, pardon me for the question, but what brings you to my house?"

If anything, she blushed some more. She was not a beauty but neither was she plain. Her brown eyes were finely drawn and shone with a lively intelligence in a face blessed with a clear, rosy complexion. He judged her to be in her late twenties or early thirties, and she was obviously a lady of quality—her green muslin gown, while not cut in the latest style, was well made and flattered her gracefully rounded figure.

"You may ask of course," she said with a nervous smile. "Mine is the house next door to this one. Please forgive my rude entrance just now. I am well acquainted with the Cranshaws, you see, from when they lived in this house. And of course, I am well used to Mr Cranshaw's visits here. When I saw the Stanton carriage outside, I assumed that it was he in here."

Daniel frowned. "I did not hear the doorbell ring."

Mrs Forbes looked even more awkward, if that was possible. "Umm, I came through the back door," she explained.

"And is it usual for your good self to have the run of my house by use of the back door?" asked Daniel frostily.

"I—I..." she stammered helplessly. She took a deep breath and tried again. "Mr and Mrs Briggs are getting on in age, and

I am in the habit of looking in on them—out of neighbourly duty."

"I see," said Daniel dryly. "In that case, I do appreciate your neighbourly duty." They were still standing and belatedly, he remembered his manners. "Please do take a seat, Mrs Forbes."

She hesitated, then with a slight nod of her head, sank into a nearby chair. By now, she had gathered her composure enough to be able to enquire, "If I may ask, is Mr Cranshaw also accompanying you on this visit, my lord?"

"He is," said Daniel shortly.

She appeared to be too happy at Daniel's answer to notice his irritation. "Mr Cranshaw, being an old friend, is in the habit of dining with us whenever he is in town," she explained. "I do hope, my lord, that you will both do me the honour of joining us for dinner this evening."

"I look forward to it," answered Daniel with polite caution, "and to making the acquaintance of Mr William Forbes."

"Ah, well you see, umm, Mr Forbes is not in residence at present. Dinner will be a small affair with just myself and my son, Edwin."

Her husband was not in residence, but she was in the habit of dining alone with Ambrose, notwithstanding the presence of some infant son. Daniel did not like the sound of this. He did not like it at all. He refused, however, to betray any emotion. With exaggerated politeness, he said, "In that case, I look forward to making the acquaintance of Master Edwin Forbes." Now that was a lie. He had no interest whatsoever in spending time with children that were no relation to him.

Seemingly unaware of his thoughts, she beamed a bright smile. "He is but seven years of age, nearly eight, but very well behaved, I assure you. And he is so very excited to see his Uncle Ambrose again—that is what he calls Mr Cranshaw," she added confidingly.

Daniel ground his teeth and pressed his lips into a firm line. It was an effort to keep the grimace off his face. Uncle Ambrose indeed. What was it with all this excess of familiarity? He did not like where his thoughts were leading him.

Mrs Forbes stood then to excuse herself. "It was an honour to make your acquaintance, Viscount Stanton. Good day for now. We dine early, at five o'clock."

"Good day, Mrs Forbes," he answered crisply. He got to his feet and made to escort her out, but she stayed him with a gesture of her hand.

"No need to see me out, my lord. I shall make my way back the way I came, through the rear entrance." She grinned. It appeared her good humour had returned after the initial shock of their meeting. He was pleased that at least she had not noticed whatever feelings of jealousy he had just been experiencing. An instant later, she had flitted out, closing the door gently behind her.

Daniel stood staring at the door, but he had little time to ponder this strange encounter because the doorbell rang at just that moment. He heard Briggs walk stiffly towards the door to open it and then Ambrose's pleasant tones as he greeted the butler. The turbulence in Daniel's breast was soothed by the sound of that voice. It was melodious and comforting, like the gentle ripple of water lapping upon a sandy shore. Daniel's lips curved into a pleased smile. Ambrose was back. It had only been an hour, but already he had missed him. The pleasure at hearing Ambrose's voice vanished an instant later when he heard Mrs Forbes again.

"Ambrose!" came her voice, loud and clear through the door, which Daniel had pulled ajar. "Finally, you're here." Her tone was warmer surely than that of a friend.

Ambrose chuckled. "I am here, finally. You are looking well, Lexie."

"And you are looking thinner than before," retorted Mrs Forbes. "I have been so dreadfully worried ever since you wrote of being ill with the influenza."

"It was not a very pleasant thing to have, but I am back to full health now, never fear," replied Ambrose gently.

"We shall have to feed you up, my dear," fussed Mrs Forbes. "Dinner is at five o'clock. There is game pie, and I have invited the viscount too."

"You have met?" Ambrose's voice sounded cautious.

"Yes, just now. He is in the drawing room," replied Mrs Forbes—or was it Lexie—still full of cheer.

"I see. Well, I had better go in. We shall see you at five then."

"Oh. Yes, of course," said Lexie, sounding a little disappointed. "I suppose we can talk more later. Goodbye for now."

There was a sound of footsteps approaching the drawing room, and not wanting to be caught eavesdropping, Daniel quickly returned to his seat and lifted the tea cup to his lips, as if he had been sitting there all along. The door opened, and in walked Ambrose.

"Ambrose," Daniel looked up, feigning surprise. "Just in time. Do join me for a cup of tea and sandwiches."

"Thank you, my lord." Ambrose came towards him, taking a seat opposite and helping himself to the refreshments. He drank his tea gratefully and said with a sigh, "Ah, that is much better, thank you."

Daniel decided to broach the subject of Mrs Forbes straight away. "We are invited to dinner next door," he said, studying Ambrose's face.

"Yes," replied Ambrose evenly. "I spoke to Mrs Forbes as I came in just now."

"I understand she is an old friend of yours."

"That is correct," said Ambrose, looking a trifle flushed. "My sister and I have known Mr and Mrs Forbes for many years."

"I am told," continued Daniel, "that Mr Forbes is absent at present. Is he often so?"

Now Ambrose hesitated. Eventually, he answered, "I really could not say."

"Ambrose!" Daniel's tone was sharp. "Do not speak fustian to me. If they are old friends of yours, then you should very well know."

Ambrose's lips tightened stubbornly, in a manner Daniel was fast becoming familiar with. "Perhaps, my lord, it is not my place to discuss the gentleman and his lady's personal affairs."

Daniel levelled a stare at his estate manager, but he did not pursue the matter any further. Experience had taught him that Ambrose would not budge an inch once he had set his mind to it, especially if he were trying to conceal his real relationship with Lexie Forbes. Nevertheless, Daniel was fully determined to get to the bottom of this mystery one way or another.

The rest of the afternoon was spent in each other's company, exploring the architectural delights of Oxford and browsing through the numerous shops. However, Daniel's good humour, with which he had arrived in this historic city, had evaporated. The more he ruminated on the friendship between Ambrose and Mrs Forbes, the less he liked it. He walked beside Ambrose as the latter pointed out various buildings and historical features, not taking much of it in. His mood was sullen; his responses monosyllabic. By the time they returned to the house, he was sure that Ambrose was feeling heartily sick of him. It was not usual for him to be such poor company, but there again, it was not usual for him to be heartbroken and riddled with jealousy either.

At the appointed time, he dressed for dinner with care and joined Ambrose in the drawing room, who was waiting to accompany him to Mrs Forbes's house. As they always seemed to do, his eyes glided over Ambrose's person, taking in the elegant line of his slim form accentuated by the simplicity of his respectable but unfashionable clothes. Daniel's gaze strayed up to examine Ambrose's silky blond locks, neatly parted to one side, exposing his noble brow and showing off to perfection the beauty of his stormy grey eyes. His breath caught in his chest. Ambrose was truly… ambrosial.

On the back of that thought came a flash of possessiveness. *He is mine. Mine!* Daniel swallowed the hard lump in his throat as reason tried to battle with the instinctive need to capture Ambrose and never let him go. If he had lived in a bygone age where a lord's word was law, he would have done just that—held Ambrose captive in a turret and refused to let him go until he submitted to him. He would have shackled the man to his bed and had his wicked way with him, plundering the delights of his body and leaving him in no doubt to whom he belonged. But this was the year 1861 in the modern era, and lords, no matter how rich, did not wield such arbitrary power.

Reluctantly putting to one side his swashbuckling flight of fancy, Daniel forced a smile and declared, "Ambrose, you are looking well, if a trifle thin. We shall have to put some meat back on your bones." The words were a conscious echo of Mrs Forbes's remarks earlier today. If anyone was to ensure Ambrose ate well and recovered his former physique, it would be Daniel, not that meddling Mrs Forbes.

Ambrose nodded his agreement. "Yes, I am a trifle leaner than before, but I fully intend to eat my way back to health. The good news is that Mrs Forbes's cook makes an excellent game pie, so I am sure to gorge myself tonight."

Daniel pursed his lips in annoyance. Not to be outdone, he replied, "And Stanton Hall's cook is second to none. I believe,

Ambrose, it is best if henceforth, you should take your luncheon at the main house with us."

"And deprive Sarah of my company for luncheon each day?" queried Ambrose with a raised brow. "I think not, my lord."

"Sarah may join us too," said Daniel quickly.

"It is extremely kind of you to extend the invitation, my lord, but the answer must be no. As it is, we are already encroaching on your hospitality quite enough with our luncheons at the house each Sunday."

A growl issued from Daniel's chest. "Must you always be so difficult, Ambrose?"

"Must you always be so forceful, my lord?" responded Ambrose in kind.

"I am merely looking out for your best interests," grated Daniel. "As your employer, it is my duty to do so. However will you fulfil the functions of your job if you are not in good health?"

Ambrose took umbrage at this. "I manage quite well, my lord, and not once have I been derelict in my duties," he protested.

Daniel's expression softened. "I know you do, Ambrose. Forgive me. I did not mean to impugn your work ethic. It is simply care and worry for you that has me speak so." He took a step towards Ambrose and placed a hand on his shoulder. "Let us compromise on the matter," he said gently. "Sunday through to Wednesday, you and Sarah will have your luncheon at Stanton Hall, and do not argue with me on this. I know that Sarah will not mind this arrangement, for I have heard her say with my own ears how well she thinks of my cook. The rest of the days, you may do as you please."

As he spoke, he moved even closer and squeezed Ambrose's shoulder gently. He watched the rapid rise and fall of Ambrose's chest. And were his cheeks a trifle flushed?

In a hoarse voice, Ambrose rasped, "Very well, my lord."

Daniel breathed a sigh of relief at winning this small battle. He should remove his hand from where it still gripped Ambrose's shoulder. All he wanted though, was for that hand to pull the man he loved into his embrace. He nearly trembled with the need to do so. With a mighty effort, he loosened his grip and stepped back. "Let us be on our way," he said thickly. Abruptly, he turned away and marched out of the room.

Together, they went out the door and walked the few paces to the next house. No sooner were they ushered in by a footman than a young boy came barrelling over to them, followed closely by Mrs Forbes. "Uncle Ambrose!" the boy cried.

Ambrose smiled and ruffled the boy's hair. "Hello Edwin," he said cheerfully. "Have you been good?"

"Yes, sir," insisted the boy.

"In that case, here is something to mark your birthday," Ambrose said, taking out from his leather bag a small package wrapped in brown paper and giving it to the boy.

The child looked delighted. "What is it?" he asked in wonder.

"You shall have to find out," chuckled Ambrose.

"But not here," Mrs Forbes hastened to say. "Edwin, please make your bow to Viscount Stanton."

At last, the boy seemed to notice Daniel. With a shy little smile, he executed a creditable bow, saying stiffly, "How do you do, sir."

"I am well, thank you, Edwin," replied Daniel.

"Please do come in," said Mrs Forbes, leading them to the drawing room.

Daniel looked about him as he entered the room. This house was similar in proportions to his, yet it had a very different feel. Instead of the stately, bordering on ostentatious décor next door, this place was homely and welcoming. Comfortable and brightly coloured furniture, slightly frayed with use, adorned the room. Books were strewn on a side table, and by the window stood an easel bearing a charcoal sketch of a steam train rendered in childish strokes. This house reminded him a little of his home back in Ohio, and for an instant, he felt a spurt of nostalgia for that faraway place he would not see again for a long time.

While Daniel took a seat, Edwin jumped to unwrapping the package excitedly, as both Mrs Forbes and Ambrose looked on fondly. From it, the boy pulled out a cylindrical-shaped object with vertical slits all the way around. Inside the cylinder was a series of drawings showing a rider on horseback. Edwin examined it curiously, then enquired, "What is it?"

"This, Edwin, is a zoetrope," said Ambrose. "Place it on the table and fix your eyes level with the slits that you see." Edwin did as he was bid. "Now look carefully," continued Ambrose. So saying, he spun the zoetrope around. It turned on its axis like a merry-go-round.

Edwin watched carefully, then cried out in excitement, "The horse is moving! It's galloping." He looked up at Ambrose and exclaimed, "It's magic!"

"No, not magic, Edwin, but science, though I am afraid I do not know enough to explain it to you. If Sarah were here, no doubt she would know. Do you like it?"

"Yes, sir, I do."

"Edwin, what should you say to Uncle Ambrose?" chided his mother.

The boy leapt to his feet and threw his arms around Ambrose in a fierce hug. "Thank you, Uncle Ambrose," came his muffled voice as his face was pressed to Ambrose's chest.

Daniel watched with a tight feeling in his own chest as Ambrose held the boy to him in obvious affection. In his twenty-four years on this earth, Daniel had never given much thought to the idea of having children. He supposed it was something that people did once they married. But now, seeing Ambrose with this young boy, Daniel was suddenly beset with a feeling of loss. Ambrose would make a wonderful father, he thought. His calm and gentle nature was perfect for the rearing of children. Daniel also knew quite well that it was a physical impossibility for two men to beget children together. The only ways for Ambrose to experience fatherhood would be for him to marry or have a mistress, both of which would take him away from Daniel.

For the first time, it occurred to him just what manner of a sacrifice would entail from a love between two men. Even if Ambrose were ever to develop feelings for him, Daniel would never be able to give him this gift of life. They would never be able to celebrate their love openly for all to see. It would be a forbidden love, tainted by secrecy. Desolation swept through him. This love he felt for Ambrose was doomed. He looked away quickly, blinking back a surge of unwelcome tears.

Around him, the other occupants of the room chattered happily, unaware of his distress. Soon, he had himself in hand enough to join in with the conversation. But though outwardly he smiled, spoke with wit and charm, even made the occasional joke, inside, he withered in despair.

They convened to the dining room where they were served with a fine meal. It could have been sawdust for all Daniel cared. Under his close scrutiny, he saw Ambrose eat heartily, laugh, tease and exchange the odd affectionate look with Mrs Forbes. His suspicions were growing that there was more to this friendship between Ambrose and Lexie Forbes.

Finally, the torture was over, and they said their goodbyes, returning to the Stanton house next door. Once inside, Ambrose turned to face Daniel and said, "I am travel weary, so I will bid you goodnight, my lord."

"Goodnight, Ambrose."

They both went up the stairs then went their separate ways, each to their rooms. Inside his bedchamber, Daniel undressed, made his ablutions, and slipped on a night shirt. He took the candle to his bedside and a book of poems by Keats. Once settled in bed, he read by the light of the candle, his melancholy mood oddly at one with the poetry on the page.

But when the melancholy fit shall fall

Sudden from heaven like a weeping cloud,

That fosters the droop-headed flowers all,

And hides the green hill in an April shroud;

Then glut thy sorrow on a morning rose…

Some unspecified time later, a sound made him stop. He put down his book and listened. There it was again—the creak of a floorboard. Someone was walking along the corridor. Without thinking, Daniel quickly rose from his bed, not bothering with a robe, and tiptoed to his door, opening it quietly. In the dim shadows, he discerned a form moving down the stairs. He followed noiselessly and looked over the stair rail. A beam of moonlight streaming in from a window illuminated briefly the figure of a man—Ambrose—walking silently down the stairs, dressed in a robe.

Daniel waited a fraction of a minute before engaging in pursuit. By the time he reached the bottom of the stairs, Ambrose had disappeared, but the light click of a door shutting indicated where he had gone. It was the rear door to the gardens at the back of the house—the door by which Mrs Forbes had entered the house earlier today. Quickly, on bare feet, Daniel went to the door and opened it, gazing out into the shroud of darkness. At first, he could not see anything, but another shaft of moonlight threw into relief the tall, lithe form of Ambrose, walking rapidly towards the house next door and disappearing inside.

Daniel waited a few minutes to see if Ambrose would return, but there was no further movement. Shivering in the cold, he withdrew back into the house and returned to his room, though not to sleep. He lay in bed, his book forgotten, painful visions in his head of what Ambrose was possibly doing at this very time. Was he undressing Lexie with meticulous care and kissing each newly exposed part of her body? Was he uttering words of love as he did so? And was he allowing that female to touch his person, to stroke every inch of his exquisite body?

A streak of irrational possessiveness flashed through him, much as it had before dinner. Ambrose was his. Nobody else had a right to touch him. Earlier, he had thought their love was doomed. Now, he was full of anger and jealousy. It did not matter if Ambrose deserved him or not. He was his.

Daniel kicked off his covers and sat up in frustration. He recalled the slim, wiry body he had sponged down not two weeks ago with love and care in every touch. The thought of somebody else gliding their fingers over that alabaster skin sprinkled with a dusting of soft, golden hair was enough to make him punch the mattress in anger. It was not to be borne, neither was the ensuing, sharply painful vision of Ambrose burying himself in Lexie's body and scattering his seed into her womb—possibly to create a new life. Damnation! Would this pain never end?

Daniel inhaled deeply, trying to calm himself. Despite the cold, his body was covered in a fine sheen of sweat, evidence of the inferno raging within him. The urge was strong to march into the house next door and drag Ambrose by the scruff of the neck back here. And then, patience at an end, Daniel would ravage that man, mark every inch of his body with the lap of his tongue and the bite of his teeth, making it unequivocally clear who he belonged to.

He was all too aware that this was mad, caveman-like thinking. Daniel buried his face in his hands, desperate to regain his sanity and a semblance of calm. His breaths were short and choppy as he fought his primitive instincts, reminding himself that he was a civilised human being, a Christian man of empathy and tolerance.

Had not Ambrose already told him he had no interest in men? Though a part of him still sensed that Ambrose was attracted to him—the earlier jealousy of Mr Templeton, for example—what man would choose that over a flesh and blood woman? He was not about to pass judgement on that lady's breaking of her marital vows. *Judge not, that ye be not judged.* Was that not the scripture his mama oft liked to quote? What did he know of her circumstances or indeed of Ambrose's? Very little. It was past time that he became a controlled, mature gentleman as befitted his new station. *"Do better, Daniel, do better,"* he repeated to himself.

After a time, enough composure returned for him to lay back in bed, the covers snug around him. However, sleep was slow to come. When it did, he drifted in and out of consciousness, unable to settle, subconsciously waiting for the creaking sound of footsteps that would signify Ambrose's return.

Chapter 19

Ambrose

Ambrose had undressed in preparation for his visit to Lexie next door and put on his robe. He had waited then for all sounds in the house to die down before venturing out of his room. While he waited, he had mulled over the events of the evening.

Daniel had been his usual charming and gregarious self. Ambrose could tell both Lexie and Edwin had been won over by him. Yet beneath the pleasantries, he had sensed a dark disquiet in Daniel's eyes. He had been morose ever since their arrival in Oxford.

No, that was not quite right. At the bank, he had been upbeat and in fine spirits. It was afterwards that his mood had soured. Trying to pinpoint the moment, Ambrose narrowed it to just after Daniel had met Lexie. Yes, that was when Daniel had become testy and uncommunicative.

Could Daniel have guessed about his relationship with Lexie? And could he be jealous? Dear Lord! Ambrose had sunk to the bed and stared at the corniced ceiling. Daniel had made no secret of the fact that he desired him. More than desired him. Ambrose recalled the words he had never forgotten. *What I feel for you is no careless passing fancy. It is deep and strong.*

Daniel was jealous. That might explain perhaps his forceful manner just before dinner, when he had insisted that Ambrose eat his luncheons with him at Stanton Hall. He had gripped his shoulder, and for a moment, Ambrose had thought he was going to pull him into an embrace. God help him but he would not have been able to resist him if he had. Fortunately, or not, Daniel had released him and walked away.

Daniel was jealous and hurt.

Ambrose had rubbed a hand to his chest as his emotions veered from guilty delight to troubled distress. The last thing he had wanted was for Daniel, a man he had come to care for greatly, to be upset. If only… No, he would not let his thoughts follow that unfruitful path. The world was what it was. Wishful thinking was not going to change it. He could not see how loving another man could bring anything but pain. Daniel would soon learn this lesson. It was best to repress such impulses and attend to other, more acceptable, forms of behaviour.

Lexie was waiting for him. He had best go to her. Ambrose had slipped out of his room, tiptoeing carefully downstairs. He had been unable though to avoid the odd creak of the floorboards under his feet. He hoped that had not wakened Daniel. Now, with quick, furtive movements, he went out the back door and by the light of the moon, hurried over to Lexie's house. He gently opened the door and walked in. In the dark, he tiptoed across to the stairs, finding his way through touch and familiarity. He silently went up the stairs and glided like a thief to Lexie's room. Without knocking, he opened the door and slipped inside.

"I was beginning to think you would not be coming," came Lexie's soft voice. She was lying in bed, a candle beside her casting a faint light over the room.

Ambrose briskly removed his robe and got under the covers, murmuring, "I had to wait to make sure the viscount had settled to sleep." He reached for her, and she came to him willingly. Her body was bare and warm to the touch. He held her to him, stroking his hands along her silky smooth skin. She sighed in pleasure. He nestled his face in the crook of her neck, breathing in her familiar fragrance and dropping light kisses. His mind, though, was somewhere else entirely. It was thinking of another person's neck, an Adam's apple and the rough feel of a day's stubble on his skin. What would it be like to bury his nose into that neck?

He had to shake off such thoughts. With a determined effort, he brought his lips to hers, slipping his tongue into her velvety mouth.

What would he taste like?

Ambrose growled in his throat and deepened the kiss, determined to cast all thoughts of Daniel aside. Burying his hands in Lexie's hair, he held her in place as he ravaged her mouth with savage kisses. She moaned and kissed him back ardently.

He turned her over onto her back and straddled her body, his mouth still clamped to hers, plundering it in a show of masculine force. When he released her lips, she whimpered, "Ambrose, I have such need of you."

"And I you," he grunted, letting her feel his long cock which was fully erect. His lips travelled down her body to find one small breast. He took the tip into his mouth and bit gently, the way he knew she liked. Would Daniel like it too? As he sucked and nipped each pebbled tip, he imagined himself at Daniel's breast, worshipping his flat nipples. The thought fired up his arousal even more. He felt his cock throb with need. It had been too long since he had fucked. "Are you ready for me, Lexie?" he rasped, his hand sliding down to test the moistness of her sex.

"So ready," she breathed.

"Turn around," he commanded. "I want you from behind."

Her eyes flared in surprise, but she did as she was bid, lying on her stomach, her knees bent under her. From this position, his cock would go deeper, he knew, and he could also be a little more forceful. He felt a need to exert power, though in his mind, it was not Lexie he wished to dominate but someone else. A someone who by day required his subservience. A someone whose orders he had to follow, whose name on his lips was "my lord". Ambrose may have exhibited an obedient front, dictated by his place in the social order, but he was not obedient by nature. At heart, he was many things he could not show to the world.

But here, in this darkened room, with his best and oldest friend, a woman he loved and trusted, he could let that beast rise out of him. In one deep thrust, he penetrated her. It felt good. Her moan told him she liked it too. "How hard can you take me?" he growled.

"As hard as you wish," she panted.

That was all the permission he needed. He thrust hard and hard again, letting his body wrap around hers, his breath hot on the back of her neck. As his cock plunged into her tight, wet heat, he shut his eyes and pictured himself holding down a tall, male body and thrusting himself deep into him, having him at his mercy, letting him feel his power. "*Oh Daniel,*" he thought. "*You know nothing of me, the real me. You charm and cajole, thinking to seduce me, but it is I who will hold you captive. I who will get your submission.*"

Fired up by the fantasy, Ambrose pumped himself into Lexie, breathing hard with the exertion, already feeling his balls retract and his cock thicken. "*You are mine,*" he raged wildly in his fervent imagining. And with one last thrust, he poured his seed into Daniel's core, his orgasm powerful and long.

It took several breaths to return to sanity. He was not straddling Daniel, but Lexie. Quickly, he pulled out and took his weight off her body, rolling to his side. "Did I hurt you?" he asked contritely.

She touched a hand to his heaving chest. "No, I am well," she whispered. Then, "You are different tonight. What has happened?"

Guilt ate at him. He knew full well what had happened. It was Daniel. He could not shake off thoughts of him, dangerous fantasies of that impossible man. He should have been thinking about Lexie, not him. "Sometimes," he said slowly, revealing something of the truth, "I feel the need to be strong and dominant. Maybe it is me fighting back against the weakness I have felt since being sick, and maybe it is me reacting to the circumstances of my life. By day, I am compelled to be an obedient servant, but with you, tonight, I wanted to be in command. Did you mind?"

She laughed and kissed his cheek. "I liked it." Pulling back the covers, she got out of the bed. "Let me clean up," she murmured.

He watched her wistfully as she wet a cloth and wiped the residue of his seed from her sex. She was beautiful, and he loved her. Why could that not be enough?

She came back to the bed and into his waiting embrace. He held her to him, feeling equal parts guilt and affection. Something, perhaps it was a need to confess, made him blurt, "It's him. Him that made me different tonight."

She pulled back to look at him. "Viscount Stanton?"

He nodded.

Looking puzzled, she asked, "How so?"

The urge was strong to tell her about the feelings he kept bottled up. He knew he should not. It would be lunacy to reveal those forbidden thoughts in his mind. It could hurt him and Daniel, Lexie too. Yet, if he could not be truthful with Lexie, his closest female friend, then every part of his life would be a lie. All at once, it became vital to have one place, one person, where he could be his true self.

He braced himself, took a deep breath, then began, "From the moment that I met Daniel, I have been subject to strong feelings. It was the same for him, except that while I kept mine hidden, he did not."

She stared at him, bewildered. "Strong feelings you say. What sort of strong feelings?"

This was it. The moment of truth from which there was no turning back. He held her gaze and uttered the words. "Feelings of desire. Feelings of love."

He watched as the truth sank in. Her eyes welled with tears. "You love him," she trembled. "You love a man."

"Yes," he said simply, his own eyes blurring.

She choked on a sob. "What of me? Do you not love me?"

"Oh, Lexie!" He pulled her into his arms and held her tightly, his own body now racked with sobs. "Of course, I love you. I always will. You are my dearest friend." Perhaps in time, he could come to love her as she loved him, but a part of him knew this was wishful thinking.

They stayed clutched together in an outpouring of mutual grief. For Ambrose, the grief was tinged also with relief and fear. He felt as if a heavy burden had lifted from his shoulder. At the same time, he worried what this would mean for his friendship with Lexie. Would she develop a disgust of him? Would it end what they had together? Tonight had been a departure from his usual cautious self. He had spoken boldly, perhaps rashly. Be that as it may, he could not regret it.

Finally, Lexie pulled away, getting out of the bed to fetch a handkerchief to wipe her face with. She came back with another for him, which he took gratefully and used on his own blotched countenance. She burrowed under the covers to her chin and sighed heavily. Then she spoke two words. "Tell me," she said.

So, he told her. From the beginning, not stinting on any truth, he told her of the feelings he had for men, of how he had tried in vain to keep them in check, especially after what had happened to John. He told her of his relief when they had started their love affair at the knowledge he was normal after all, not a freak. "Of course you are not a freak," she interrupted. He smiled in gratitude, kissed her lips and continued his tale. He made sure to tell her that he loved her—not quite in the same way as he loved and desired Daniel, but love all the same—and how very much she mattered to him. How their monthly trysts had given him comfort, relief and a safe haven of loving warmth. And then he told her about Daniel and everything that had occurred between them until this day.

After he finished his speech, there was a long silence. When finally she spoke, it was to seek reassurance. "When we are together like this, in bed, do you feel any desire for me or has it all been pretence?" She gazed at him with wounded eyes.

In response, he took her hand and placed it on his flaccid penis. "Would I be able to fuck you, Lexie, with a cock as soft as this?" he asked.

"No," she mumbled.

"Then that is your answer, darling. When we make love, my desire for you has my cock swell and harden. None of that is pretence. I love you, my beautiful Lexie, and holding you in my arms is always a pleasure."

She was not fully convinced. "When you are with me, do you pretend in your head that I am someone else?"

He grimaced at this. "Usually, no."

"But tonight—"

"Tonight, yes, he was in my head as I fucked you. Forgive me."

She nodded as if in confirmation of what she already knew. "I thought something was different about you," she said under her breath. She shot him a look and added, "Yet tonight, I felt more pleasure in our union than ever before. When you held and entered me so powerfully, so possessively, it made me feel desired. Now I see how wrong I was." She took a steadying breath, then asked, "What now between us?"

He studied her face apprehensively. "We carry on as before," he said.

Her eyes flew to his in surprise. "How can we, when it is not me you want but him."

"I cannot have him," he said softly.

"And am I to be your consolation prize?"

"Never that!" he snapped, an arrow of pain digging into his heart.

She huffed in frustration. "I do not know what to think anymore. What you described of your feelings for Daniel sound nothing like what you feel for me. Be truthful, Ambrose. If you could have a choice, it would be him."

He turned to lie on his back, staring at the ceiling as if it would provide him with answers. Haltingly, he said, "We do not live in a world where that can ever be. We are both in the same boat, Lexie. You are stuck in a loveless marriage, abandoned by your spouse, and I live in a world where to display my feelings for Daniel would leave me open to ostracism, penury and possible imprisonment. We cannot change these circumstances we are in, but we can make the best of what we have, which is a deep love and friendship. Can you not be happy with that?"

"You propose an affair of convenience then."

"It is more than that, Lexie, and you know it," he told her, a little hurt. But then he reminded himself that it was she who had every right to be hurt, not him. He took her hand and kissed it. "What I propose," he went on, "is for two dear old friends to provide love and comfort to each other as we have always done. Whatever feelings I have for Daniel will remain forever hidden. I can never let him know of my desire. Eventually, he will tire of hitting his head against a brick wall and will seek greener pastures, I guarantee it. And I promise you this, Lexie. You will always be the only woman for me. Between us there will always be truth. And I will make it my priority to focus on you and only you when were are together like this."

She thought about it, her brow furrowed in concentration. Finally, she said, "Will you promise to tell me if ever your feelings change?"

"I have promised you only truth from here on."

She took his hand then and placed it on her heart. "Friends forever?" she asked.

"Friends forever," he confirmed.

She smiled tremulously. "Very well then."

In that moment, he felt a powerful wave of love for her at her acceptance of him. She so easily could have rejected his friendship in revulsion after he had made his confession, but Lexie was a special human being. He had always known it. And now, seeing the uncertainty on her face, he felt a need to reassure.

Using his thumb, he wiped an errant tear that had escaped down her cheek. He put his lips to where that tear had been and tried to kiss it better. Then, he asked softly, "Will you let me make love to you, darling? This time, I promise all my attention will be on you."

"Yes," she breathed.

He brought her into the circle of his arms and kissed her, gently at first, then with increased ardour. This was his Lexie, he told himself, the same person who had offered him comfort and love all these years. He stroked the softness of her skin and breathed in the familiar scent of her. With another hand, he pumped his cock, feeling it swell to a state of arousal. Then, he positioned himself above her, face-to-face this time. With infinite care, he entered Lexie until he was fully seated in her lush heat. There, he stayed, deeply lodged. "Feel me inside you," he murmured.

"I do."

He kissed her lips gently, still buried in her heat. "Do you know how beautiful you are?" he asked her.

"I am not a beauty," she demurred.

"Oh, but you are to me." He pulled back and thrust deeply with the long length of his cock, reaching a spot that made her gasp. "Feel me, darling," he grunted, spearing her once more. "Feel me loving you." He kissed her then as he continued with his slow, deeply penetrating thrusts. For a long time, they continued this dance of love, alternating between looking into the other's eyes and kissing as their two bodies were intimately joined. They took their time, building up a crescendo of pleasure until he knew she was close to achieving her release. "Do it," he encouraged. "Spend your pleasure around me. I want to feel your sex choking my cock."

She looked helplessly into his eyes, unable to withstand the command in his voice. Moments later, he felt the unmistakable tightening of her moist walls around him in a pulsing sensation. "That's it, my lovely," he groaned and let himself go, spilling his seed into her. He held her then, both of them spent, unwilling to break the connection. Eventually he pulled out and went to fetch the cloth, tenderly cleaning away the wetness between her legs. He got into the bed again and gathered her into his arms, weary with relief. He had not lost her. She had not taken a disgust of him after hearing his confession.

He held her close until the sound of her breathing told him she had fallen asleep. He stayed where he was for a long time, gazing at her sleeping face and thinking over what had been said. Had he made the right choice, both to tell her and to continue with their love affair? He could not be sure. He knew he needed her still, but he felt guilt too for not being able to love her as she deserved. As for Daniel, he told himself there was no hope there. As much as he could, he would have to put him out of his mind. At the first light of dawn, he left Lexie with a gentle kiss to her forehead and returned to his own room.

Chapter 20

Daniel

Daniel awoke the following morning to a gloomy day with rain and hail lashing at his window. It was every bit as miserable outside as he felt in his heart. Their journey would be slow today on the muddy rutted roads, he realised, but he was determined they should be on their way. He hated to admit to himself that part of the reason for his haste to be gone was a wish to take Ambrose away from the presence of Mrs Forbes.

Weary and downcast, he made his way down to the dining room. A breakfast was laid out for him on the table. "Good morning, my lord," Briggs said, walking into the room with a pot of fresh coffee. He poured it into a cup and placed it fastidiously before his master.

"Good morning, Briggs," responded Daniel with a semblance of a smile. "Has Mr Cranshaw already breakfasted?"

"Yes, my lord," replied the butler. "He is in the Forbes house visiting at present but asked me to tell you he is ready to depart whenever you are."

Spending more time with his mistress, of course—or merely avoiding him? "Please send word to him that I shall be ready to leave in half an hour," instructed Daniel.

"Yes, my lord," said Briggs and left to do just that.

Daniel ate his breakfast, ruminating on the events of the past night. All the evidence suggested that Ambrose and Mrs Forbes were lovers. His fingers tightened dangerously on the knife and fork he held in his hands. Then he thought of his promise to himself to act like a gentleman and not some uncivilised madman. He tried to relax his grip on the cutlery. Perhaps it was a casual affair that would soon extinguish itself, he told himself. At any rate, he would be polite with Ambrose, cordial even. He would act as if all was well.

Breakfast complete, he went up to his room to get himself ready, coming back down with his travel case within the half hour he had specified. The rain, thankfully, had eased, and the carriage was outside ready to leave. Ambrose was already inside, waiting for him. Daniel said his goodbyes to Mr and Mrs Briggs, then boarded the carriage.

"Morning, Ambrose," he said, settling himself opposite him.

"Good morning, my lord," came the response.

"I trust you slept well?" he enquired.

"Like a log, my lord," claimed Ambrose, not quite meeting his eyes.

At this, Daniel raised his brow but forbore to say anything more. The carriage clip clopped along the cobbled streets of Oxford, then onto the country road that would take them back home. Inside, silence reigned for several minutes, until Daniel could stand it no more. Throwing caution to the wind, he declared, "I heard you last night."

"My lord?"

"I saw you too. Going next door to pay a visit to Lexie Forbes."

Ambrose wore a guilty expression. "My lord, you are mistaken," he began.

"I only mention it," continued Daniel, "because you returned to your bedchamber a long time later, near dawn. It strikes me as unlikely, therefore, that you could have slept like a log."

To this, Ambrose had no response. At his silence, Daniel spoke again, unable to erase the accusation from his voice. "She is your mistress, is she not?"

"My lord, I do not think it right to discuss personal matters," said Ambrose uneasily.

"I disagree. Now answer me, Ambrose. Is she or is she not your mistress?"

"She is," said Ambrose softly.

He had known it already, but the admission still brought a painful stab to his chest. He exhaled a long breath, then continued the inquisition. "And her husband, what of him?"

"They have long been estranged," replied Ambrose, seemingly resigned to revealing the truth. "He lives the life of a bachelor in London and rarely if ever visits his wife and son."

"How long have the two of you…" he could not go on and say the words.

Ambrose understood his meaning, answering shortly, "Seven years."

Daniel reeled at the revelation. Seven years her lover? That was an age. His hopes that this was a casual, short-term arrangement foundered there and then. He forced himself to ask, "Do you love her?"

Ambrose did not catch his eye as he replied, "Yes, I do."

"If she were free, would you marry her?"

Ambrose appeared to be trying to maintain a calm voice with his next words. "Yes, I would."

Daniel inhaled sharply and looked out the window, battling to keep his eyes from welling. His voice not quite steady, he said, "I am sorry, Ambrose, to have importuned you with my unwanted advances. I understand now how unwelcome they were." He breathed deeply, trying to calm himself. The evidence was there, plain for him to see. Ambrose was not and would never be interested in him. All those little clues he had so hungrily grasped at—the blushes, the hesitations, the avoidance of his eyes—were not signs of hidden desire but of something else entirely. Ambrose was in love with Lexie Forbes. It was time at last to accept this unpalatable truth.

After a while, Ambrose's voice intruded on his turbulent reflections. "I see this causes you pain. For this I am sorry."

Daniel shook his head adamantly. "You have nothing to be sorry for, Ambrose. The fault is entirely mine. Do please forgive me. We will speak of it no more."

They continued their journey in terse silence. Then Ambrose spoke again. "I once recall you asking if we could be friends."

Daniel laughed shortly. "I recall you saying friendship had to be earned."

"Yes, I did," agreed Ambrose, "and I believe we both have earned the right to call each other a friend. Do you not agree?"

"I will always be your friend, Ambrose, even if I cannot be more." Daniel forced a smile.

"Then as your friend, Daniel, let me say this to you. Friendship is not something to sneer at or a poor substitute for love. It is precious and worth having. While I cannot reciprocate the sentiments you have expressed towards me, I can be many things to you. I can be the person you talk to whenever you are in need of companionship. I can be the person who you come to when you have a problem to solve. I can be the person you share good news of your successes with, and the person to help lift you out of your sorrows. All these things I can be for you and you can be for me. What say you to that?"

Daniel felt the import of Ambrose's words. In them was a promise which was in its way as precious as the one he wished he could hear. Eyes glistening, he held out his hands. Unhesitatingly, Ambrose gripped them firmly in his. "I say yes to that," said Daniel, his voice gritty with emotion.

Ambrose squeezed Daniel's hands and said, "Then the matter is settled." Releasing him, he sat back, a gentle smile on his beautiful face.

"Thank you," said Daniel thickly.

The rest of the journey was accomplished in a far more cordial and relaxed manner. This friendly cordiality persisted over the next several weeks as Ambrose and Daniel settled into the parameters of their new relationship. With each day, their bond deepened and their platonic affection grew. Daniel became accustomed to having Ambrose in his home each day, working together on estate business or sharing a luncheon with their respective siblings. Saturday was the one day that Daniel did not see Ambrose, as he took the day off and spent it at home. Consequently, Saturday soon came to be Daniel's least favourite day of the week.

He could not extinguish the attraction he felt for Ambrose nor the yearning he had for him, but he managed to put it to one side, and very nearly to convince himself that he was satisfied with the status quo. As time went on, however, he could not stop the gnawing need he had for sexual release. He had been celibate ever since his arrival in England last November, and his hands were growing weary from pleasuring himself each night to visions of Ambrose. He supposed he should find himself some willing wench to dally with, but he could not find the appetite for it.

One Wednesday in early April, Ambrose and Daniel sat in his study, going over the terms of some tenancy contracts that required renewal. It was a lengthy and wearisome process, but necessary. Finally, when the documents were all complete, Ambrose stood gathering up the papers. "If that is all, Daniel," he said, stifling a yawn, "then I shall take myself home and prepare for my journey tomorrow."

"What journey?" wondered Daniel then quickly realised. Tomorrow would be the first Thursday of the month, the day when Ambrose went to Oxford to deposit funds at the bank.

Jealousy surged in Daniel's breast. In Oxford, there was Lexie. Ambrose would soon be indulging in a night of passion with his mistress while Daniel had nobody to share his bed. It was insupportable. On impulse, he said, "And I shall go to London. Mr Templeton has already kindly agreed to help me with some introductions there."

Ambrose pursed his lips and nodded. "Then I wish you a safe and prosperous journey. Might I enquire, Daniel, when you shall return?"

Daniel considered the matter. "I shall be gone a few days at least," he finally replied. "I will send word, but I would think to return on Monday or Tuesday."

"Very well," Ambrose nodded, placing the documents in his leather case. "I shall bid you farewell."

"Farewell, Ambrose, and may your journey prosper too," responded Daniel. My, my, how civil they both sounded.

Once Ambrose had gone, Daniel sat down to jot a quick note to Mr Templeton, enquiring if the latter would join him on a trip to London the following day. He rang the bell for the footman and handed the missive to him, instructing him to have it delivered to Graveley, Mr Templeton's home, without delay. An hour later, a response arrived. Mr Templeton would be delighted to join Viscount Stanton on the 10:15 train to London the following day.

The following evening

Daniel took a sip of his cognac and answered yet another query about his home in America. He was at White's, where Mr Templeton, or Philip as he now called him, had been as good as his word, introducing him to various high ranking individuals. Some had been witty and interesting company, others were stuffed shirts with little of import to say.

All, however, had been fascinated by Daniel's history, wanting to know about America. Daniel had obligingly provided a carefully curated portrait of his family's estate in Ohio. He was already aware that he could not disclose how informal his life there had been nor how much of it had involved manual labour with his own bare hands. That would not do at all in the snobbish circles he now found himself in.

Another talking point had been the political situation in America. He had lost count of how many times he had been asked which state was likely to next secede from the Union. He wished he knew. It was a worrying state of affairs, causing his father no small amount of concern, judging from the last letter he had received. Daniel had spoken of it to Ambrose on numerous occasions. Together, they scrutinised the papers for every scrap of news from America and discussed the implications. He was more glad than ever to have him as a friend. Thinking of Ambrose gave him comfort in these slightly discomfiting surroundings.

Determinedly, he returned his attention to what his interlocutor was saying—some lord, whose name Daniel could not immediately recall. This same lord had volunteered to take Daniel to the House of Lords on Monday. Daniel would go merely as an observer this first time, but would get an opportunity on his next visit to make his maiden speech, though about what it would be, he had as yet no idea.

At last, after what seemed like hours of enforced civility, Mr Templeton stood and made their excuses. Together, they walked out into the drizzly April evening, their coats buttoned up against the cold. "Where to now?" wondered Daniel.

Philip gazed at him speculatively. "I can offer you two choices," he said.

"And they are?"

"The first," said Philip, "is a card party being held at Lord Marchmont's house. I have an invitation and secured one for you too."

A card party. It sounded very dull to him. "How about the second?" asked Daniel.

"The second one is a delicate matter," replied Philip enigmatically. Daniel raised a brow, and Philip continued with a smile, "That first time you paid a visit to my house—you had, I believe, recently returned from a trip to Oxford—and we got a trifle tipsy together. You regaled me then with tales of your many and varied adventures with the opposite sex."

"I did? That I do not recall. I must have been well into my cups."

Philip sniggered. "I think you may have been."

"And what has any of this to do with the second choice?"

"It has to do with it because it is a private members' club, but nothing like White's." Philip hesitated. "I am not in the habit of taking anyone there whom I have not known for a very long time and can trust with the confidentiality that is required."

Daniel was intrigued. "And yet you are willing to trust me?"

"It is a hunch I have that you would like this club, Daniel. It is called Tremayne's, and it is a place of revelry, nay debauchery. Do you get my gist?"

Daniel narrowed his eyes. "Let me understand this fully. When you talk of debauchery, do you mean by that excessive imbibing of alcohol and the smoking of opium, or do you mean sexual frolics?"

Philip grinned wickedly. "I mean the latter. Would you like to see it and partake in the revelry?"

Daniel thought of Ambrose, in all probability partaking in revelry with his mistress at this very moment. Still, he hesitated. It was Ambrose he wanted, not anyone else. A voice whispered in his ear, *"But you cannot have Ambrose, so what will you do? Remain celibate the rest of your life?"* He needed to end this bout of celibacy, and he had no wish to romance anybody or play any seduction games. Surely this place, Tremayne's, was one step better than paying to be with a whore? He took a deep breath and answered, "Yes, I would."

"That's my man," said Philip approvingly. "Well then, let us go. It is only fifteen minutes' walk from here."

A short stroll later, they arrived at an unremarkable looking four-storey building. On ringing the bell, the door was opened by a stiff-looking butler who ushered them into a neatly furnished hall. He took their hats and coats, then enquired, "What name shall I put down, sir?"

"My guest's name is Viscount Stanton," replied Philip equably.

"He will have to sign the declaration," went on the butler.

Daniel eyed Philip curiously. What on earth was this declaration? Philip was quick to elucidate. "The declaration is merely a document in which you promise to abide by the rules of this establishment. As I said to you before, this is a very private club where confidentiality is of the utmost importance."

"I see," replied Daniel. "Well then, show me this declaration."

It was brought out, and Daniel read it through from start to finish. He was not to mention the name Tremayne's to anyone outside these premises. All occurrences inside the club were to be treated with the utmost discretion and never spoken of outside these walls. All visitors and members were to be respectful to one another. Physical violence in any form would not be tolerated. Daniel realised, of course, that there was no legal recourse should a person break the signed terms of this declaration. As far as he could see, it functioned on an old-fashioned honour system. After one, final moment of hesitation, he signed his name at the bottom of the document. The butler bowed, taking the paper from him, and then invited them to go up to the dining lounge on the first floor.

"Are you ready?" asked Philip with a smile.

"As ready as I will ever be," responded Daniel.

"Then come." And up the stairs they both went, then entered a richly furnished room filled with two dozen or so people sitting at dining tables and conversing casually. It did not look subversive in any way. Philip chuckled at Daniel's obvious bafflement. "This is what it says it is, merely a dining lounge where members can eat and drink before beginning their revelries. Are you hungry, Daniel?"

Daniel smirked. "I am, Philip, but not for food."

Philip clapped him on the shoulder with a laugh. "Then come with me." He led Daniel to a door at the other end of the room, nodding to acquaintances along the way. Once at the door, he winked and said, "Here we go." He pushed the handle and opened it.

Daniel followed Philip inside, trying not to stare openly at what he saw. The room was large and dimly lit, though it was light enough to see perfectly well what was going on. Naked men and women were cavorting everywhere, on strategically placed couches, on a small central stage, and up against the walls. His eyes bulged as he spied a man on his knees, sucking another man's cock. If only Ambrose could see this, came the unbidden thought. Nearby, two men were fucking the same woman, one in her cunt and the other in her mouth. Oh Lord, what was this? He felt his cock thicken with instinctive arousal.

Just then, a young maid came over to them. "May I undress you, sir?" she asked.

"Of course," beamed Philip.

Daniel watched agog as she deftly disrobed him, folding his clothes in a neat pile onto a table by the door. Next, she came to him. "Sir, may I undress you?"

He nodded his acquiescence and watched in wonder as she took every stitch of clothing he wore and stowed it away on the table. He was naked in a room full of people. He should have felt an ounce of shame at the lack of modesty, but curiously, all he felt was wild abandon and lust—a great deal of lust. His cock stood proudly to attention, raring to go.

Philip glanced down at it. "Good man," he said. "Looks to me like you are ready for some revelry." His eyes twinkled. "Go forth, Daniel, and enjoy yourself. Once you are done, this lovely maid here will fetch your clothes for you, and we can meet up again in the lounge for some refreshment. Adieu!" With that, he walked off and was soon swallowed up by the crowd of revellers.

Cautiously, Daniel stepped forward into the room, unsure of the protocol in finding himself a partner to cavort with. He need not have worried. A curvy female with large, pendulous breasts came to him with a delighted smile, followed by another female with high, pert breasts and—if his eyes were to be believed—a totally hair-free cunt. The first female called out to her friend, "Oh goody, fresh meat."

The friend looked him over and smiled knowingly. "Fresh meat indeed. Would you like to have some fun with us, sir?"

A smile spread slowly over Daniel's face. "I rather think I would."

They took him by the hand and led him to a nearby couch. There, the large-breasted female lay with him, allowing him to fondle her while she stroked and kissed his upper body. Her friend, meanwhile, went straight to work on his cock, stroking it with soft hands, then replacing her hands with the touch of her mouth. It felt very good indeed, so good that he was in danger of finishing in her mouth if he did not stop her soon. Gently, he pushed her away, saying, "I am not ready to climax just yet, lovely lady."

The woman laughed. "Oh dear, we cannot be having that. Perhaps we can give your cock a rest while you pleasure my cunt instead."

"I am at your service, madam," replied Daniel.

With a sultry look, she stood and came round to the other end of the couch where his head lay. With slow deliberation, she straddled him, lowering her bare cunt to his face. He licked her then, getting a first taste of her tangy essence. Encouraged, he began to lap at her, then as her arousal became more pronounced, he took her engorged clitoris in his mouth and sucked until he felt her spasm under his tongue, a warm wet flow of her juices gushing out.

She sighed happily, shifting her body off his face. "I think we need to reward this good work with a fuck," she told her friend, who was busy sucking on his nipples.

Her busty friend paused in her ministrations and looked up. "I think we should," she concurred. "Me first!"

Quickly, she slid down his body to his long, thick length, squeezing it admiringly with her hand. Then in one lithe movement, she positioned herself atop him and lowered her cunt, inch by inch, on his throbbing shaft. He felt pleasure engulf him as he slid all the way inside her. It had been too long, and his need was great. He took a calming breath, not wanting to embarrass himself by climaxing so soon.

She began to ride him, her large breasts bouncing hypnotically before his eyes. But soon, the sight was too enticing for his self-control. He closed his eyes and breathed deeply, willing himself not to spill his seed. Her movements atop him quickened, and the walls of her cunt tightened around him. She was close, he knew, and he had to help her over the edge. Bracing his feet on the couch, he began to thrust up into her, hitting a spot inside her cunt that made her gasp. "Yes!" she cried. "Oh fuckity fuck yes." Her walls clamped around him as she screamed her climax out loud.

With one final pleasurable sigh, she stilled, then climbed off him. "My turn," said her friend, who had been watching them lasciviously. Said friend now climbed onto his cock and swallowed it up into her welcoming cunt. Oh Lord, this was too good. He was so ready to burst, but as if reading his thoughts, she gazed at him severely. "Oh no, sir, you will not. At least not until I have orgasmed one more time." And then she too began to ride him.

He stared up at her pert little breasts, bouncing frantically in time with the rest of her body. Too arousing. Once more, he closed his eyes and tried to think of something that would take his mind off his agony—the first thing springing to mind was the tenancy contract he and Ambrose had reworded just yesterday.

Ambrose. No, he must not think of him. No, no, no. Ambrose was lost to him as a lover. He was merely a friend. Ambrose was busy fucking his precious Lexie at this very minute. And that thought alone was quick to bring Daniel back from the precipice, his cock deflating at the painful vision. No, that would not do either. He had to perform at least long enough to give the lady pleasure. He opened his eyes again and stared at her breasts. They were so very pretty. He kept his gaze there, not looking at her face and purposely not thinking of Ambrose. His cock stiffened once more, and as with the previous lady, he decided to help her along to her climax by thrusting up, looking to find that venerated spot inside her cunt that brought so much pleasure. He heard her gasp. Good. He was striking the right place. Sweat forming on his brow from the effort, he pulsed up into her cunt in a rapid motion that soon had her walls spasming around him. With a long, loud moan, she went over that precipice.

And then, finally, it was time for him to achieve release. He fucked into her, over and over until he could take no more. Then, in one swift move, he lifted her off him and sat up, his hand wrapped around his shiny, throbbing cock. He stroked his shaft rapidly just as the large-breasted lady crouched before him. "Spend on my titties," she encouraged.

With a frantic cry, he did just that, spurting streams of his pearly emissions onto her heaving breasts. The relief was intense but short-lived. At long last, his five-month drought was over, but it was not Ambrose that had quenched his thirst. He pushed away a twinge of guilt. He did not owe Ambrose fidelity. They were friends, that was all. And this impersonal, unsentimental fucking was just the thing. Never again would he romance anybody else, for his heart belonged to Ambrose for posterity. His body though, was another matter.

"Oh my, what a pretty sight that was," purred a voice beside him.

He turned sideways and for the first time noticed the slight, fair-haired man standing by the couch and watching them. The man searched his eyes before asking, "Sir, may I clean you up with my tongue?"

Once upon a time, Daniel might have jumped with excitement at the thought of a man touching him intimately. But now, he made a small addendum to his previous considerations. His heart belonged to Ambrose, and while his body was another matter, it would never belong to any other man but Ambrose. His lips pressed into a firm line. "I think not," he replied.

The man shrugged in evident disappointment. "What a pity," he said and walked off.

Meantime, his two lady friends had disappeared too, most likely to go clean up. Daniel was left alone, though he knew by now it would not be for long. He'd had enough for one night though. Coming to his feet, he strode to the maid and requested his clothes, swiftly getting dressed once she had brought them over. Then, he left the room and walked back into the dining lounge. Finding an empty table, he sat and ordered a plate of steak and potatoes.

He was busily eating his meal when finally, Philip joined him, he too ordering a similar repast. "How did you like it?" asked Philip.

Daniel set down his fork. "I liked it well enough," he said.

Philip beamed, evidently pleased to have inducted someone new into his debauchery. "I come here once every month," he said. "You are welcome to join me."

"Thank you, I think I will," replied Daniel. They continued their meal peaceably, and once they were done, he insisted on taking care of the bill. Then, replete at last, they took a hansom cab to their respective homes.

As Daniel slid under the fine cotton sheets at Stanton House, he reflected one last time on the evening he had just had. This was the way it would be for him from here on, he thought. His days would be spent in loving friendship with Ambrose, and once a month, when Ambrose went to his mistress, he would come here and assuage his physical needs at Tremayne's.

There would be no affairs, no messy relationships, just simple fucking. And as soon as those needs were met, he would return home to bask in Ambrose's company once more. He would forever be unsatisfied romantically and sexually, but there was nothing he could do about it. These were the cards that capricious fate had dealt him, and he would play them out the best he could.

Chapter 21

Ambrose

Ambrose made good time, reaching Oxford just before eleven o'clock. As was his wont, he stopped first at the bank to divest himself of the large sack of coins secured in his leather bag. Once that important task was complete, he visited several shops on the High Street, ordering necessary supplies for Stanton Hall. It was nearly one o'clock when he reached the house on St Michael's Street.

"Good day, Briggs," he greeted the butler with a smile. "How do you do today?"

"Can't complain, sir, can't complain," replied the old retainer.

Taking his case up with him, Ambrose went to his room where he made use of the commode and washed quickly, then returned down the stairs. He decided to go next door via the back. As he let himself into Lexie's house, he spied a passing footman and called out, "Stibbs, where is Mrs Forbes?"

"In her private parlour, sir."

Ambrose thanked him and made his way eagerly to the room in question. He knocked briefly, then went in. He found Lexie sitting in her favourite armchair, staring pensively at the fire in the hearth. She looked pale and worried, and immediately, Ambrose sensed that something was wrong. He went to her quickly, enfolding her into his arms. "Darling," he murmured. "What is it?"

"Ambrose," she said softly, then again, "Ambrose."

"Yes, darling. Speak to me."

She levelled her expressive brown eyes at him. "I am with child," she said simply.

He took a sharp breath in. With child. They were going to have a child. His first reaction was panic. This could mean trouble for Lexie, and by extension, for him. How would William take the news? And Daniel? On its heels came another, surprising reaction. It was joy. He was to become a father. He endeavoured to tamp down his excitement and to focus on the problem at hand. With a calm he did not entirely feel, he said, "We always knew this was a possibility. It is surprising, in fact, that it has not happened before."

"Yes, I know," she said on a breath.

"We spoke of this eventuality. Have you written to William?"

She nodded. "I have. He is due to arrive this afternoon."

"Does he know why you have summoned him?" queried Ambrose.

"No, but he will soon. I am sure he must suspect." Lexie's bottom lip trembled. "Now the time has come, I am fearful, Ambrose."

He took her hand and kissed it. "I will be there with you, darling. You will not face him alone."

She took a steadying breath, trying to smile. It broke his heart. He pulled her into his embrace and held her tight. "We are going to have a child of our own," he said. "A beautiful girl or boy. We are blessed, Lexie. Truly we are."

"Yes," she said, and held on to him. After a while, she recovered enough to pull back and ask, "Have you eaten luncheon?"

"No," he replied, "but I am too worried to eat."

"Then sit here and hold me," she pleaded.

He settled himself on the settee and pulled her against him, leaning his chin on the top of her head. "Where is Edwin?" he now asked.

"I thought it best to send him to Mother and Father," she murmured.

"That was well thought, though I shall miss seeing him."

"He will be back in the morning," Lexie reassured him.

They stayed together in the parlour, whispering words of encouragement and taking only some warm tea for sustenance. It was around another hour later that the bell rang. They heard Stibbs go to answer the door, then the sound of a male voice. They both sat up straight and waited. A moment later, there came a knock, and then Stibbs announced, "Mr Forbes is here, madam," before stepping aside to let William in.

Both Lexie and Ambrose stood as William strode in confidently. He paused on seeing Ambrose, then snorted, "I should have known you would be here, Ambrose." He turned then to his wife and bowed. "Lexie, good day. As you see, I am come and would appreciate you tell me straight up what this is about."

Lexie turned anxious eyes to the door. Understanding her meaning, Ambrose strode quickly there, opening and shutting it to make sure nobody was within earshot. He nodded encouragingly at her. Gathering her courage, she addressed her estranged husband. "I am with child, William."

He nodded, looking anything but surprised. His eyes landed on Ambrose once more. "I take it you are the father?"

"Yes," replied Ambrose and Lexie at the same time.

There was a pause. "And what is it you wish me to do?" enquired William. "Pass off the bastard as my own?"

Ambrose clenched his fists but forced himself to remain silent. Lexie spoke with difficulty. "If you could stay overnight, then it would quiet the gossip about the origins of this child.

And yes, William, he or she must take your name. You know he must, or be an outcast from society for ever."

Her husband regarded her coldly. "Very well," he said at last. "I have no wish to invite unwelcome gossip where you are concerned. I will do as you say, and you can then plausibly claim the child as mine. However, I am not going to pay for your by-blows, Ambrose. Lexie will receive the same funds as before, not a penny more."

"That is quite alright," said Ambrose quickly. "I will take care of any additional expenses."

"And do not expect this child to inherit a penny from me." William stood, the matter dealt with. "Have dinner ready within the hour, Lexie," he said crisply. "I am tired and hungry."

"Yes, of course," she murmured. She hurried out of the room to speak to the servants, leaving Ambrose alone with her husband.

The latter turned to him with a sneer. "So, how long have you been fucking my wife?" he demanded.

Ambrose rose to his full height, responding in a chilling tone, "Considering you have fucked your way through London society, William, I do not think you are in any position to ask such a question. Good day to you." He swept out of the room and went to find Lexie. She was busy instructing a housemaid in the proper way to lay out the dinner for the master of the house. She looked up distractedly at Ambrose and said, "You should go now."

"Will you be safe with William on your own?" worried Ambrose. "I do not like to leave you so."

"I do not think he will harm me, especially with you being nearby," she said with a frown. "But it is best you should go now. I shall see you in the morning."

Reluctantly, he did as he was bid and returned to the Stanton house, knowing he could not set foot next door again until William had left. He spent the evening alone, alternating between worry and excitement. He was going to be a father. He would never be able to acknowledge that child publicly, but he would know, and so would Lexie, that it was his. He would love this child and nurture him or her to the best of his power. Already, he had put away funds for this possible eventuality. Whatever happened, this child's future would be secure. He would make sure of it.

He went to bed early that evening, though sleep was elusive. His mind was filled with thoughts of this child. He thought of Daniel too, in all probability having a fine time in London in the company of Mr Templeton and his cronies. Perhaps Daniel had found himself some lightskirt to dally with, or worse even, a man to ravish. Ambrose's fingers dug into the coverlet, jealousy shooting through his body. He had no right to be jealous, especially with the knowledge that he had impregnated Lexie. Ambrose had sent Daniel on his merry way, making it clear that there could never be anything more than friendship between them. How could he then blame him for finding joy in the arms of someone else?

Rationally, he could reason it all, but instinctively, he felt rage at the thought of Daniel taking a lover. He tried to calm his turbulent thoughts. He had better get used to this. This would be the first of many times, he was sure, that Daniel would visit the great metropolis, and in all likelihood engage in sexual trysts of one sort or another—for such was the corrupting influence of London. Ambrose could only wish that these sexual exploits were confined to the great city and never to Stanton Hall. He did not think he could bear it otherwise. It would be a case of out of sight, out of mind, he told himself. He would manage to live with the jealousy that way.

Next morning, he waited for William's carriage to leave before hurrying over to the house next door. He found Lexie sitting listlessly at the breakfast table. He went and sat beside her. "How did it go?" he asked.

"As well as could be expected," she replied. "It was not a happy affair, dinner last night, but finally it came to an end. We retired to bed at the same time, and William made a show of entering my bedchamber. He did not stay long, though. He slipped back into his own room a short time later, and then first thing this morning, he left for London." She let out a long breath. "I think it will work," she said hopefully.

He pressed her hand. "I believe it will."

"William has promised to return for the christening of the child. Other than that, he made it clear that he has no wish to set eyes on me or Edwin." Her voice wobbled on that last word. Eyes sparkling with unshed tears, she went on, "I can bear that for me, but poor Edwin. It is hard for him to know that his own father cares so little for him."

"It is hard for him," agreed Ambrose, "and horribly unfair that William has not shown any affection for his own son. I want you to know, Lexie, that I love that boy like my own."

"I know you do," she said, kissing his hand. "And at heart, I think he knows it too."

Ambrose lingered another day and night in Oxford. Daniel was in London and would not be there to welcome him home, so there was little need to return too soon. That night, he made gentle love to Lexie and held her close, holding a whispered conversation late until dawn about this new life that was growing in her womb. He left her then, urging her to write to him daily and keep him informed of everything that occurred. Then, he climbed aboard the carriage and began the journey back to Stanton Hall.

Chapter 22

Ambrose

Back at Stanton Hall, Ambrose and Daniel resumed their everyday life of easy companionship and fond friendship. Neither made any mention of what had transpired in their individual trips away from home, and Ambrose was glad of it, allowing himself to put into practice his "out of sight, out of mind" approach when it came to Daniel's love life.

Lexie wrote to him daily about her progress with the pregnancy. All seemed to be well, apart from her bouts of queasiness, but these were known to be a common effect of being with child. At times, Ambrose burned to share the news of his impending fatherhood. It felt far too big an event to be kept secret. Nevertheless, better counsel prevailed.

Sarah, for all her scientific knowledge, was not well versed with the ways of the world, and he was not sure she would understand or empathise once she knew of his affair with Lexie. He felt very bad keeping it from her, but decided it was the only way. Daniel was another matter. Several times, it was on the tip of his tongue to tell him, but there seemed to be an unspoken code between the two of them that whatever happened away from Stanton Hall was not to be discussed. Ambrose was minded too of Daniel's feelings in the matter. He recalled only too well his hurt at learning of the affair with Lexie. That hurt would only be compounded by the knowledge that there now was a child on the way. It was better, therefore, to keep this knowledge to himself.

In May, the following month, they each went their separate ways once more, he to Oxford and Daniel to London, where he was due to give his maiden speech in the House of Lords. They had worked on it together, after Daniel had sought his guidance, both deciding that it should address the current situation in America and what Britain's position should be in case the conflict escalated between the Union and the Confederacy. As they said their farewells, there came into Daniel's eyes a wistful look. "Ambrose," he said. "I do wish you were coming with me to hear my speech."

Ambrose merely responded with a weak smile, "I am sure it will go very well."

These monthly separations would not be easy, but this was their life now, and they were both playing by the rules of the game. Daniel smiled, wishing him a prosperous journey. He smiled in return, wishing him a successful maiden speech. And then they parted ways.

Another month passed, and they were now in the first week of June. One Monday morning, Ambrose arrived as usual at Stanton Hall and went up to Daniel's study, where they were in the habit of meeting to discuss estate matters at the start of every week. He found Daniel sitting in an armchair by the hearth, staring pensively into space. He knew at once that something was wrong. "Daniel, what is it?" he asked, going to sit before him.

In response, Daniel reached into his pocket and took out a folded sheet of paper. "This arrived today from Benjamin," was all he said, handing the letter to Ambrose. He took it and read it quickly.

April 30th, 1861

Dear Daniel,

I hope this letter finds you well and in good spirits. I am sure by now you will have heard the news about the Confederacy's attack on Fort Sumter and the fact that we are now in a state of war.

I have thought hard on the matter and have decided that as soon as the call comes, I shall volunteer for a cavalry regiment. You would do the same, I am sure, if you were in my shoes, for I cannot see either of us standing by and not answering the call when the security of our way of life is at stake.

I have not yet told Ma or Papa of this, and fear they will not take the news well. However, I am firm in my decision. I will fight for the Union.

Now don't be getting any quixotic notions of joining me in this fight. Your place is in England with Isabella, and Papa will not thank you for abandoning her to her fate. Besides, isn't it time I got the glory for once? Let me do this one thing alone, without you. Wish me luck, brother.

With love,

Benjamin

Ambrose sighed and put the letter down. He gazed at Daniel anxiously. "I do hope you are not getting any quixotic notions of volunteering to fight in this war," he said, echoing Benjamin's words.

"Rest easy, Ambrose, I am staying in England," said Daniel flatly.

"Good," murmured Ambrose, relieved. "It is the right thing to do."

"Is it?" asked Daniel with a sardonic twist to his mouth. "That I do not know, but I will abide by my family's wishes."

"And my wish too," Ambrose ventured to say, looking away. He wanted to say more but could not do so without expressing all that he felt.

Daniel's brown eyes softened a fraction. "I know," he said. "Though it does not make it any easier to be a bystander here, in the safety of Stanton Hall, while over on the other side of the ocean, my brother and countless others are soon to be risking their lives."

"No," agreed Ambrose, "it is not easy. I know you feel helpless in this position, but perhaps you may make your own contribution to the effort through any influence you may wield in London—your maiden speech was well received, I hear."

Daniel shrugged impatiently. "My influence is minimal, Ambrose, and you know it. Besides, the British government is much too beholden to the cotton and tobacco trade to want to sever ties entirely with the Confederacy."

Ambrose acknowledged the truth of this statement. "You are doing this for your family then," he said instead. "Isabella needs you here. She is but nineteen, Daniel, and cannot live alone and unchaperoned. And the last thing you would want is to take her back to America when a war has just been declared there."

"I know this, Ambrose," said Daniel irritably. "It is why I am staying. But damn it to hell, can I not be mad about it?"

"Of course you can."

Daniel took a calming breath and exhaled. "I am sorry, Ambrose. I do not mean to take it out on you."

"And I am sorry, Daniel, if it seems like I am haranguing you. The frustration you are expressing is understandable, but it also gives me a fear that you may someday take it upon yourself to go and join the Union army. Please, as a friend, I beseech you not to." Ambrose looked away again and tried to slow the pounding of his heart. He was coasting dangerously close to showing his hand, acting like a lover rather than as a friend.

In response, Daniel reached across and placed a hand on his thigh, squeezing it affectionately. Ambrose felt that touch like the heat of a brand. It sent a warm tingle of pleasure and arousal through him. He cleared his throat and swallowed. The hand fell away. Daniel sat back in his chair and was quiet a moment. Then, he said, "What did you think, Ambrose, of Benjamin's words about letting him have the glory for once?"

Ambrose chose his words carefully. "It appears there is some rivalry between the two of you."

"Not of my making," said Daniel shortly.

Ambrose could not be so sure of this. As much as he loved working with Daniel, Ambrose was all too aware that his title and fortune represented a barrier to their friendship. It was not too much of a stretch, therefore, to understand how this too could have caused a distance or rivalry to form between Daniel and his brother. He owed his friend a truthful response. "Perhaps not directly so," he said, "but inadvertently, you may have contributed to this rivalry. Pardon me, Daniel, but I must point out that you have inherited a title and a fortune, while your brother must content himself with still being dependent on his family for his income."

"Yes, I know," answered Daniel morosely. "However, Papa is changing the terms of his own will so that Benjamin will be the sole inheritor of all his lands in Ohio. He will get the share I once was to have had."

"But still," pointed out Ambrose, "there is a difference between being already in possession of a fortune and being in line to inherit one after your father's passing."

"There is not much I can do about that," replied Daniel wryly, "unless you wish me to pray for my papa's hasty demise."

"Nothing of the sort!" protested Ambrose. "If you recall, I said you may have stoked the fires of rivalry inadvertently, not through any direct action. But surely you must own that your elevated position in life places those around you, whose station remains well below yours, somewhat at a disadvantage." Ambrose had meant to talk of Benjamin but somehow ended up speaking of himself. He hoped this would pass Daniel's notice.

"Yes," murmured Daniel, looking at him fixedly, "I begin to see that." After a moment, he looked away and huffed in frustration, "But I am not sure that the matter of the inheritance is the sole reason for the feelings Benjamin has expressed with regards to me."

Here too, Ambrose had to tread carefully. He did not want to hurt his friend's feelings, but he thought he had an inkling of what was going on with Benjamin. "No," he agreed. "It is not all due to the inheritance. There is also the matter of… how shall I put it?"

Daniel regarded him quizzically. "Go on, Ambrose, do not spare my feelings."

Ambrose sighed. He had put his foot in it, so he may as well continue. "When I first met you, Daniel, I was most struck by… erm, by the autocratic nature of your character. You are fearless and decisive, going after whatever it is you want as if it is your right. And Benjamin, from what I saw, is not like that at all."

Daniel stared at him. "You mean," he said slowly, "the way I went after you."

Ambrose did not respond at first, then murmured very quietly, "I suppose so, yes, though that is not quite what I meant."

Daniel huffed, "Well in that case, I have well and truly been taught a lesson, for I went after the thing I wanted and got my fingers burned."

"*And burned me too in the process,*" thought Ambrose. He could not say this of course. Instead, he forced a smile and murmured, "Humility brings one closer to God."

There was a pause. Neither man looked at the other. "I would wish it brought me closer to Benjamin," Daniel said softly.

"In time, perhaps it will," responded Ambrose gently.

Then Daniel seemed to remember something. He stood and went to his desk, opening one of the drawers. From it, he took a sealed missive. "This came for Sarah," he said. He gazed down at it soberly, adding, "By the thickness of this packet, it is clear Benjamin has far more to say to your sister than he has to me, his own brother." With that, he handed the letter to Ambrose who carefully placed it in his leather bag. He would give it to Sarah on his return home later that day.

Daniel went back to his chair and stretched out his legs before him. "What do you think of this friendship between Sarah and Benjamin?" he wondered.

Ambrose shrugged. "To be honest, I do not know what to think. She maintains they are merely friends, but I cannot help but think there is more to it than that."

"I am tempted to agree with you," replied Daniel thoughtfully. "I have never before seen Benjamin behave like this. He has had his fair share of amorous adventures, but they have always been light-hearted and short-lived. This feels different."

"How do you feel about it?" asked Ambrose curiously.

"If you are asking if I would welcome Sarah as my sister-in-law, then Ambrose, you must know the answer is an emphatic yes. I am very fond of your sister. She is quite the character, and I think she would suit Benjamin admirably well. The real question, to my mind, is how do *you* feel about it?"

Ambrose ran a hand through his hair distractedly, then was immediately annoyed with himself. He did not like his neatly combed locks to be in disarray. "I am not sure what to think about it," he replied honestly. "You know my sister far better than I know your brother, who I only met on a few brief occasions." He added to himself, *"But if he is anything like you, Sarah will be the happiest woman in the world to be married to him."* Aloud he said, "There is also the problem of him living in America and volunteering for war, with no prospect of returning here for a long while."

Daniel's countenance hardened at the reminder that his brother was to join the Union army. Then he forced himself to relax. With a humorous twinkle in his eye, he declared, "Then they shall have to court each other via a long-distance correspondence. It could be quite the romance, you know. And eventually, I would hazard a bet that Benjamin will realise the depths of his feelings and come for her."

"There is also another problem," said Ambrose.

"Oh? What would that be?"

"The problem," went on Ambrose, "is that Sarah has harboured a secret attachment to someone else for quite some time."

Daniel sat forward with a frown. "Who?" he demanded.

"Mr Templeton."

Daniel reared back in shock. "What did you say?"

"You heard me quite well the first time," replied Ambrose.

"I did, but I am still finding it incomprehensible. Mr Templeton? Why he is the very last person a gentlewoman should contemplate for a husband."

"Really?" Ambrose raised a brow. "I distinctly recall you saying he was a charming and amiable fellow."

"Well that he is," said Daniel uncomfortably, "but I would not deem him suitable as a match for my sister, let alone yours."

"Would you care to explain why?" queried Ambrose.

"I—I..." Daniel was speechless. Ambrose narrowed his eyes at him. There was definitely something that Daniel was holding back. But then his friend seemed to gather his thoughts and explained, "He has something of a reputation when it comes to the ladies."

Too bad. For a moment there, Ambrose had thought Daniel was about to enlighten him as to what he and Mr Templeton got up to on their jaunts to London. Though perhaps, it was better he did not know.

"In any case," said Daniel, "I sincerely hope she is cured of that attachment, and soon. I may be biased in the matter, but Benjamin is a far better prospect for her."

Ambrose smiled. "These things are not in our hands, Daniel. We shall have to see how things go. Now, did we not have work to do?"

Daniel smiled ruefully. "Indeed we do, Ambrose. Let us get to it."

Chapter 23

Daniel

June 1862, one year later

The train steamed into Oxford station several hours later than scheduled. There had been an exasperating delay some two thirds of the journey in from London while a broken rail was attended to. And now, with darkness falling, he still had to endure a two-hour carriage ride back to Stanton Hall. Daniel considered for a moment stopping at his Oxford house for the night and resuming his journey in the morning but discarded the idea.

With a sigh, he descended from the train onto the platform. He was travel weary, and all he wanted was to be back home and to see Ambrose again. Over this past year, they had continued to go their separate ways at the start of each month, but the separation had not become any easier. He missed his friend desperately.

The London season had been in full swing. Daniel had attended various balls and soirées, danced with countless aspiring debutantes and exchanged pleasantries with the doyens of high society. Then of course, there had been his obligatory visit to Tremayne's. It had achieved its objective. He had slaked his lust until the same time next month. But the whole thing—the society balls, the debauched frolics and London in general—had left an unpleasant taste in his mouth. He wanted to be home. He wanted to be with Ambrose.

Briskly, he walked down the platform, travel case in hand, looking for his coachman. He had sent word to Stanton Hall to have the carriage waiting for him at the station. He looked all around but could see no sign of it. He made enquiries with the clerk in the ticket office and the porter on the platform. Neither of them had seen any sign of his carriage. He huffed in frustration. There was nothing for it. He would have to walk to his Oxford house on St Michael's Street and bed there for the night. It was only a few minutes' journey away.

He set out, walking rapidly, wanting to get there as soon as he possibly could. At last, he turned into his street and reached his front door. Taking out his pocket watch, he scrutinised the time. Nine o'clock. He wondered if Mr and Mrs Briggs were still up, or if they had retired for the night. Well, it could not be helped. He had to stop at the house.

Daniel found the doorbell and rang it. There was a long delay, during which no doubt Briggs was getting himself out of bed, before the door opened and Briggs's suspicious face peeked out. On seeing his master, his expression relaxed into a perplexed smile as he held the door open. "My lord, welcome," he said. "We were not expecting you."

"A train delay, Briggs," replied Daniel laconically. "I am sorry to put you out of bed, but could you see to having my room prepared and some water brought up?"

"Yes, my lord," replied the aged butler. "I will get to it at once. Please do come into the drawing room. I shall ask Mrs Briggs to bring you some tea, and a bite to eat perhaps?"

Daniel smiled at the butler gratefully. "Thank you, Briggs."

"Of course, sir," replied the butler, lighting a taper and taking it through to the drawing room, where he proceeded to illuminate the room. He left then to do his various tasks, leaving Daniel alone in the richly furnished chamber. He sat down in an armchair and idly reached for a book that had been left on a side table, no doubt by Ambrose. He looked at the spine. *A Tale of Two Cities* by Charles Dickens—a favourite of his. He had mentioned it to Ambrose some time ago. Was that why Ambrose had taken the volume out of the Stanton Hall library to read? Daniel smiled at the thought.

He leafed through the book, reading passages to pass the time until a knock at the door heralded the arrival of Mrs Briggs, bearing a tea tray and sandwiches. "My lord," she said as she entered the room. "It is good to see you."

"And you, Mrs Briggs," replied Daniel. "I hope you are well?"

"As well as can be expected," mumbled the housekeeper. She set the tray down on the table then said, "Your bedchamber will be ready presently, my lord. Is there anything else I can get for you?"

"No, Mrs Briggs, I thank you," replied Daniel pleasantly. "This is all more than enough."

She bobbed a curtsy and left him. Putting the book back down on the table, Daniel helped himself to some tea and a plate of sandwiches. Ah, that was much better, he thought some minutes later. He stretched his legs out and sighed. He supposed he should head upstairs to his room. With an effort, he got to his weary feet, taking a candle with him to light his way. He stepped into the hallway, catching sight of the back door, and paused, remembering that fateful night he had followed Ambrose as he sneaked out to have his tryst with his mistress. Something made Daniel go to that door now. The key was in the lock, so he twisted it open and let himself out into the quiet of the night.

A welcome breath of fresh air fanned his face as he stepped out into the garden. Just three nights ago, he thought miserably, this would have been Ambrose moving furtively in this space, going to visit Lexie Forbes. Daniel looked towards the next house, imagining it. He knew he should stop. He was merely torturing himself, thinking about Ambrose and his mistress. But just like a tongue returning repeatedly to lick a cut lip, he had to revisit the site of his wound.

That was when he heard it—a faint noise coming from the next house. He listened carefully. Was that the cry of a baby? The noise came again, a little louder this time. From where he stood, he saw the door open in the next house, and a white-robed figure step out into the night. She held a fractious child in her arms and was busy trying to soothe it.

Without conscious thought, his feet took him forward. As he got closer, he saw who it was. "Mrs Forbes," he called out.

She turned to him with a start, holding her child protectively, expression fearful until he was close enough for her to recognise him. "Viscount Stanton," she said tremulously. "You gave me quite a fright."

"Pardon me. I did not mean to do so." His eyes were glued to the child she was holding. "And who is this little one?" he ventured to ask.

She looked down at the bundle in her arms, an affectionate smile lighting her face. "This is Emily Seraphine Forbes, my daughter," she said proudly.

He came closer and peered down at the little scrap of life being bounced in Lexie's arms. "How old is she?" he enquired.

"A little over five months," came the reply.

Daniel stared at the baby's wide grey eyes and fuzzy mop of blond hair. Pieces of the jigsaw were falling rapidly into place—Ambrose's febrile excitement last January and his anxiousness to be gone to Oxford. Daniel had chalked it to impatience to be with his mistress, but that was not what it had been. He had been impatient to see his newborn baby. Daniel did some quick mental calculations and realised that this child must have been conceived on that fateful night he had followed Ambrose out into the garden. The knowledge had him dumbstruck for a full minute while he continued to stare. The baby had ceased her grousing and taken an interest in the tall stranger addressing her mother as well as in the bright candle he held in his hand.

This was Ambrose's daughter. A myriad of emotions swept through Daniel as he stood glued to the spot. Ambrose had a child, a beautiful little girl. This was the child Daniel could never have given him. Instead, it was Lexie who had gifted him with this miracle. Jealousy, envy and joy swirled in his chest, followed by a deep sadness for Ambrose. This was his daughter, yet he would never be allowed to claim her publicly as his.

"She has his eyes," he said huskily.

Lexie did not pretend to misunderstand him. "Yes," she agreed softly, "she has."

He stepped closer and ran a finger along the baby's soft, downy cheek. "She is perfect," he whispered.

"And stubborn, just like her father," added Lexie.

Emily batted her fists at him in excitement. He touched a finger to one small, delicate hand and found it engulfed in a surprisingly strong grip. He laughed in delight. He looked up at Lexie and asked, "Please, may I hold her?"

She hesitated a fraction, as if wondering if he were angry at the discovery that Ambrose had a daughter. Something in his expression must have reassured her, for she said, "Yes, of course."

He placed the candle he held onto a wooden bench and put his hands out. With great care, he took the small bundle of life into his arms, gathering her close to his chest. He rocked her gently, smiling down into those wide grey eyes.

"You are a natural with children, my lord," said Lexie approvingly.

He grinned. "Would you believe it if I said this was the first time I have ever held a babe in my arms?"

"I would not!" she retorted. "You do it so well."

"A part of me always thought he would be a father one day. Not me, though," he said, his eyes still glued to the child in his arms.

"Why not, my lord? You are still too young to write off your future in such a way."

He looked up at her then. "Call me Daniel," he commanded. Abandoning all pretence, he added, "Ambrose has spoken to you of me, I suppose—of my feelings for him."

She did not answer immediately, seemingly unsure what to reveal. Finally, she murmured, "He has told me everything."

A sharp stab of pain cut into his heart. Of course, Ambrose would confide in the woman he loved. Daniel leaned down to kiss Emily's little forehead. "Then you will understand," he said quietly, "why it is I say that I will never marry."

"Do you love him that much?" asked Lexie softly.

"He is everything to me." Daniel's chest heaved with the emotion he was trying to keep in check. His voice thick with pain, he added, "But you have nothing to worry about in my regard, Lexie. He is all yours. He merely allows me into his life as a friend."

He rocked the baby gently, leaning down to breathe in her sweet scent. She was a part of Ambrose. And just as he loved Ambrose fiercely, he knew too that he would love this precious child of his. Looking up, he caught Lexie's troubled gaze and smiled sadly. "It is alright, Lexie," he assured her. "There is no need for tears. As long as he is in my life somehow, as a friend, then I can be satisfied with my lot. There is much to be thankful for, foremost of which is the miracle of this beautiful girl. How precious she is."

Lexie nodded, her eyes glazed with the tears he had asked her not to shed. "You know he cares greatly for you," she said hesitantly.

"I know. I am truly blessed to have him as my friend." Daniel smiled widely, trying to ease her worry. Lord, he had not come to Oxford to inflict his woes on this kind woman.

"May I ask something, Lexie?" he added quickly.

"Of course."

"Would you mind if I came to visit?" he asked her. "I would not do it at the same time as Ambrose, so you may have your private time with him. But on other occasions, may I come to see you, and Emily? I would wish to be a part of her life, if you will allow me."

Now the tears were flowing freely down her cheeks, God forgive him. She took a deep breath in and replied, "I would welcome your visits, Daniel, and so will Emily."

"Thank you," he whispered. "You are kind-hearted, Lexie, and I quite understand why Ambrose loves you so much."

She nodded, if anything looking more distressed. He glanced down at the babe in his arms one last time. Her eyes had fluttered shut, long dark lashes fanning her face. "I believe she has fallen asleep," he murmured very softly.

"Your voice must have lulled her to sleep. It is the same when Ambrose is with her." She held out her arms, and with the greatest care, he gave back that precious bundle. She held her baby close and whispered, "Well, I shall bid you goodnight."

"Goodnight, Lexie and God be with you."

With one final smile, she turned and made her way back inside. Daniel lingered a few moments more in the stillness of the night. Then, heaving a long breath, he picked up the candle and returned to his house.

Chapter 24

Ambrose

The following Monday morning, Ambrose arrived at Stanton Hall, as was his wont, and headed directly to Daniel's study. He had seen him yesterday at a luncheon hosted by the Sedgwicks at Mulverley Grange. Daniel had only just returned from his trip to London, a day later than planned, explaining that his train the previous evening had been delayed, necessitating an overnight stay at his house in Oxford. Ambrose's curiosity had been aroused, but Daniel had studiously ignored his gaze, addressing his remarks to Sarah instead.

All through luncheon, Ambrose had observed him keenly. Something was different about Daniel, but he could not quite put his finger on it. Ambrose's stomach lurched at the idea of Daniel knowing about Emily. Had Daniel discovered the truth? Would he reject their friendship? But there was relief too at the thought of Daniel knowing. For months, Ambrose had been longing to tell him his news. Perhaps now, with this opportunity for private discourse, Ambrose would find out how things stood with his friend. He knocked on the study door and entered.

Daniel smiled at him from behind his desk. "Ah, good morning, Ambrose. You are looking well," he said cheerfully.

"And you," replied Ambrose, coming to sit opposite him. "I was sorry to hear about your train on Saturday," he said casually.

"Yes, it was rather tiresome," responded Daniel. "I had to wake Briggs from his bed, poor fellow."

"Did you happen, by any chance, to meet anyone else?" enquired Ambrose.

Daniel threw him an amused glance, not immediately answering him. "What is it you really want to know, Ambrose?" he asked instead. "Out with it."

Ambrose felt himself flush. "Nothing," he protested. "I was merely enquiring generally."

Daniel leaned forward, his palm on his cheek. "I have been thinking, Ambrose," he began.

"Yes, Daniel?"

"I believe it would be beneficial if you were to increase the frequency of your visits to Oxford from once a month to once a week," declared Daniel.

"Why so?" demanded Ambrose suspiciously.

Daniel ignored the question and continued his speech. "Except on the first Thursday of every month, when you must keep your fixed appointment at the bank, I think it would be best that you travel there on a Friday afternoon and return Saturday evening. I do not see you on Saturdays as it is, so it will not be a great loss of your company for me, and as for Sarah, I shall ensure that she spends her time with Isabella and me during your absences, so you need not worry about her."

"Is a weekly trip to Oxford not a trifle excessive?" asked Ambrose uncomfortably.

Daniel raised a brow. "Do you consider seeing your child once a week excessive, Ambrose?"

The jig was up. "So, you know," said Ambrose quietly.

"I know," confirmed Daniel. His expression hardened. "When were you planning to inform me that you were a father, Ambrose?"

"I thought to keep this side of my life private," he said, twiddling nervously with his thumbs.

"And I thought we were friends," said Daniel flatly.

"We are!" flashed Ambrose.

"Friends confide in one another," continued Daniel.

"I have been dying to tell you. It has been on the tip of my tongue a thousand times," said Ambrose defensively.

"Then why didn't you?"

"Because," said Ambrose softly, "I did not want to cause you pain."

Torrid dark eyes fixed their gaze on him. "You think finding out about Emily would cause me pain?"

"Didn't it?"

Daniel sighed aloud. "Maybe a very little. Mostly, it gave me great joy. She is beautiful, Ambrose."

He smiled proudly. "Yes, she is my princess."

"If I may ask a delicate question, how did William Forbes react on hearing the news?" wondered Daniel.

Ambrose grimaced. "It was not a pleasant interview. I was there for it. He agreed to give Emily his name and nothing else. I shall be the one to provide financially for her. I am already putting aside funds every month."

"Then double those funds, Ambrose, with a contribution from me. Whatever happens, rest assured that her future will be provided for," said Daniel earnestly.

"Why should you?" demanded Ambrose. "She is not yours."

Daniel winced at the choice of words, and Ambrose regretted them instantly. "No," Daniel agreed, "she is not mine, but she is yours, and that matters to me. You matter to me. Do not argue with me on this, Ambrose. As it is, I am hardly likely to marry or have children of my own, so I might as well put aside some of my fortune for your daughter."

A swell of bittersweet emotion swept through him at these words—guilt and sadness for Daniel mixed with pleasure that no one else would have him. He had feared that one day, his friend would bring a bride to Stanton Hall. But Daniel was young still to be making such pronouncements, not yet six and twenty. How could he be so sure that he would never marry? Ambrose looked into Daniel's eyes then, seeing the swell of emotion in his dark gaze, and he knew of course, although he could hardly admit it to himself. Daniel still loved him. His chest swelled with happiness and pain. For this changed nothing. The two of them together as lovers was an impossibility. There could be nothing between them but what they had now.

"Thank you. That is very kind," he said stiffly to Daniel, and the subject was closed.

Chapter 25

Daniel

August 1863

A year had passed since that fateful visit to Oxford had uncovered the existence of Ambrose's daughter. Daniel had kept his promise to visit Emily and Lexie at odd times when he knew Ambrose would not be there. Often, he caught an earlier train from London on his return from the great metropolis, with the express purpose of spending time in Oxford with them.

He brought gifts with him, rattles and other small toys, delightful little outfits and books (for when she was older of course, he told the little girl). He spent hours playing with Emily, walking her in the gardens or singing her lullabies to put her to sleep. He could see so much of Ambrose in her—the grey eyes, the pouty mouth, the blond locks. It was obvious to all that he was smitten with this child.

Of course, Ambrose was well aware of his visits to Oxford. They could hardly be kept secret when his many gifts to Emily were strewn about the room. Ambrose had refrained from comment on the matter except for remarking once on the dangers of spoiling children, but Daniel had scoffed. If he wanted to buy Emily gifts, then he would. In any case, Daniel perceived that, despite his token protests, Ambrose was secretly pleased about the gifts.

Ambrose's friendship and the visits to Emily were the only bright spots on Daniel's horizon these days. They were the ones that kept him sane as the desperately worrying news trickled through from America. Sometimes, Daniel felt as if he existed in a vacuum from one letter that he received to the next. The war in America had been dragging on for over two years now, with little end in sight. Letters struggled to find their way to him. His parents wrote to him and so did Benjamin, but it took months sometimes for the missives to arrive. God knew how many were lost upon the way.

He worried constantly about his brother. He was alive still, in one piece, but that was all he knew. Benjamin's letters to him had become sparse and factual, sparing him very few details of his life. Daniel could only imagine what his circumstances truly were from piecing together information in newspaper reports. Late last month, news had come through of a large engagement of forces at Gettysburg. It was painted as a victory for the Union, pushing back the Confederacy's advance on Washington. Yet the news also told of mass casualties, soldiers on both sides perishing in their thousands.

Had Benjamin fought at Gettysburg? Was he one of those many thousand casualties? The worry gnawed at Daniel. Every day, he looked out for the post. Every day, he was disappointed.

Ambrose was the rock that sustained him in these difficult times. On days when worry consumed him, his friend listened in sympathy as he ranted and fulminated about how badly the war was being prosecuted. When letters came, he enquired about his family's news and gave sound counsel. When letters failed to arrive, he provided comfort and encouragement. What would he do without Ambrose? He had become his right hand, not just in the management of his estate affairs, but in nearly all aspects of his life.

This August morning was no different from most other mornings at Stanton Hall. He had awoken in a hot sweat, his covers kicked to the end of the bed. A sponge wash had cooled him down—just. Then, he had dressed and come down to the dining room for his breakfast. Isabella was already there, buttering a slice of toast. "Morning, Bella," he said, taking a seat. "Has the post arrived yet?"

"No, not yet," she replied. "I have a good lookout of the window from here, so I will see the mail coach when it arrives."

Disappointed, he poured himself a cup of coffee, then took his plate to the sideboard where a vast array of meats, eggs and cheeses were laid out. He served himself then returned to his seat and began to eat.

"Are you going to Netherwick Hall today?" he enquired of his sister.

"Yes," she said, taking a sip from her tea. "Ambrose is taking me there at nine o'clock. We will be showing the house to a prospective new tenant, Mr Wilson, a factory owner from Manchester who has retired on his riches and wishes to live the good life. I am told he is a widower with two young children. To be honest though, I am not sure that someone in trade will make an appropriate tenant for Netherwick Hall."

"And why should that matter?" rebuked Daniel. "I will have you remember, Bella, that your own father made his fortune through the toil of his hands."

"I am well aware of that," she countered, bristling at the reprimand. "It is not the same though. Papa was a gentleman to start with. I simply fear that this Mr Wilson may be vulgar and uncouth. Though Ambrose says that what matters most is the man's good character."

"He would be right!" concurred Daniel. "Has he checked this Mr Wilson's references? What do we know of this person?"

"It is all well in hand," said Isabella airily, "and for your information, Ambrose has made enquiries which have all checked out. Mr Wilson is a respectable business owner, a widower with two young children and a large fortune. These are the salient facts. We shall know the rest on meeting him today. Ambrose tells me it is important to trust one's instinct on meeting a person, as he believes that we can tell naturally if such a person is trustworthy or not."

"Ha!" said Daniel, much diverted. "I had not thought Ambrose to be one to believe in such things as instinct."

"Perhaps then you do not know him as well as you think," replied Bella tartly.

"You may be right," smiled Daniel. "I shall quiz him on it next I see him. And I wish you luck with Mr Wilson today."

She smiled back, mollified. "Thank you, Daniel." Something at the window caught her attention. "The mail coach is here," she said, jumping to her feet. "I shall go see if there is something arrived." With that, she hurried out of the room.

He continued to eat his breakfast, his heart pounding a little faster than usual as he set to hoping today would be the day some news of Benjamin finally came. He had just finished a slice of beef steak when the door flew open and Isabella rushed in. With shaking hands, she held three missives, all written in the same unmistakable scrawl. One for him, one for Bella and one for Sarah Cranshaw. Daniel broke the seal on his letter, his hands not shaking any less than Bella's, and pulled out one lone folded sheet. He read it quickly.

July 8th, 1863

Dear Daniel,

Perhaps you have already heard news of our latest engagement at Gettysburg. The Confederate advance towards Washington has been halted, and they are now in retreat. The price for this has been steep, with heavy loss of life on both sides, including, I am sad to say, our dear friend Jimmy, from a gun wound to the shoulder. Although the surgeon was able to

Daniel put the letter down, gulping air into his lungs. Benjamin was alive and well, but Jimmy, the stable boy who had joined the cavalry regiment with Benjamin, was dead. He looked across at Isabella, whose face was flooded with tears. "Jimmy is gone," he said.

She sniffed. "Yes, it says so in the letter. Poor Jimmy!" She wiped at her eyes and added, "Is it wicked of me to be relieved that it is him and not Ben that is gone?"

Daniel went to his sister, drawing her into the circle of his arms. "I had the very same thought," he said. "It is not a very Christian reaction, but it is understandable. I cannot tell you how relieved I am that Ben is unharmed."

"Me too," she mumbled into his chest.

"Benjamin's letter was so dry and factual. I do wonder why he is shutting us out and writing to us as if to strangers," he went on. "It pains me."

"I know," agreed Bella. "It pains me too."

Daniel spent the day veering between elation that his brother was still alive and being disconsolate at Jimmy's death and at the cold tone of Benjamin's letter. He wished he could repair his relationship with him, but he was powerless to do so until this war was over. It frustrated him to be in such an impotent position.

That afternoon, Ambrose came by to see him and bid him farewell before he travelled to Oxford, for it was a Friday, the day he went to visit his daughter. It was clear he had already heard the news about Benjamin from Bella. He knocked on the library door and came in, finding Daniel in his shirtsleeves, due to the heat, lounging on his favourite armchair by the open window, reading a book.

Daniel put the book down at Ambrose's entrance and watched his friend, face flushed from the summer heat, take a seat across from him. The ripe air carried a faint aroma of Ambrose's clean sweat mixed with his bergamot and orange scented cologne. It was a heady scent that made Daniel's cock perk up with interest. He willed it down the best he could and smiled at his friend. "Come to say goodbye?" he asked.

"Actually," said Ambrose, "I came to see how you are. Isabella told me about Benjamin, and your friend Jimmy. I was sorry to hear of his passing."

"I have been thinking of Jimmy all day," replied Daniel, "dredging up old memories of good times we spent together. He always wore a smile and never a word of complaint crossed his lips."

"A terrible waste of a good life," murmured Ambrose.

"Yes," sighed Daniel. "And then amidst the pain, there is also joy at the news that Ben is unharmed."

"Yes," agreed Ambrose. "That is a relief." They sat in companiable silence for a minute, then Ambrose went on, "I knew as soon as I heard the news that I would find you here, moping, and I do not like to leave you in such a state. Therefore, I have a suggestion. Will you come with me today to Oxford? We can visit Lexie, Edwin and Emily together. I am sure it will help cheer you up."

Hope rose in Daniel's chest. What he would give to spend time right now with Ambrose and Emily. Yet he hesitated, not wanting to be in the way. "You do not mind me being there with you?"

"Of course not," reassured Ambrose.

"I would not want to deprive you of, erm, the opportunity for intimacy with Lexie," mumbled Daniel.

Ambrose did not look at him as he said, "It is quite alright, Daniel. I visit every week and have many other opportunities for, erm, intimacy."

"In that case, I would be delighted to join you," smiled Daniel.

Chapter 26

Daniel

They left some twenty minutes later. As they galloped along the country road, Daniel pulled the carriage window open as far as it would go, willing some cooling breeze to enter their confined space. He kicked off his shoes and undid his necktie, then loosened the collar of his shirt, trying to cool himself down on this scorching summer's day.

"This heat is intolerable," he grumbled. Casting a look across at Ambrose, he added, "Do take off that necktie. It is making me hot just looking at you."

"I do not like to be dressed casually when I am out in public," demurred Ambrose.

"You are in a closed carriage," contradicted Daniel, "and nobody but me can see you. Now for the love of all that is holy, do it, and take off your shoes, even your stockings. We can put them back on once we are close to Oxford." He gave Ambrose a hard look when it looked like his friend was stubbornly going to refuse. With a huff, Ambrose complied, removing his necktie and untying his shoes, placing them neatly to one side. The man was obsessively tidy. "The stockings too," he said, when it looked like Ambrose was going to stop there.

With a sigh, Ambrose did as he was bid, baring his pale feet to Daniel's gaze. He studied them covertly. They were long and narrow, the toes perfectly formed. Above the ankle, he detected the beginning of a sweep of dark blond hair. He could not take his eyes off that hair, wishing he could run his hand along

Ambrose's calf and up that ankle, and feel the texture of it. Would it be rough to the touch or soft?

He had never before found himself aroused by the sight of someone's feet. He supposed there was a first time for everything. There again, every part of Ambrose's body was tantalising to him. He had been infatuated with him for two and a half years, and there was no sign that his feelings were ever going to abate. For the second time that day, he felt his cock thicken in Ambrose's presence. He decided to start conversing about anything to keep his mind from obsessing over Ambrose's deliciousness.

"So," he said, "what is this you have been telling Bella about trusting your instinct about someone you meet. I had not thought you one to believe in such intangible things."

"In the nearly thirty-two years I have been on this earth, I have learned a thing or two," replied Ambrose, amused. "And that is one of them. I agree it may sound illogical, but I cannot dispute the findings of my experience."

"And your instinct has always been right about people?" queried Daniel.

"Almost always," Ambrose concurred.

"You were wrong about me though, admit it. The first time you met me, you thought I was an entitled, arrogant pup, did you not?" teased Daniel.

Ambrose raised his brows as he scrutinised Daniel mockingly. "And how exactly was I wrong?"

"Well, I suppose I was that," said Daniel, feeling a trifle flustered. "But you did not see the other, more positive things, did you?" He listed them on the fingers of his hand. "My very clever mind, my kindness, my undying loyalty to those I love, my charming sense of humour." He raised his eyes challengingly at the sound of Ambrose's soft laughter.

"Pardon me, Daniel, but for a moment there you sounded like some mama extolling her daughter's virtues in the hope of finding her a good husband."

Daniel quirked his lips, acknowledging the hit. "Touché," he said softly, then, "It is not far from the truth, you know. I am always trying to prove my worth to you."

Ambrose's grey eyes lost their merriment. "You are my dearest friend, Daniel," he said firmly. "There is no need for you to prove your worth."

"And yet I do have this need. It is in the forlorn hope that someday, you might come to feel about me the way I do about you," thought Daniel to himself, looking away to hide the sadness of his gaze.

Nothing more was said after that. Daniel put his head back on the plush leather of his seat and closed his eyes, resting for the remainder of the journey. He fell into a light doze, only to be awakened sometime later by a light tap on the shoulder. "Daniel," came Ambrose's voice. "We are nearing Oxford."

With a start, he sat up and quickly began to repair his clothes. He had only just finished tying his shoelaces when the carriage drew up in front of his Oxford house. They alighted and brought their cases into the house, greeting Briggs who came to open the door. Each then went up their bedchamber to freshen up, before convening once more in the drawing room, where they partook of some reviving iced lemonade. Daniel put down his empty cup and said, "Shall we go see them then?"

Ambrose nodded and stood, not needing to be told twice. Without a word, they filed out of the room and by mutual consent headed for the back door. They walked the few paces to the next house and let themselves in. "Uncle Ambrose!" cried Edwin's voice. A moment later, he had launched himself at Ambrose, who embraced him warmly.

"I have been on the lookout for your arrival," said the young boy earnestly.

"And here I am," replied Ambrose, adding, "and I have brought company too. Say your greetings, Edwin."

Edwin made a bow in Daniel's direction. "Good day, my lord," he said most correctly.

Daniel was having none of that formality. "Good God!" he exclaimed. "Do not 'my lord' me, young man." He lifted the boy into his strong arms and chided, "I have told you before to call me Uncle Daniel."

Edwin gurgled with laughter. "I forgot!" he crowed.

"See that you do not do so again," replied Daniel with mock severity. "Now lead us to your mama."

Together, they entered the drawing room, where they found Lexie bouncing a tearful Emily on her knee, trying to ease her fussing. She smiled at them distractedly, "She does not like this heat, poor child. I cannot seem to calm her down."

"Let me," said both men at once, holding out their arms. Daniel was the quicker, taking Emily and lifting her up high above his head, making her squeal with laughter.

"Well," said Lexie in amusement. "That is one way to stop her cries." She turned to Ambrose as he folded her into his arms, kissing her lightly on the lips. "Hello, darling," she murmured.

Daniel was busy with Emily, but he did not miss the affectionate embrace. He tried not to feel envy, he did, but he was only human. To ease the ache, he turned his back to them and kept his eyes on the sweet little girl in his arms. She was laughing out loud now, as he swooped her into the air. He felt a little proud at his prowess in calming the child. That pride was soon pierced by Lexie's next remark.

"Your arms will tire, Daniel, and when they do, the poor thing will start her fussing all over again, just mark my words." She tempered the comment with a smile. "But it is good to see you," she added.

He brought Emily down to his hip, holding her securely as he smiled back at Lexie. "It is good to see you too, and looking so well. Being out in the sun has added some fetching colour to your countenance."

She touched her cheek self-consciously. "You mean it has brought out my freckles," she said.

"I do not hold with the current fashion for wanting females to look pale and wan. You look delightful, Lexie," said Daniel, using the same flattery that worked with Isabella. In his arms, Emily began to grouse once more.

Ambrose stepped over to him. "Enough with your flirting, Daniel, and my turn now. Give her to me."

Reluctantly, Daniel released his precious charge and watched Ambrose take his daughter, cooing softly to her. She quieted immediately. Ambrose looked up triumphantly. "See, that is how it is done," he said with a hint of smugness.

Lexie burst out laughing. "I see I shall be treated to a contest between the two of you as to who is best at calming Emily. But please do carry on, as it will give me some welcome respite."

And indeed, the two of them spent the rest of the day vying for Emily's attention. Whenever she began to get fractious, the other would hold out his arms, saying, "Give her to me now." It was an amicable contest though, for being with Emily brought them too much joy and relief from their cares for any real enmity to develop. It was Ambrose who soothed his daughter to sleep with a soft lullaby later that evening. Daniel sat close by, watching his friend, awash with soppy sentimentality. After Ambrose had taken Emily upstairs and placed her gently in her crib, the two of them said their goodbyes and returned to the Stanton house.

Walking into the dim hallway, Daniel turned to Ambrose and said softly, "Thank you for bringing me here. It has been the most joyous of afternoons." It had indeed been joyous, but at times like these, Daniel wondered if this familial closeness with Ambrose would be enough. He could not prevent himself from wanting more.

Ambrose pressed his shoulder gently. "I am glad, Daniel. Goodnight, my dear friend."

"Goodnight." They parted ways, each going to their separate rooms and to a night of mostly restful sleep.

Chapter 27

Ambrose

September 1865, two years later

Ambrose woke early, dressed and went down to eat his usual breakfast of buttered bread and cold slices of meat, washed down with a cup of coffee. It was a bright morning, rays of sun already peeking in through the window. As he ate, his thoughts turned to Daniel, as they always did. And as with most mornings, he wished his friend could get reprieve from his constant worry about his family in America.

The end of this war between the Union and the Confederacy was drawing near. They had all celebrated when, last April, news had reached them of General Lee's surrender. After that, it had been a waiting game for them, as they looked to receive news of Benjamin's safe return home. Daniel, however, refused to forego his daily prayers for Benjamin's safety. He had heard too many tales of soldiers surviving long wars only to fall at the very last hour. Ambrose hoped with all his heart that this would not be so for Benjamin.

Breakfast over, he left the house, setting out on foot for his first destination of the day. This morning, he had to pay a call at Gorston Manor, one of the late earl's great houses, which had been granted to Elizabeth Stanton, Daniel's cousin, as part of the four-way split of the Stanton inheritance. Beth Stanton had returned to America with her family all those years ago, but Ambrose had continued to manage the estate on her behalf. The house itself had been let out last year to a retired naval commander named Colonel Collins, who had settled there with his two daughters. His sister, Sarah, tutored these daughters several mornings a week in French, literature and classics.

However, the purpose of his visit today was to check on a leak in the roof that had occurred after some heavy rain showers earlier in the week. Colonel Collins had sent word to him late yesterday evening about the leak, and he had promised to investigate the matter. The walk to Gorston Manor was not long, only a matter of fifteen minutes. It was just past eight o'clock when he crossed the gravel driveway and rang the bell.

He was shown to the front parlour by a servant, who promised to fetch the colonel. Ambrose was not kept waiting long. A brisk step announced the arrival of the colonel, a florid gentleman of around sixty with a bluff manner of speaking. "Ah, Mr Cranshaw, good day to you," said Colonel Collins.

"Good day, colonel," replied Ambrose. "I received your note and came as soon as I could."

"Good man, good man. Follow me and I will show you the damage. It is not great, I assure you, but it will require some work soon to prevent it worsening," explained the colonel.

"I will send some workers over to make the repairs just as soon as I have assessed the damage," promised Ambrose, walking up the stairs after the colonel. They reached the top floor and headed down a corridor towards one of the rooms. The colonel knocked briskly on the door, and when there was no answer, opened it to let them in. It was a bedchamber, probably used by one of the house servants, but currently empty. Ambrose saw the damage immediately. One wall of the room was streaked with damp brown stains. He went to it and placed his hand on it, feeling the moisture. His hand came away wet and glistening.

Curious to find the source of this moisture, he went to the window and pulled up the sash. With agility and long experience of doing such things, he climbed out of the window and perched on the narrow sill, holding his balance as he glanced up at the roof. He saw the problem immediately. One of the guttering pipes had snapped and was gushing water onto the wall, which was seeping into the internal walls of the house. Satisfied he had a clear picture, he climbed back inside and wiped his hands on his handkerchief. He enjoyed getting to the root of a problem and solving it.

"Well?" asked the colonel.

"A broken guttering pipe," answered Ambrose. "I will arrange for someone to come today and sort it out."

"Splendid, splendid," replied the colonel with a smile letting them out of the room. As they negotiated their way back down, he spoke again. "While I have you here, Mr Cranshaw, there is another matter I wanted to discuss."

"Of course, sir. I am at your disposal." They reached the front parlour again, and the colonel invited him to sit.

"I have received word from my sister, Mary, that her husband has sadly passed away from an attack to his heart," said the colonel.

"I am sorry to hear it, colonel. Please accept my condolences," replied Ambrose politely.

"Yes, yes, it is the way of the world. What can you do? The reason why I bring this up is that Mary is now alone, with three young children to care for. I do not like the thought of her being without any family nearby—she lives in Gotherington, you see, a village some miles north of Cheltenham. She wrote to tell me that there is a house on the outskirts of the village newly to be let out. I went there last week to examine it and, the long and short of it is, we shall be moving there at the end of October."

"I see," murmured Ambrose, sighing to himself. He would have to look for another tenant to rent this place.

"I will of course see that the rent on Gorston Manor is paid up to the end of the tenancy period which still has another eight weeks to go," continued the colonel, "but I shall not be renewing the tenancy."

"I do understand, colonel," said Ambrose. "At times like these, it is important for families to stay together." His mind drifted to Daniel and Benjamin, and the toll of their long years of separation.

"Indeed, indeed," nodded the colonel. "Much as we have enjoyed our stay here, and the wonderful tutoring from your dear sister. We shall be sad to leave."

"And we shall be sad to see you go, sir." Ambrose stood and made his farewells, then started the walk to Stanton Hall in a pensive mood. So, Gorston Manor was to lie empty soon, unless he could find a new tenant for it. Unbidden came a thought. It would make a wonderful home for Lexie and the children. The house was spacious, without being too grand, and the grounds extensive with plenty of room for the children to play outside. It was also but a short walk from Ivy Cottage, so he could see them every day if he wished.

He snorted, pushing aside the fantasy. William Forbes would never allow it. The man kept his wife and child housed in his Oxford home, and paid a far from generous stipend for their upkeep. He was not about to agree to the expense of uprooting them to another home, all so that they could have more room to play and so that they could be close to Ambrose.

How about if he himself were to cover the expense of their move to Gorston Manor? Could he afford it? In his mind, he made the calculations and sighed. It would require some significant economies and make inroads into the savings he had put by for Emily's future. And then, there was another issue.

Would Daniel mind having Lexie and the children live there? He could not say for sure. Daniel was devoted to Emily, perhaps even more so than him, but surely he would not appreciate having Ambrose's mistress live so close by.

If the shoe were on the other foot, he was sure he would not like it one bit if Daniel were to bring a mistress to live in his home. But that was to suppose that Daniel still cared about him that way. They had not spoken of their feelings in a long time and had settled into a fond camaraderie. Ambrose's own feelings for Daniel had been constant, but he could not be sure of what Daniel felt for him, except for a deep and lasting friendship.

As his steps took him to Stanton Hall, he chided himself for building his hopes up. Next month, he would put an advertisement in the paper and seek out a new tenant. He hurried up the steps and rang the bell. As the butler let him inside, he said cheerfully, "Good day, Siddons. Is the viscount in his study?"

"Yes, sir, he is," replied the butler.

Ambrose handed over his hat and coat, then hastened up the stairs to see Daniel. He knocked briefly on the door, then let himself in. Daniel looked up from the letter he was writing, a smile lighting his face. "Ambrose, good morning to you," he said.

"And a good morning to you," came Ambrose's response as he settled himself in a chair. Then, as he always did, he asked, "Any news from America?"

Daniel pursed his lips and shook his head. Ambrose did not pursue the subject. Instead, he told Daniel the news about Gorston Manor. "That is a shame," said Daniel once he had finished. "They are a good family, and I know Sarah has enjoyed tutoring the two young Miss Collinses."

"Yes," agreed Ambrose. "Sarah will be disappointed when I tell her the news."

Just then, there was a knock at the door. "Come in!" called Daniel.

The door opened to the anxious face of a young footman. "This has just come for you, my lord," he said, coming forward and placing a folded sheet of paper on the desk.

Daniel glanced at it and paled. "Thank you," he said, dismissing the footman. Once the door had closed, he picked up the note with a shaking hand. "A telegram," he whispered, staring at the paper in his hand but not making a move to open it. Ambrose stared at it too. This could go one of two ways, he thought. Either way, he would be there for Daniel, whether it was the best or the worst of news.

Daniel glanced at him, a plea in his eyes. "You read it," he said, handing it over.

Ambrose quickly took it and broke the seal. Inside was a short message:

Benjamin home safe and well STOP Come soon STOP Papa

With a quiver in his voice, he read it out loud. Daniel stared at him in disbelief, so he handed over the note for him to read. He took it from his hand and read it several times. "He's home," Daniel murmured in a daze.

"Yes," beamed Ambrose. "Our prayers have been answered."

Daniel nodded. He placed the note carefully down on his desk, unable to speak. And then it happened. A sob escaped from his chest. Then another. Soon, the floodgates had opened. Daniel buried his face in his hands as his body shook with the force of his emotions.

It tore at Ambrose's heart. He watched for a moment, helpless, then quickly stood and went round to the other side of the desk. "Shh, it's alright," he soothed, touching Daniel's shoulder gently. Daniel's body continued to convulse, and Ambrose could take it no more. Wrapping his arm tightly around Daniel's heaving body, he murmured huskily, "Don't cry, love, all is well." He could not stop himself from kissing the top of his head and crooning, "It is only shock, my love. Don't cry, please don't cry."

Daniel turned and buried his face in the comfort of Ambrose's chest. Ambrose stood bent towards him, holding him tight. He stroked his hair and gentled him with words of love. When that was not enough to stop the sobs, he pulled at Daniel, landing them both on the wooden floor in a kneeling position, their arms wrapped around the other. "My darling, darling love, it's alright," repeated Ambrose over and over, kissing the top of Daniel's head, his brow, his wet cheek, desperate to comfort him.

Eventually, the sobs subsided. Ambrose rubbed gentle circles along Daniel's back, still kissing wherever he could, his need to comfort warring with another need that was making itself felt. For five years he had known this man, desired him, loved him, and for five years he had held back from showing how he truly felt. But now, a thunderbolt itself could not have stopped him from making his feelings known. He buried his fingers in Daniel's hair, pulling up his face to his. Daniel's glistening dark eyes stared back at him, filled with a need he recognised. He did not hesitate. In one quick swoop, he captured his lips and kissed him.

He did not just kiss. He plundered. He ravaged. He claimed. This was an act of possession. With this kiss he transmitted loud and clear, *"You are mine to comfort and cherish."* Five years of frustration and need was poured into this kiss. His tongue swept into Daniel's mouth with the possessiveness of a wild animal entering its den. He licked, then sucked, then in a fit of wanton passion, he bit Daniel's lip, drawing blood. And then, he soothed the wound with his tongue.

After an initial moment of shock, Daniel had kissed him back with equal fervour. Each wield of Ambrose's tongue and nip of his teeth had been met with wild moans and a grind of Daniel's hips against him. Daniel's cock, solid and large, rubbed against Ambrose's groin, making its presence felt. Ambrose was no less hard, jutting his stiff peak into Daniel's taut abdomen. He ate Daniel's mouth, thrusting his hips into him, wanting nothing more than to rip off his clothes and drive himself inside him, laying claim on him once and for all.

He was about to do just that, throwing all caution to the wind, when suddenly, Daniel ripped his mouth away and shoved at his chest, sending him flying to the floor. He lay panting on his back, staring at Daniel in shocked surprise.

"What," grated Daniel, his eyes accusing, "is the meaning of this?"

Ambrose had no words. Daniel's expression hardened while his breaths subsided. "I asked you, Ambrose, what is this? For years, you have given me to understand that you do not feel desire for me. So, what is this? Explain yourself."

Ambrose sat up on his elbows and tried to regain control over himself. With each heaving breath, he realised with horror that his mask had been ripped off. There was no hiding any longer who he was. "Is it not obvious?" he barked, furious now both with himself and with Daniel. "What do you wish to hear? That I too am a sodomite?" He snorted. "What if I am? It shan't make a blind bit of difference to our situation."

"All these years," Daniel growled softly, "I have bared my heart to you, made my desire known, only to be met with rebuff after rebuff. Why? For the love of God, why?"

"Why?" cried Ambrose in fury. "Are you so dense, Daniel, that you cannot see why?"

"You could have been honest with me," accused Daniel in turn. "Not let me mope and pine and wallow in despair."

"What if I had told you? What then?" demanded Ambrose, getting to his feet and dusting off his trousers angrily. "All it would have done was put temptation in your path each day. Because my feelings in this do not matter. I could love you, worship you, desire you until my body ached with it, but still it would change nothing. We cannot be lovers, Daniel, not ever. This world we live in does not allow it. You do not know what level of shame would be rained upon you if it became known what we are."

Now Daniel was on his feet too. He took two steps forward and grabbed Ambrose by the shirt. "You are wrong!" he spit out. "We can do whatever we want as long as it is behind closed doors and we are discreet. Yet instead, you chose to break my heart, you bastard!"

Ambrose snorted in derision. "You think we can hide this from prying eyes? Are you so naïve that you think people wouldn't know, wouldn't gossip?"

Daniel let go of him and strode to the other side of the room. Then, he turned and faced him with a frosty expression. "We could have been together without anyone being the wiser, but you never gave us a chance. You were happy to let me wither in despair."

"Never happy! Never that," Ambrose pleaded, wanting to be understood.

"I would have pledged myself to you, Ambrose, and given you my fidelity." Daniel shook his head in disgust. "Instead, in my sorrow and need, I sought sexual release in the arms of strangers. For years, I have debased myself in London, fornicating without heart, without feeling, when I could have been faithful to you if you had only let me."

Ambrose looked away, the truth of Daniel's words hitting him hard. He hated knowing that Daniel had given his body to others. It fuelled a rage that roiled in the heart of him.

"And what of Lexie?" continued Daniel. "What is the truth of that?"

"I love her," replied Ambrose. "I did not lie about that."

"So you are like me, desiring both men and women?"

"No, I do not think so," said Ambrose truthfully. "I have never looked at women like that. The thing with Lexie started as friendship and it grew into love. I have found comfort with her and a semblance of normality, but I have never desired her the way I burn for you."

Daniel's eyes flared for a moment, then they went dull. "So," he drawled, "Lexie is another person you have lied to."

Ambrose sighed. "Actually, no. I told her the truth years ago."

Daniel's lips tightened. "You could tell her, but not me, is that it?"

Ambrose's eyes pleaded for forgiveness. He wanted to explain but could not. "I am sorry, Daniel," he croaked. His pleas fell on deaf ears.

There was a heavy silence, broken only by these cold words from Daniel: "I no longer wish to be in your presence, Ambrose. You have lied to me and betrayed me. As soon as it can be arranged, I shall leave for America. And frankly, I do not know when or if I shall ever return. Now please, leave, and do not show your face here until after I am gone."

Ambrose stepped towards him. "Daniel," he implored, "do not be like this. Please. I am so sorry. Forgive me."

Daniel crossed his arms on his chest and when he spoke, his voice was like cold shards of ice. "I said: leave."

Ambrose stared at him a moment more, willing him to change his mind. Daniel's stance did not change. "Very well," Ambrose said finally. Head hanging, he left the room.

He descended the stairs, stiffly accepted his hat and coat from Siddons, and walked out of the house. He could not contemplate doing any work or even returning home to face Sarah's questions. Instead, he walked aimlessly through the gardens, then over the vast parkland of Stanton Hall, then to the banks of the lake where he dropped down onto a wooden bench.

For hours, he sat in stillness, staring at the gleaming water as if it could provide him with answers. He had hurt Daniel dreadfully through his cowardice. For years, he had convinced himself that he was doing the right thing, protecting both himself and Daniel from the opprobrium of being shamed for their love. But really, it had been cowardice, pure and simple. And now he had lost Daniel. It was possible Daniel may never forgive him. He did not know if he could ever forgive himself. He still believed their love was impossible, that it could never have been as Daniel had described it. But he could have been truthful. He could have let Daniel know he was not alone. That had been wrong of him.

At last, with a despairing sigh, he came to his feet and slowly began the journey back to Ivy Cottage. At the gate, he paused and composed himself. Then, he walked into his house and sought out his sister. She needed to be told about Benjamin. "Sarah, good news," he said quickly. "Daniel received a telegram from America today. Benjamin is back home from the war."

She rose to her feet and stared at him. "He's home? Really home?"

He forced a smile. "Safe and sound back in Ohio."

"Oh thank the Lord!" she cried and burst into tears.

For the second time that day, he consoled a loved one in his arms. He gathered Sarah to him and let her cry it out, patting her back soothingly. She must love Benjamin very much, he thought. He hoped with all his heart that her story would have a happier ending than his.

Chapter 28

Daniel

The journey to Ohio took two and a half weeks. With him travelled Isabella, his cousin, Grace, and her family including her husband, Benedict, their two young children and her father-in-law. It was a convivial and merry group, and by necessity, Daniel had to force a cheer he did not feel when he was around them. The smiles and the teasing ceased the moment he was alone. Then, all he felt was an unremitting ache for Ambrose, the love of his life who had betrayed his trust in such a hurtful way.

Oh, he fully understood why Ambrose had hidden his feelings so completely for the last five years. He knew Ambrose well—his need for order, for respectability, and his fear that the secure life he had spent years to achieve could crumble at the drop of a hat if his love for another man were ever to be discovered. Conversely, it was because he understood that he felt so betrayed. Ambrose should have trusted him with this most precious of secrets. Ambrose should have known that Daniel would have kept it safe, kept *him* safe.

They arrived in Ohio one afternoon in early October. It was an emotional reunion between family members that had not seen each other for over five years. Of course, they had become much changed in that time. His ma and pa had aged considerably, lines of stress and worry etched on their faces. The greatest change, however, was in Benjamin. This gaunt, scarred man with leathery skin and a silver-streaked beard was nothing like the younger brother he had known. Haunted dark eyes, full of anger, stared into his own, no less angry gaze. Whatever had happened to his sweet, joyous brother?

With firm purpose, he went to Benjamin and clasped him tight. *"You may have kept me at arm's length all this war, little brother, but no more,"* he thought as he held Benjamin's stiff body to him. At last, his brother yielded, returning the embrace for a brief time.

The next hours were a mix of lively conversation, tears and embraces as the Stanton family celebrated their reunion at long last. Throughout it all, Daniel kept a close eye on Benjamin, who said little and smiled not at all. He was the first to notice when Benjamin slipped away from the gathering and went outside to the stable. Daniel drew close to his papa and asked under his breath, "Where is he going?"

Frank Stanton looked out the window at his departing son, his expression sad and resigned. With a sigh, he replied, "He has bought old Jim Shaw's cabin and the land around it with the money he inherited from your grandfather. He wants to build a house there and live alone, away from everyone."

Daniel's lips tightened. "I am going after him," he declared. Since his friendship with Ambrose was broken, he could at least try to mend his friendship with Benjamin.

"Do it, please," said his father. "He will not talk to me. Perhaps he will with you."

Daniel nodded and quickly put on his coat and hat before striding off to find himself a horse. A short time later, he was galloping away. He rode with purpose, determined to find his brother and to break that wall of silence between them. The land Benjamin had purchased was not very far away, but it was positioned on high ground and isolated, surrounded by woods on one side and a wide, flowing stream on the other.

Once he had reached his destination, Daniel dismounted and tied the reins of his horse to a nearby tree. From where he stood, he saw the ramshackle old cabin that had been built by Jim Shaw, and sitting on the front steps was Benjamin, sketching something on a sheet of paper. He walked over to him. "I thought I would find you here," he said conversationally. Then, looking over at the drawing that Benjamin had made, he asked, "Are these your plans for rebuilding the cabin?"

"Just some initial ideas."

Daniel noticed something on the side of the drawing and pointed to it. "What's this?"

"A large rectangular barn," Benjamin replied. "I'm thinking of using it as an engineering workshop where I can design and tinker with machinery."

Daniel nodded, scrutinising the landscape around him. It was different from what he had become used to in England—but no, he would not think of that. "It's good land," he remarked. "There is water, a steady supply of wood, green pasture for your cattle. I always thought old Jim could have made a lot more out of this place."

"We'll see if I can do any better," muttered Benjamin. "I've a great deal of work to do—knock the cabin down, dig the foundations and rebuild. I don't know how much I'll get done before the snow comes this winter."

It would get done, if Daniel had anything to do with it. His brother had better understand that he was no longer alone. "I can help you," he said simply.

Benjamin snorted. "And ruin those perfectly groomed hands, viscount? I think not."

This was how it was going to play out? Daniel laughed to himself. Manicured hands be damned. Without another word, he went to pick up an axe that was leaning against the wall of the cabin. Gazing coolly at his brother, he taunted, "We better get started if we want to get anything done before dark."

They began their work. Together, they toiled for hours, demolishing over a third of the cabin's structure. It felt good once more to labour with his hands, though it was exhausting too. He was out of shape and needed to build up his strength, but Lord was he glad to shake off the trappings of his aristocratic privilege. Moreover, the physical work helped to take his mind off his heartache over Ambrose.

When the sun had begun to set over the horizon, they laid down their tools and rode home, still without a word. Although they had not spoken, something precious had blossomed between them—a re-connection reminding them that they were brothers and that they loved one another. Daniel remembered that evening to give Benjamin the letter that Sarah had written and entrusted to him. He hoped that now the war was over, the odd relationship between his brother and Ambrose's sister, which had been conducted via letters for so many years, would finally bear fruit.

Sarah's letter did not seem to have made Benjamin any happier, for the next day he was grim-faced as they toiled side by side, dismantling the old cabin. Daniel watched him discreetly, as he hacked furiously with his axe, rage emanating from him in waves. It was a rage that echoed in Daniel's breast whenever he thought of Ambrose's betrayal. At last, Daniel could take it no more. "Benjamin!" he called out, but his brother barely heard him. He tried again. "Benjamin! Will you stop?" Still, Benjamin lifted his axe and thrust it into the wooden planks before him. Daniel moved to get as close as he could and cried sharply, "Benjamin, put it down!"

Finally, his brother attended to him and stopped wielding his axe. And with the cessation of Benjamin's rage, so too came a lessening of Daniel's anger towards Ambrose. It was as if the frenzied wielding of that axe had purged the anger from his body. Feeling light-headed, Daniel guided his brother gently to the front steps and sat him down. Breathing deeply, he recovered his self-possession and focused his attention on Benjamin. What had happened to cause such despairing rage? He wished he knew, but he would wait until Benjamin was ready to speak of it. In silence, he watched his brother as he buried his face in his hands. In his mind, he whispered the words, *"I am here, Ben. Talk to me."*

It was as if Benjamin heard, for he looked up and said in a gritty voice, "I apologise. It is the way with me these days. My temper gets the better of me."

In response, Daniel squeezed his shoulder in sympathy. He hoped his brother would open up about what was causing him such pain. Patiently, he waited.

Benjamin glanced at the remains of the cabin behind them. "We have done well today," he said, sounding more composed.

"We work well together," agreed Daniel.

"Think you we can make fast work of the new building?"

Daniel considered the matter. "It depends how long the dry weather holds up," he replied. "Is it of great import that we finish this build quickly?"

"Yes," murmured Benjamin.

Daniel prodded a little more. "Will you tell me now what it was that had you so upset?"

At first, Benjamin did not answer. Then, exhaling loudly, he asked, "Do you recall what you said when you handed me Sarah's letter yesterday?"

"About her still being unmarried?"

"Yes."

All of a sudden, Daniel understood. "You want to build this house for her," he stated.

"Yes."

"And you mean to go to England."

"As soon as I possibly can," replied Benjamin.

And there it was. Yet another Stanton in love with a Cranshaw. Oh the irony! Daniel regarded his brother with curiosity. "So, you are more than simply friends."

"There is something more," said Benjamin tentatively. "However, nothing has been declared."

Daniel gave an unamused laugh. He understood this all too well. How many years had he believed Ambrose to be just a friend while the truth was hidden from him? "Believe me," he said dryly, "I am well acquainted with such a thing."

This seemed to pique Benjamin's interest. Turning to Daniel, he demanded, "What do you mean? Who?"

Daniel shook his head. This was not something he could be open with his brother about, much as he would have liked to. Out of respect for Ambrose, the secret of their love would have to remain just that. However, an idea had begun to germinate in his mind. "It is of no import," he stated, "except in one respect. I have good reason to want to stay away from England for a considerable time—three months at least, perhaps more. It would make sense, Benjamin, if you were to step into my shoes and take over the reins at Stanton Hall while I remain here. It will not be too arduous a task, as the estate is well managed by Ambrose. And it should give you time to woo the delightful Sarah."

Benjamin glanced doubtfully at the ruined cabin behind him. "What of the house?"

Daniel held up his hands in front of him, saying mockingly, "Not so perfectly groomed any more. Will you trust me to build it for you? I am well capable of following a set of your drawings." Daniel warmed to the idea as he set out his plan. He needed to be away from Ambrose, and Benjamin needed to be with Sarah. What better than to trade places? Spending the next few months in hard manual labour, building a beautiful home for Benjamin and Sarah, sounded like just the thing—an act of penance to the brother who had suffered so much already, and a way for Daniel to find relief from the gnawing ache in his heart.

Benjamin hesitated. "She might not want me as a husband, or to live in America, so far from her family."

Daniel pressed the point. "And you'll only know for sure once you ask her. Go to England, Benjamin, and win her hand. I'll build your house."

No further convincing was required. "When?" asked Benjamin.

Daniel's smile spread across his face. "Tomorrow, dear brother. You leave tomorrow, and do not worry about Mama or Pa or anyone else. I will manage them for you."

And indeed, that was what he did. On their return to the house, he convened the rest of the family in the front parlour and laid down the law. "Benjamin is to go to England to see Sarah," he stated, staring hard at his ma and pa. "You will not question this decision or try to stop him. This is what he needs to do. It is what is right for him, and so he shall do it," he said with some asperity. Then he added, "He leaves tomorrow, and while he is gone, I shall build his house. I will appreciate any and all help to accomplish this task in the time we have before he returns."

They all stared at him in astonishment, but nobody argued. He felt fired up with purpose. He would do everything to help ensure that Benjamin and Sarah's story had the happy ending that had eluded him with Ambrose. That evening, he sat to write a letter to his estate manager, explaining the situation. Benjamin could hardly swan into Stanton Hall and take over without his express written permission. The letter was short and to the point.

Dear Ambrose,

I will be staying on in America indefinitely. In my absence, Benjamin is to take on the running of my affairs in England. Please report to him as you did to me and assist him in any way possible. Should there be any matter of great import that requires my consideration, you may write to me of it. Otherwise, please direct all your queries to my brother.

Yours,

Daniel Stanton

He sealed the letter, leaving it on his desk until he could give it to Benjamin on the morrow. Undressing quickly, he extinguished the light and got into bed. Sleep, however, would not come. He went over the text of his letter in his head. He had not yet forgiven Ambrose, and his words had been curt, reflecting his anger. He knew they would be hurtful to Ambrose when he read them, and he did not have it in his heart to wound the man he loved. Late in the middle of the night, he sat up and lit a candle. Then, breaking the seal on his letter, he added a postscript.

P.S. I will return eventually, and then we shall talk. I am still angry at you, Ambrose. I miss you all the while I rail at your obstinacy in having kept your feelings a secret from me. You stubborn, foolish man. We could have had five years of happiness together. Think on it!

P.P.S. Please help my brother as best you can. As you will see, he is not in the best of spirits. Be kind to him. Lend him a listening ear. Give him your best counsel. And Ambrose, however you can, support his efforts with Sarah. He loves her so. Perhaps there can be one Stanton/Cranshaw love story that ends with joy.

Sealing the letter once more, he put it aside and went back to bed. The next morning, with little fanfare or fuss, Benjamin left for England, and Daniel began the work on Benjamin's new house.

Chapter 29

Ambrose

Three months later

Ambrose woke and stared at the ceiling, willing himself to find the strength to leave his bed. It was that way with him these days. He forced himself to go about his day with little vigour and little enthusiasm—for the day was another twelve hours of enduring life without Daniel. Then night came, and he could claim the blessed peace of sleep once more.

It had been three and a half months of gloom and misery since Daniel left, made only worse by the situation with regards to his sister. Sarah, foolish darling Sarah, had gone and gotten herself engaged to none other than Philip Templeton—though he should not cast aspersions, for no one had been more foolish than him when it came to Daniel.

For some obscure reason beyond Ambrose's comprehension, Templeton had decided to start courting Sarah some months ago, after years of ignoring her affections. This had culminated in a proposal of marriage which Sarah had accepted with alacrity, refusing to stop and consider that perhaps it was another man that owned her heart.

Ambrose could not be sure of it, of course, for he did not have a mirror into Sarah's heart, yet his power of observation told him that she was not immune to feelings for Daniel's younger brother. For five years, she had waited eagerly for letters to arrive from America, devouring them in the privacy of her room and emerging dreamy-eyed the following day. Long epistles were written and sent to America in return, until the war had put a stop to that. If this was not love, it was definitely… something. But it had not been enough to prevent Sarah from making the catastrophic mistake of promising herself to Templeton.

Ambrose was as sure as sure could be that Templeton would not bring happiness to his sister, yet he could not stand in her way once she had made up her mind. She was a grown woman of thirty who could decide matters for herself. And then Benjamin Stanton had arrived, tormented by his wartime experience and lovesick for Sarah. Still she had not been able to see the wood for the trees. It had put him quite out of sorts with his sister the other day, and they had exchanged cross words for the first time ever. He felt as helpless for her as he did for himself.

Ambrose had tried to support Benjamin's efforts with Sarah, in accordance both with Daniel's wishes and his own, but there was only so much he could do. There came a point where people had to help themselves if they wanted a chance at happiness. He was no cupid, shooting arrows into other people's hearts. In any case, he was ill qualified in the field of love. Had he not made the biggest mistake of all and betrayed the trust of the man he loved? He could not be trusted to help anyone else when it came to affairs of the heart.

The only bright spot on his horizon was his sweet girl, Emily, who would be four years old next month. He continued to visit every week, and those hours he spent in the company of Emily, Edwin and Lexie were always a balm for his battered soul. After Daniel's departure, Ambrose had confided all in Lexie, crying his heartbreak on her willing shoulder, and she had comforted him the best she could.

That night had heralded a change in their relationship. Now that his feelings were out in the open with Daniel, it no longer felt right for him and Lexie to be lovers. In all honesty, it had not felt right for a long time. After he had dried his tears, he had looked into Lexie's kind eyes and finally admitted the truth, "Lexie," he had said, his voice gruff. "I cannot be the person you need—the one who will desire you and put you above all else. I wish I could have been that person for you, but it is not in me to love a woman that way, and I do not think it fair for either of us to continue with the pretence."

Lexie had stroked his cheek lovingly. "I know," she had said. "I have long thought it too but have been too comfortable in the arrangement to make the change."

Miraculously, they had defaulted to an affectionate friendship with little recrimination. He still made his way to her room sometimes at night, when he needed the comfort of an embrace and a kind ear to listen to his woes. Their clothes, however, stayed resolutely on.

At night they talked of what was in their hearts, of Edwin and Emily, both of whom Ambrose now considered his children, of the future. Ambrose often voiced his concerns about Lexie. With no husband to speak of, and with his own failure to be a good lover to her, he feared she would grow lonely, as he himself felt alone. "What will you do with yourself?" he had asked her just last week.

She had shrugged. "The same as you, darling. I wake each day and face it the best I can. I am fortunate in that I have both Edwin and Emily to keep me company. They are the greatest comfort to me, you know."

"Yes, I know," he had murmured. "But how about the other thing. I mean to say, how about your physical needs, Lexie? I know I was but a poor lover to you, but the communion of our bodies brought us both some pleasure. What shall you do now?" A thought had occurred to him then and he had stared at her in horror. "Please do not say you shall take another lover."

Her laugh had been genuinely amused. "No, Ambrose, I have no plans for another lover. It is grim at times, I do admit, but I have learned to live with it. I have ways to pleasure myself, by the use of my own hand if you must know."

He had blushed, yes blushed. "I see," was all he could say.

"Ambrose, darling, do not look so surprised. Is it not what you do too, in the privacy of your room at night?"

"Yes," he had admitted. "It is. I had not realised that it was something women did too."

"Well, now you do," she had smiled. "See what an education I am providing you with into the private practices of females."

His face had fallen as he had thought of another female close to him. "Do you mean to say that all females…" He had lost the power of speech. No, he would not let his mind go to such an uncomfortable place.

Lexie had laughed. "I cannot speak for all females, however, it is a distinct possibility."

"Stop, Lexie, please do not put such thoughts into my head. It is most disconcerting."

She had taken pity on him then. "Very well, let us talk of other things," and thankfully the subject had been dropped.

Now, as Ambrose stared at the ceiling, he thought of the day that lay ahead. It was New Year's Eve, and both he and Sarah had been invited to celebrate it with a dinner party at Stanton Hall hosted by Benjamin. This would be followed by an overnight stay at the great house.

Ambrose was not particularly looking forward to spending an evening with Templeton fawning over Sarah centre stage while Benjamin watched pain stricken from the wings. His friend, Benedict Sedgwick, would be there too with Grace, his wife. That was something, he supposed, though those two were very much in love, and no doubt would get more amorous as the night progressed and the alcohol flowed. It seemed at times as if everyone but him was paired up with another. He could not help but feel wistful that those around him could express their love outwardly while this privilege was denied to him and Daniel. It was enough to set him wishing he could stay abed. But no, it was not to be. Reluctantly, he lifted the covers and stepped onto the cold wood floor to go get dressed.

The day passed slowly and drearily. Eventually, it was time for Sarah and himself to make their way to Stanton Hall. Once there, they were ushered into their private bedchambers where they were to dress for dinner. Ambrose prepared himself for the night ahead, donning his best formal clothes for the occasion.

Before leaving the room, he stood for a moment and gazed at his reflection in the mirror. Unlike the heroines of romantic novels who faded into wraiths upon their heartbreak, his trajectory had gone in the opposite direction. Weariness and lassitude had decreased his level of activity, and in the cold of winter, he had sought comfort in food to help get through the dreariness of each day. It had resulted in an increase in girth around the waist. It was not enough to have been noticed by all around him, but it was apparent to him. He was not young anymore, nearly five and thirty, and the thick blond hair of which he was inordinately proud was also beginning to thin ever so slightly. *"Daniel will have a disgust of me when next he sees me,"* he thought glumly. It was enough to make him want to hide his head under the covers of his bed and never come out again.

With a sigh, he turned away from his dispiriting reflection and went down to join everyone in the drawing room. Dinner was an elaborate meal of ten glorious courses—Stanton Hall's cook had truly excelled herself. Benjamin had also sent for the finest wines from the cellar.

However, no amount of excellent food and wine could make this evening anything but excruciating. Watching Templeton make unctuous love to Sarah, showering her with compliments and taking her hand to kiss one time too many, while beside them Benjamin gnashed his teeth in frustration, was really not something Ambrose wanted to experience again. He was beginning to despair of Sarah. When would she realise that marriage to Templeton was a mistake? He feared she would leave it much too late. It must be something that ran in the family, he thought. A Cranshaw inability to find success in love.

Dinner was followed by dancing—well, not for Ambrose, who was called upon to play some tunes on the piano. On and on the evening dragged until finally, the clock struck twelve midnight. There were cheers and applause as the party gathered congratulated one another. Ambrose held his arms open for Sarah, and they embraced fondly. "Happy New Year, Sarah," he said. "May it bless you with joy."

"Happy New Year, Ambrose," she smiled, "the best brother in the world." He laughed at that and kissed her cheek. He doubted that very much, but he did love her. And then, it was time to go up to bed and seek blessed sleep.

The following morning, bleary eyed, he went down to the dining room for breakfast. He was not the only one suffering from the consequences of the previous evening's overindulgence. Benedict clutched his head and bemoaned his intemperance, while a pale-looking Grace rested her head on her husband's shoulder and refused any food, contenting herself with a cup of tea. But it was Sarah that captured his attention. She sat furthest away from Benjamin, avoiding his gaze and looking haunted. What on earth could be the matter with her?

The time came to say their goodbyes. Benjamin's face looked bereft as he bid Sarah farewell, all the while she refused to meet his eyes. They climbed into the carriage for the short journey back to Ivy Cottage. There, Sarah spoke not a word, clutching her hands together and looking distraught. Ambrose watched her in concern and dismay. Something must have occurred last night, after they retired to bed, but what?

Once they reached their home, Sarah went straight up to her room, ostensibly to unpack her overnight bag. Ambrose went to his study and waited patiently for her to come back down. Eventually, he heard her soft footsteps taking her to the back parlour, which was her own private space. He went to find her there. She was placing a locomotive on her miniature railway, her back turned to him. He studied her a moment then asked gently, "Do you wish to talk about it?"

She shook her head then changed her mind and nodded. He laughed and pulled her into his embrace. Then, he led her to his study, ordering a pot of tea from Elsie upon their way, and sat her down to talk. At first, she said nothing, so Ambrose conjectured, "So, it is Benjamin."

"Yes," she replied softly. "I have been very foolish."

He could hardly disagree. "Yes, you have," he said gently, "but we all have it in us to be extremely foolish at times." He knew that better than anyone.

She glanced at him. "You knew, didn't you?"

He suppressed a sad laugh. Of course, he knew. It was plain for anyone with a beating heart to see. But all he said was, "It was not my place to tell you, Sarah. You had to find it out for yourself."

"And so I have," she murmured under her breath.

He smiled encouragingly. "So you have. What is it that happened last night? Will you tell me?"

"After we all went to bed, I could not sleep and decided to go to the library," she replied, looking distressed. "I will not go into the details, but I saw Benjamin. We kissed, and he declared his love for me."

And that was a bad thing? God save him from the vagaries of females. "So why the long face?" Ambrose enquired.

Sarah looked at him crossly. "It was an immoral thing to do, Ambrose, as long as I am betrothed to Philip."

"Yes," he agreed, "it was, but you can do something about it."

She was quiet for a moment. "I shall have to go see Philip," she said finally.

"*Hallelujah,*" he thought.

Ambrose sat up and refilled his cup of tea. He took a long sip and put it down. "The poor man was not looking quite the thing this morning," he said casually. "I suggest you wait until later this afternoon to speak to him. Do you wish me to come with you?"

Sarah stood and came over to him, placing her arms around his shoulders. "I do not deserve you, Ambrose," she said. "But no, thank you. This is something I should do myself."

Later that afternoon, Ambrose waited a trifle anxiously for his sister's return. He berated himself for letting her go alone to see Mr Templeton. What if the man had become angry on hearing his betrothed break off the engagement? Why had Ambrose not insisted on accompanying her? He walked back and forth in his study, peering out the window every so often, impatient to see Sarah return.

At last, he heard a pounding on the front door then the sound of voices. "Get my travel case down from the wardrobe,"

Sarah was instructing Elsie breathlessly. "I need to pack for a journey."

"Miss?" their maid asked doubtfully.

"Do it now!"

He opened his study door and went to see what the commotion was all about. "Sarah, what is it?" he asked in concern, but she was too emotional to speak. Instead, she handed him a letter which he perused quickly. It was a farewell note from Benjamin. After she had rebuffed his advances last night, he had given up in despair and decided to return to America. He was already long gone.

He looked back at his sister in commiseration. "Oh, my dear," he said. "I am so sorry."

"I must go to him," replied Sarah, having finally regained the power of speech.

His gaze turned to alarm. "Sarah, my love, consider. All this can be resolved in time. Write to him now and explain."

"No!" cried Sarah sharply. "There is no time to be lost. I am going after him, Ambrose, whether you like it or not."

Had she lost her wits? He gathered himself up and spoke sternly, "I cannot let you go chasing after him all on your own. It would not be right. In any case, how on earth would you catch him up? I believe he already has quite a head start on us."

His sister's eyes burned with fierce determination. "There is a way. I have it memorised from *Bradshaw's Guide*. If we use the Great Western route to Birmingham, then we could get a mail train connection to Liverpool and get there by morning."

"The mail train! Sarah!" Ambrose was aghast.

But Sarah was beyond listening, marching into his study. "How much money do we have? I will need funds for the journey."

"Sarah!" Ambrose remonstrated again. She could not seriously be thinking of gallivanting across half the country after a man. What would people think? What would they say? It was not to be borne. He was about to put his foot down and insist she stay home when, in that instant, he heard a voice in his ear as if Daniel were there in person chastising him. *"Stop being such a pompous ass, Ambrose. So what if people talk? Is her happiness not worth more than cheap gossip?"*

He stared at her a few moments more, realising that the imaginary Daniel was right. Sarah loved Benjamin and wanted to catch him up before he sailed for America. How could he stand in her way? Resigning himself to this madcap expedition, he sighed, "Very well, if that is what you mean to do, we shall both go."

That was how he found himself, several hours later, lying uncomfortably on top of a set of mailbags as they rode the overnight mail train from Birmingham to Liverpool. It was a most uncomfortable journey. What had he been thinking to agree to this? Throughout the long night, he cast reproachful glances at a mutinous Sarah, who refused to be cowed. At long last, they arrived at Liverpool station just after eight o'clock the following morning, rumpled and ill-tempered—at least in Ambrose's case. They hailed a carriage that took them to the docks and made their enquiries about ships sailing to America, being pointed towards a steamship called *The Scotia*.

But of course, their adventure had not ended there. Oh no! The steward they spoke to would not let them board the ship to speak to Benjamin, not without a ticket, and there were only a few precious minutes to go before the ship set sail. So, of course they had to go and purchase a passage for America at unimaginable expense. He supposed he could have said no to Sarah and pretended there were not enough funds—but there were, for he had taken the precaution of bringing a bag of two hundred sovereigns with him. Seeing the desperation on her face, he had not had the heart to stand in the way of her happiness. Besides, there was a reason why he wanted to go there too. So, on the ship they had sailed to America.

Sarah and Benjamin had been married just over a week ago by the ship's captain. And here they all were, about to dock at New York harbour. For hours, Ambrose had debated with himself about what to do next. He could not absent himself from Stanton Hall for long, nor from Lexie and Emily. He should find a passage aboard a ship returning to England at the soonest opportunity. But finally sighting land in the distance, and knowing that Daniel was somewhere on that land, he knew with a certainty that he was not going to turn back. It was as if a magnet were pulling him inexorably towards Daniel. To Ohio he would go.

Chapter 30

Daniel

January 1866, Ohio

They were just about to start dinner when they heard the sound of hooves clattering on the gravelled drive outside the house. It was unusual enough a sound to make Isabella rush to the window to take a look. She peered sideways towards the main entrance to the house, then gasped, "He's back!" She turned to her family in excitement. "It's Benjamin. He's back, and Sarah is with him!"

All at once, everyone was hurrying out of the dining parlour and going to the front porch, anxious to greet the prodigal son and his bride, for surely that was what Sarah was now. In the ensuing melee of cries and hugs and warm wishes, Daniel did not at first notice the tall, slim man that emerged last from the carriage. He was about to clap Benjamin on the shoulder in delight when he caught sight of the man. He stood for a moment, arrested in shock. Then a surge of blood pumping through his veins had him stride towards Ambrose and cry, "You! What in all hell's name are you doing here?"

Anger was quickly replacing shock, fuelled in no small part by the force of his longing for this man. Without thinking, he grabbed Ambrose by the lapels of his jacket and roared, "Answer me! Why are you here?"

White-faced, Ambrose could not speak. Instead, it was the sound of his mama's voice, heavy with disapproval, that made itself heard. "Daniel! Stop that at once. Is that any way to greet a guest?"

Too late, he realised what he was doing. His chest felt constricted, his breaths heavy. With an effort, he loosened his grip on Ambrose's jacket and dropped his hands. His mama stepped forward quickly, holding out her hands to Ambrose, though not before casting Daniel the most castigating of looks. "Mr Cranshaw," she said. "I do apologise for my son's rudeness. It is both a surprise and a great pleasure to see you here. Welcome sir, welcome."

Ambrose took her hands and bowed over them. "Lady Stanton, I am honoured to be here," he replied, his voice not quite steady. He looked shaken and shocked by the force of Daniel's angry outburst, but not surprised.

Then it was his papa coming forward and speaking with authority. "Mr Cranshaw, it is indeed a pleasure to welcome you here. I am sure there is much to be discussed, but please let us not do it out here in the cold. Do come inside."

With a withering look at his son, Frank Stanton ushered everyone into the house. Coats, hats and bonnets were taken off their guests, suitcases brought out of the carriage, and servants sent to put additional place settings at the dinner table. All the while everyone exclaimed over Sarah, who looked pretty as a picture and flushed with happiness, the wedding band on her finger obvious for all to see. Despite his own shock at encountering Ambrose, Daniel, like the rest of the family, was full of questions. When had they docked in New York? Where had they married? On board the ship? How romantic! That last was from Isabella, who cooed in delight and clutched at her heart.

When a servant came to pick up Benjamin's travel case to take it upstairs, his brother put out his hand to stop him, glancing across at Daniel. "Is the house ready?" he asked.

"It is," Daniel answered proudly, for a moment pushing to the back of his mind the surprise of Ambrose's presence. "We put the finishing touches on it just this week and had some simple furnishings brought in. It is ready for occupation."

"Then after dinner, I shall take Sarah there," declared Benjamin.

Dinner was a joyous, boisterous affair for everyone except Daniel and Ambrose. Daniel could not stop his stares, studying the changes in Ambrose since last he saw him. He was pale and hollow-eyed, as if from lack of sleep. The golden whiskers on his face were longer and not as neatly trimmed as before. His glorious hair too, did not have its usual bounce, though it was still parted to the side. His fingernails were bitten to the quick. It pained Daniel to see Ambrose like this, sad and diminished. It put salt on an already bleeding wound. He knew it was his doing, but a part of him was still angry at what Ambrose had done. Damn it all to hell! None of this would have happened if Ambrose had only been honest with him.

Despite all these changes, Ambrose was still the most beautiful man he had ever seen. Daniel continued to examine him as pudding was served, his anger slowly turning to wistfulness as he realised something. He was never going to fall out of love with this stubborn, impossible man. For the rest of his days, he would pine for Ambrose Cranshaw. Yet still he did not know how he was going to find a way to forgive him.

They all rose when dinner was over and bid Benjamin and Sarah farewell as they departed for their new home. Servants had already been dispatched there with essential supplies of food, fuel and linens. Daniel hoped Benjamin would appreciate the house he had built for him.

It had taken three and a half months of hard work from dawn till dusk. Daniel had enlisted the help of his cousins and men from the local village, but he had been chief amongst them in putting in the effort to get the house built. Each night, he had put himself to bed with muscles sore and aching from the exertions of the day. He knew he had grown bulkier as a result of that manual labour. He wondered if Ambrose would appreciate the changes in him. More importantly, he wondered how the both of them were going to put past hurts behind them. They would need to talk soon and finally have a reckoning.

The opportunity to do so was taken from him, however, as no sooner had Benjamin left with Sarah than his papa turned to him with a stern countenance and commanded, "Daniel, in my study, now. We need to talk."

Reluctantly, Daniel followed his father to the back of the house where his study was located, casting a last, frustrated glance at Ambrose before he left. Frank Stanton said little as they entered the room, shutting the door behind them. He went to fetch the sherry decanter from a sideboard. Then in silence, he poured them each a shot of the liquor and brought the drinks back, gesturing for his son to take a seat on one of the chairs. Settling across from him, he took a sip of the amber liquid and stared at it reflectively for some minutes before speaking.

"What was the meaning, Daniel, of that unprecedented display of ill manners earlier?" he demanded.

Daniel bit his lip. What could he say? Finally, he stuttered, "It was ill-mannered, Papa, and I do apologise."

Frank continued to scrutinise him severely, expecting more. Falteringly, Daniel added, "It was a shock to see Ambrose here, that is all."

Frank Stanton's lips curled. "Do not take me for a fool, Daniel," he said flatly. "Now tell me, what is going on between you and Ambrose Cranshaw?"

Daniel's nostrils flared as he took in a deep breath. He looked away from his father, fixing his eyes on the clock that ticked on the far wall of the room. He could not tell his father the truth, or could he? Not without risking the very fabric of their relationship. Hadn't he sworn to himself never to fall out with his family the way his father and grandfather had fallen out with each other? No, he could not speak of this. But he would have to think of something to say. "Well?" his papa asked.

"It is complicated," ventured Daniel.

"Indeed? Well, I am sure I have the intellectual capacity to grasp this complicated state of affairs, so please do explain yourself."

Daniel brought his gaze back to his father's, his brain feeling sluggish. Slowly, he began, "We have been friends for a long time, and then something happened which meant we were no longer friends."

Frank Stanton said nothing, waiting for his son to continue. Damn it. These heavy silences were one of his papa's strongest weapons. Daniel was no match for them. He could never fathom what his parent was truly thinking. Perforce, he went on, "I... I discovered something about Ambrose which soured our friendship."

Now his papa frowned. "Do you mean, Daniel, that you were slow to discover that Ambrose is one of those men, what society calls sodomites? And what possible business could that be of yours?"

Daniel stared at his father in shock. "Do you mean you knew, Papa? How?"

Frank Stanton snorted in disdain. "For goodness' sake, Daniel, of course I know there are men like this. I was not born yesterday! And back in England, I caught the way he looked at you a time or two, then quickly tried to hide his regard. The more salient question is how on earth *you* did not know all these years."

"I..." Daniel spluttered, too taken aback to formulate coherent speech. Finally, he gathered his senses enough to be able to go on, "I had long knowledge of Ambrose's affair with a gentlewoman in Oxford, one that resulted in a child. Those are not the actions of a man who desires other men."

Frank leaned forward on his elbow, his eyes furrowed. "Let me put this to you," he said. "If you were a person with a certain desire that you knew society disapproved of, what would you do?" He raised his brow in enquiry.

Comprehension was beginning to dawn. "I would throw people off the scent," stated Daniel.

His papa sat back, having made his point. "Precisely," he said.

"So, you think Ambrose embarked on an affair with Lexie Forbes in order to convince people—or perhaps himself—that he did not desire men?"

"Lexie Forbes? Do you mean the Forbes family that occupies the house next to ours in Oxford?" enquired his papa.

"Yes," Daniel said.

"Hmm, that would make sense. To answer your question, Daniel, I cannot say for certain, only that it is a distinct possibility."

Daniel let out a breath. "All these years," he said bitterly, "I believed that Ambrose was in love with her."

"Perhaps he was, who are we to say? Again I ask you, what business is it of yours?"

Daniel finally gathered the courage to make his confession. "What if I were to tell you, Papa," he said very softly, "that I too am a man that desires men?"

A heavy silence descended on the room. Daniel lifted his eyes to his father, bracing himself for the look of disgust that was bound to be on his face. But Frank Stanton did not look disgusted, only perplexed. "Forgive me, Daniel," he said at last, "but are you sure? I do not like to talk of such things, but I am well aware of your many dalliances with the fairer sex. Why there is hardly any maiden between here and the next town that you have not seduced."

"It is not that bad, surely," protested Daniel.

"You have the reputation of being something of a Don Juan," replied his father with severity. More gently, he added, "Son, it has never crossed my mind that you would entertain those kinds of desires."

Now that the Pandora's Box had been opened, Daniel felt a compulsion to talk and explain. "I have always enjoyed the company of women," he said, "and except for one time many years ago, I have never looked at men that way."

"So, what happened to change this?"

"Ambrose," said Daniel simply.

His papa huffed in annoyance. Upon further reflection, as if trying to make sense of a conundrum, he declared, "You met Ambrose at a challenging time in your life, and you have had to rely greatly on his expertise to run the affairs of the Stanton estate. He is a very clever and able man. It is not surprising therefore that you may have developed some sort of hero worship for him. It does not signify."

At this, Daniel scoffed, "It is not hero worship, I assure you. I am well aware of all Ambrose's faults. And pardon me, Papa, but I have had five years and more to become fully acquainted with my feelings for him. I love him."

His father gave an irritated snort then began to remonstrate with him, "Daniel, you have always been headstrong, going after whatever you please. But do consider. Such a love as you speak of has no possible hope of bringing you happiness. No marriage or children. Always having to hide your feelings for each other. Always keeping it a secret."

"I know, Papa, of course I know."

"I am saying these things, Daniel," continued his father sternly, "not because I think there is anything wrong with you, or for that matter with Ambrose. I am saying this because the path you seem to be choosing is a difficult one that will bring you great pain." He shook his head in frustration. "Why condemn yourself to this, when by your own admission, you enjoy the company of women and could in time find yourself a good lady to be your wife?"

Daniel was silenced for an instant then came back with the rejoinder, "I cannot control what my heart wants, Papa, and it wants Ambrose."

His father was not convinced. "Then make yourself stop wanting him," he insisted. "Stay on here for a few months more, and in time, with distance apart, your feelings may fade."

Daniel leaned forwards on his elbows and challenged that statement. "Now I have a question to put to you, Papa," he said. "Years ago, if Grandfather had said to you, make yourself stop wanting Charlotte Harding. Stay apart from her for a few months and soon your feelings will fade, what would you have said?"

There was no answer to that. Frank Stanton smiled wryly at his son, relenting, "You make your point well, Daniel." With a sigh, he rose to his feet and went to fetch the sherry decanter. Coming back to his seat, he refilled both their glasses and took a gulp of his. "I shall be needing several more shots of this sherry to grapple with your revelations tonight," he added on an afterthought.

Daniel took a great gulp of his own glass, his heart pounding rapidly in his chest. Reaction was beginning to set in. He had told his father about Ambrose. The truth was out in the open between them. "So," he said shakily. "You are not going to disavow me? Sneer in disgust and tell me to leave this house?"

"Oh Daniel," murmured his papa. He poured himself another drink. After a while, he said, "Five years of war is a long time for reflection on this life we have been given. If there is one thing I know for certain, it is this. Nothing matters more to me than to know my wife, my sons and my daughter are safe and sound. Everything else is a minor consideration."

Daniel nodded, his chest tight with emotion. His eyes refused to remain dry. He took a deep breath, trying to rein in the tears. He had not cried since that awful, wonderful day over three months ago when he had learnt about Benjamin's return and Ambrose had kissed him. He would not allow himself to do so now.

A hand gripped his knee, and he looked up into his father's eyes, so like his own. It was too much. A sob escaped him. The next moment, his papa was holding him tight. No words were exchanged. They simply held each other for a long, long time.

Later that evening, drunk on his fifth glass of sherry, he told his father the whole story of him and Ambrose, from the very start. Then, late into the night, he went up to his room on swaying feet and collapsed onto his bed, barely able to remove his shoes. His head was woozy, but he had one last thought before sleep claimed him. He did not know what was to happen with him and Ambrose, but at least he knew, with the deepest of certainty, that his family would always be there for him. There was great solace in that. And tomorrow, he and Ambrose would talk. With that, he slept the sleep of the dead until he woke next morning with a pounding head.

Chapter 31

Ambrose

Ambrose had retired to bed, tired and dispirited. It had been a mistake to come to Ohio. He could see that now. Daniel did not want him here—had made it clear to everyone. He had thought perhaps they were going to talk in private and have a chance to argue out their feelings, but shortly after dinner, Daniel had gone to his father's study and not returned for the rest of the evening. Ambrose had waited to speak to him, all to no avail. He was beginning to see how little he mattered to the family—and to Daniel—too little to be even afforded a private audience.

Now, several hours into the night, the sound of heavy footsteps alerted Ambrose to Daniel's presence in the corridor outside. The footsteps stopped and a door close by slammed shut. Ambrose was being put up in Benjamin's old room, vacant since his brother-in-law now had a house of his own. It had not taken much deduction to realise that this room was next to Daniel's.

He waited some tense minutes to hear further sounds, but all went quiet. Getting to sleep became impossible, knowing that Daniel was lying on a bed just next door. Eventually, he gave it up with a sigh and threw off his covers. He had to speak to him. In bare feet, he tiptoed to the door of his room and stepped into the corridor.

He had to find his way by touch, as it was dark as pitch. When his hands found the next door, he knocked softly and waited for a reply. None came. He hesitated some more then, trying to maintain his courage, he turned the handle and let himself inside. He could not see much in the dark, but immediately, he could perceive the familiar clean scent of Daniel. He listened closely and heard the sound of deep breathing.

Slowly, he let his eyes accustom themselves to the dark. He made out the shape of the bed, and on it, a figure lying prone. On soft feet, he approached. A sliver of moonlight came through the window, illuminating his path. Daniel was fast asleep, still in his clothes, on top of the bed. For a long time, Ambrose watched him, watched the steady rise and fall of his breaths. Finally, he came closer and lifted the edge of the bedcovers, tucking them loosely over Daniel's body. Then he left quietly and returned to his room.

Next morning, he lingered in bed in a hazy state between slumber and sleep. He ought to get up, he knew. A noise caught his attention. It was Daniel's door, opening and shutting, then the sound of footsteps which paused outside his door. He held his breath. A moment later, the footsteps continued and went down the stairs.

Ambrose released his breath. He did not know whether he was relieved or disappointed. There was no point in dilly dallying in bed though. He threw back the covers and hastened to wash and dress. Once he was ready, he opened his room door and stepped out into the corridor, intending to make his way downstairs. Something though, made him hesitate. He turned around and stared at Daniel's door. He could not say why his feet took him to that door nor why he quietly let himself into the empty room.

He cast a quick glance around. The bedcovers were mussed and yesterday's clothes thrown in a heap on a nearby chair. He sniffed the air, taking in Daniel's scent. He wanted more. With the furtiveness of a thief, he went to the bed and put his nose to the pillow, breathing in deeply. There it was. He would never tire of that scent. He let himself have a minute, just breathing it in.

Eventually, he sat up and looked about him. He knew he should leave, but he could not make his feet move. Being in Daniel's space was both intoxicating and calming. Slowly, he drew open the bedside drawer, studying its contents. He picked up a book—a collection of Tennyson's poems. He smiled to himself; it was a favourite of his. As he went to put the book down, something fluttered from within the pages. It was a sheet of paper with some words written in Daniel's recognisable script.

I can be the person you talk to whenever you are in need of companionship. I can be the person who you come to when you have a problem to solve. I can be the person you share good news of your successes with, and the person to help lift you out of your sorrows. All these things I can be for you and you can be for me.

Then below, at the bottom of the page, Daniel had added one last sentence.

Is that enough for me?

Ambrose remembered once saying those words to Daniel. It had been the basis upon which they had built their relationship, these last five years. But it seemed this was no longer a satisfactory arrangement for Daniel. Was it enough? He had always thought it would have to be. What other choice was there? The question sent fear spiralling through his body. If Daniel wanted more from him and Ambrose could not provide it, would Daniel consider looking for love elsewhere, finding himself a wife and starting a family with her? He was twenty-nine, a good age for marriage—certainly too young to want to be shackled for life in an unsatisfactory relationship with him.

Carefully, Ambrose inserted the sheet back in the book and returned it to the drawer. The only other item in there was a small glass bottle. Ambrose unstoppered it and sniffed—some kind of viscous oil, most likely castor oil. He carefully replaced the lid. On an impulse, he slipped the bottle into the pocket of his jacket. He stood then and shut the drawer.

He had come here wanting to feel some connection with Daniel, knowing he would soon have to begin his journey back to England. He could not linger here anymore without risking discovery. On tiptoes, he trod to the door and listened. When he was sure the corridor was clear, he slipped out of the room and hastily made his way down the stairs.

He headed to the dining parlour, from where he could hear voices. Upon entering the room, he found Daniel, Isabella and Lady Stanton lingering over the remains of their breakfast. "Good morning," he greeted. "I seem to have overslept," he added by way of apology for his tardiness, avoiding Daniel's gaze.

Lady Stanton smiled at him kindly. "That is quite alright, Mr Cranshaw. You have had a long journey to get here and no doubt were very weary. Do come sit here beside Daniel." She pointed to a chair on Daniel's right.

Feeling flustered, he pulled the chair back and took the seat indicated, eyes cast down. Guilt flooded him at the knowledge he had just now been in Daniel's room uninvited. A clinking noise made him look up. Coffee was being poured into a cup for him. "Thank you," he murmured as Daniel added a dash of milk, just the way he liked it. Next, Daniel reached for a platter of cold meats and began serving him, putting a generous amount on his plate.

As he did so, he said casually, "After breakfast, Ambrose, I should like to take you on a walk around the estate. I am sure you will want to see it after the many things you have heard me say about it over the years." He cut a thick slice of bread and gave it to him, then passed the butter dish, adding, "It will also give us an opportunity to discuss matters."

"Of course," acquiesced Ambrose. So, they were going to have a private talk after all.

His reflections were interrupted by Isabella exclaiming, "What a good idea! I think I shall join you too."

"No, you will not," said Daniel shortly.

His sister gave him an injured look. "I can see where I am not wanted," she muttered.

"Isabella, my love," interjected Lady Stanton diplomatically. "Remember you were going to help me organise the books at the school today and to choose some to take to Mr Wilson's children."

"Yes, of course, Mama," she replied, still sounding stung.

Ambrose gazed at her apologetically as Daniel huffed, "Bella, don't take on so. I simply need to talk to Ambrose in private."

"Far be it from me to stand in your way, Daniel," she said haughtily. Taking a final gulp of her tea, she stood and made her excuses. "I shall go get myself ready, Mama."

Lady Stanton too rose to her feet, beaming at Ambrose. "It is dry and not too windy out there today," she assured him. "I am sure you will enjoy the walk. Now please do excuse me."

Ambrose stood politely to see her out. When they were alone again, he sat to eat once more, still not looking at Daniel.

"I am sorry about yesterday," Daniel began.

Ambrose waved a dismissive hand. "You were well within your rights to demand why I am here," he stated. "But fear not," he went on, "I shall soon be returning home. I simply wanted to ensure Sarah is well settled before I leave." Despite Daniel's apology, he could see there was no path to real reconciliation between them.

"We shall all return together," Daniel stated firmly. "But first, you and I must talk."

"Yes," said Ambrose. He finished his last bite of bread and drank up his coffee.

Seeing this, Daniel said, "I shall meet you on the front porch in five minutes. Will that be sufficient time for you?"

"Yes, of course."

They both stood and left the dining parlour, going up to get themselves ready. Five minutes later, they met as planned on the front porch. Ambrose followed Daniel down the steps and then strolled beside him as they took a curving path that began just beyond a group of outbuildings. "Over there is the vegetable garden and a glass house," Daniel said, pointing to the right. "On the other side are ten acres of pasture land. We keep a livestock of eighty heads of cattle here, in addition to the two dozen pigs in the pens back there."

Over the next half-hour, they continued their tour, Daniel pointing out the main features on the estate. It was large, though not as massive as the Stanton lands back in England. Everything looked neat and orderly. Daniel's father and uncle had done well for themselves here.

After a time, Ambrose noticed that they were now walking in woodland. The natural landscape was somewhat different to what he was used to. Tall pines dotted their path, the tips still bearing wisps of snow that must have fallen some days ago. The air was cool and fresh, but not unpleasant. They had not met a soul since they had left the cultivated fields and made their way to this wooded area. It gave Ambrose a curious feeling of liberation. Here, nobody could judge him. Social and class distinctions fell away, as did morality judgements. In this space, there was only him and Daniel.

Presently, he felt Daniel sigh gently beside him. "We can talk at ease here," he said, "with no fear that anyone will overhear us. There is a lake a mile further down, which we swim in during the summer."

They walked on, gathering their thoughts. This then was to be their talk. Where to start? Remembering the words Daniel had written, Ambrose blurted out, "Being just friends, is it enough for you?"

Daniel gazed at him quizzically. Unable to help himself, Ambrose went on, "I saw what you wrote on that sheet tucked inside the book of poems."

"So, you have been poking around in my room," huffed Daniel.

"It was wrong of me, I know."

"Yes, it was," agreed Daniel. "There again, in your shoes, I would have done the same."

"I am sorry," Ambrose said. "I should not have entered your room uninvited. I—I also came in during the night to speak with you, but you were fast asleep."

"So, you were the one to tuck the covers around me. I did wonder," mused Daniel.

"My behaviour has not been quite what it should. I will blame the upheaval of the past few weeks for my impaired judgement."

Daniel snorted but did not comment. They kept on walking. Up in the distance, Ambrose detected the faint glimmer of the water in the lake. He glanced at the man beside him. "You did not answer my question," he reminded him. "Is friendship with me enough?"

"Is it enough for you?" Daniel countered. Then he blew out a frustrated breath. "It will have to be enough if it is all you will allow me, but you know that I would like there to be more between us."

"Does that mean you have forgiven me?" asked Ambrose hopefully.

"Oh, I am a very long way from having forgiven you, Ambrose, but I am working on it. It does not take away from the fact that I still want you."

Ambrose's pulse quickened. His breaths came short and sharp. With an effort, he reined in his excitement. "I have not changed my mind on the matter," he said hoarsely. "We cannot be lovers."

"No?"

"No."

"Ah well," said Daniel, and was silent, a grim turn to his mouth. They had reached the lake by now. It was not large, more like an oversized pond. Reeds grew tall along one bank. On the other side, water lapped at pebbly ground. Ambrose stopped and looked around. To their left was a small wooden cabin with a thatched roof. "What is that?" he asked, pointing to it.

"It is just a cabin my family uses when we come to swim at the lake. Mama and the girls change in there." Daniel shrugged. "When it is just the men, we do not bother. We simply throw our clothes to the ground and jump into the water."

"Do you not wear bathing suits?" asked Ambrose, much perturbed.

"Whatever for?"

"For modesty of course!" protested Ambrose, though in his mind, he imagined what it would be like to swim here naked with Daniel. He felt an involuntary twitch of arousal.

Daniel laughed. "There is no need for it. We have all seen each other bare. Before we had the new bathing room built into the house, we were in the habit of washing in the tub outside."

Ambrose shuddered at the thought. Daniel's smile widened. "You really are so very prim and proper, aren't you?" he teased.

"I am the son of a clergyman after all," demurred Ambrose.

"Yes, so you are. You would be a fish out of water at Tremayne's," pondered Daniel.

"Tremayne's? What is that?"

Daniel seemed to regret the slip of his tongue. He tried to dismiss the question with a casual explanation, "Oh, it is simply a members' club that Philip Templeton took me to."

"What sort of a club?" prodded Ambrose, his curiosity growing.

"Just an ordinary club, nothing of great interest," Daniel evaded.

But Ambrose was not to be fobbed off. "Then why do you say that as a consequence of being a clergyman's son, I would be a fish out of water there?" He tried not to imagine what this could mean.

Daniel huffed irritably, "It is simply not the kind of place you would frequent, Ambrose."

He was hiding something, he just knew it. Ambrose faced him, hands on hips. "You will explain that," he said softly.

Looking uncomfortable, Daniel prevaricated some more. "It is a place of jollity and high spirits," he said.

"And why would I not enjoy a place of jollity and high spirits?" demanded Ambrose.

"Because you are modest, Ambrose, that is why!"

Ambrose narrowed his eyes dangerously, feeling his ire grow. "What do you mean by that?" he hissed.

Daniel threw up his hands in exasperation. "I mean, Ambrose, that people go about in this club without a stitch of clothing on."

"What?"

"On first arriving, a maid removes all my clothes and I then cavort naked with everyone," said Daniel, hardening his tone.

Ambrose's eyes nearly bulged out of their sockets. "Cavort?" he roared.

"Fornicate. I go to Tremayne's to fornicate, Ambrose."

White hot fury surged through Ambrose's veins. He grabbed Daniel by the collar of his coat. "Why?" he snarled.

"Why do you think?" spat out Daniel. "It is because I have needs, and the man I love refuses to fuck me. It is because I will not engage in romantic seductions with anyone but him. Why else do you think I would debase myself so each month?"

"I suspected you might have some hussy in London who you visited, but never in my wildest imaginings did I entertain the idea that you would fornicate with multiple people in a public space," grated Ambrose, the flames of his anger still burning bright.

"Well," mocked Daniel. "I am sorry to disappoint you, but that is the way it is. And as you still refuse to be my lover, Ambrose, I will have to resume my visits to Tremayne's just as soon as we return to England."

Ambrose was still holding on to Daniel's coat, but now, his anger boiled over. Shoving him backwards until his back hit the wall of the cabin, he yelled, "You will do no such thing!"

"And how will you stop me?" taunted Daniel.

"Like this!" Ambrose grabbed Daniel by the throat. A moment later, his mouth clamped down onto Daniel's lips in a savage kiss.

He had fought against this. Lord how he had fought. But he could not resist the lure of this infuriating man a minute longer. The hands that were around Daniel's throat slid upwards to bury themselves in the soft strands of his hair. Ambrose pulled his face closer and kissed him with desperate desire. "Like this," he repeated, sucking Daniel's bottom lip into his mouth. His tongue traced a line along his luscious lips then dived inside for a taste of paradise.

But he was not alone in this kiss. Daniel's hands gripped his head close as his tongue too came out to play with his. It was Daniel now that took the lead, stroking his tongue inside Ambrose's mouth and giving light nips to his lips. At last, they drew back to gasp for air. "You will never go to Tremayne's again," ordered Ambrose.

Daniel merely responded with another kiss. It distracted Ambrose for a time, but he drew back again, breathless, and rasped, "Promise me!"

"I promise," moaned Daniel. "Now kiss me."

Ambrose could not refuse when he was desperate for another kiss. Their lips met again and again, their hunger unrelenting. Their breaths fused and became one. "You are mine," Ambrose mumbled against Daniel's lips. "Say it!"

"I am yours. I am yours," chanted Daniel, punctuating each sentence with a kiss.

"I want you," groaned Ambrose, licking a path along the velvet softness on the inside of Daniel's lip.

"Yes," breathed Daniel.

"I want to claim you." More licks. More kisses.

"Then claim me," invited Daniel.

"Have you ever—had a man fuck you?"

"No," Daniel panted. "Never."

"Me neither. I have read about it though." Ambrose drew slightly back to look into Daniel's blazing eyes.

"So have I," whispered Daniel. "And once at Tremayne's, I saw two men do it."

"Do not mention that place again," growled Ambrose, but Daniel smiled mischievously.

"If it makes you do what you just did, I will keep mentioning it," he quipped.

Ambrose distracted him with another kiss. "So," he murmured against his lips, "will you let me?"

"Yes," came Daniel's breathless response. "Now?"

"Yes, now. In the cabin." With a firm hand on Daniel's arm, he led him to the cabin's door. It was unlocked, though the hinge was stiff, and it needed a few pushes to get it open. Inside it was dim, with only a few rays of light coming in through the small glass window. The cabin was sparsely furnished—a small chest of drawers, a wooden bench.

Daniel pulled a drawer open and took out a towel. "We may need this," he grinned. Then, nerves coming to the surface, he bit his lip. "We will need lubrication," he said hesitantly.

"Do not concern yourself with that, Daniel. Undress. Now."

Daniel did not immediately comply. "How about you?" he asked.

"You first. I want to see what kind of show you gave them at Tremayne's." Their eyes met for a long moment, then Daniel smiled ruefully. He unbuttoned his coat and took it off, laying it flat on the bench. Next it was his jacket, then his necktie and finally his shirt. Ambrose watched in rapt concentration. Daniel's naked chest was broad, dusted with dark hair, the muscles sinewy and strong from all the work he had been doing. He stood for him now, hands open by his sides. "Do you like what you see?" he asked, a trifle uncertainly.

"Yes, I do," murmured Ambrose. "Keep going. Do not stop."

Daniel kicked off his shoes, then slowly, he unfastened his trousers and pulled them down. Keeping his eyes fixed on Ambrose, he lowered his drawers and exposed his jutting hard cock, which rose majestically from a thick patch of dark, curling hair. Ambrose took a sharp breath, his eyes glued to Daniel's magnificent penis. He stepped forward, his chest heaving. "*Oh my*," he thought.

Next moment, his legs folded beneath him as he dropped down to his knees and buried his face in Daniel's groin, breathing in the musky scent of his sex. It was glorious. One hand crept up and cupped the two heavy sacs that hung like ripe fruit, while the other hand wrapped itself around Daniel's thick length. "Oh, you beauty," Ambrose murmured under his breath. He looked up into Daniel's scorching eyes. "Will you let me put my mouth to it?"

"Yes. Please, yes."

Ambrose bent his head and kissed the tip of Daniel's cock, which dribbled small amounts of his seed. He licked it, not wanting to see any of it go to waste. It had a musky tang with a trace of saltiness. He came back for more, licking it with increased fervour. Daniel groaned. Encouraged, this time Ambrose opened his mouth and sucked the tip in. "Ah," cried Daniel. Ambrose sucked another inch into his mouth, then another and another until he could take no more. The skin felt satiny smooth under his tongue as he pulled back, letting Daniel's cock slip out of his mouth with a pop.

He was letting himself get distracted when he had a task to do. Slowly, he got to his feet again and stared into Daniel's needy eyes. He asked one more time. "Will you let me claim you?"

And once more, Daniel replied, "Yes."

"Then turn around, my love, and lean on the bench with your elbows."

Daniel licked his lips nervously. "Will you take care of me?" he pleaded.

"Always," Ambrose promised. "Now do as I say."

Exhaling a deep breath, Daniel turned to face the bench and leaned on it with his elbows. His firm buttocks, brushed with a soft layer of downy hair, were raised up into the air in invitation. Ambrose looked on hungrily. He laid a gentle hand to that firm swell, stroking towards the curve of Daniel's lower back, where he was delighted to see two small dimples—a match for the ones on his face.

With determination, he put his hands to each buttock and pulled them apart, exposing the entrance where he was going to lay his claim. On impulse, he leaned forward and kissed that spot. He heard Daniel let out a whooshed breath. "Do you like that?" he whispered.

"Yes," breathed Daniel.

So, he kissed that spot again. Then, he straightened and took out the bottle of oil that was in his pocket. Had he known that he was going to use it on Daniel? Maybe so, in the far reaches of his mind. He poured a few drops of oil into his palm, then greased Daniel's puckered entrance with it. "Oh!" groaned Daniel. "What was that?"

Ambrose held out the bottle for Daniel to see. "I took a little memento from your drawer this morning," he explained.

Daniel huffed, "You devil! Was this your plan all along?"

Ambrose chuckled darkly, "So it seems. I did not know it then."

Daniel laughed. "I always knew you were no angel, Ambrose Cranshaw."

"Hush now, and let me do my business," chided Ambrose. He began to stroke that puckered entrance again. Then, bravely, he pushed one greased finger until the entrance gave way, and his finger was sucked inside the tight heat of Daniel's body. *"Oh my,"* he thought again. *"This is what will envelop my cock."* He felt his shaft pulse with excitement.

Slowly, he let his finger plunge in and out of that puckered hole. He poured a little more oil, then tried to insert a second finger. Daniel gasped, so he stopped at once. "Did I hurt you, love?" he asked worriedly.

"No, it is fine. Keep going," urged Daniel.

His fingers resumed their task, slowly widening and stretching that passage. Could a third finger fit? He tried, and Daniel took a sharp breath. "Too much?" queried Ambrose.

"Give me a moment," panted Daniel.

Ambrose waited patiently. "Do it again now," said Daniel.

Very slowly and looking out for any sign of pain, Ambrose pushed three fingers into him. There was a tight ridge which obstructed their passage at first, but with a little persistence, his fingers were able to push through. "How does that feel?" he wondered.

"It feels good. Very good," breathed Daniel.

"Will you let me take you now?" asked Ambrose.

"Do it!" barked Daniel.

Wiping his fingers on the towel first, Ambrose undid the fastenings of his trousers and pulled them down together with his drawers, releasing his long, slender cock. "Look at me, Daniel," he commanded.

Daniel turned his head and his eyes landed on Ambrose's erect penis. "You are long!" he exclaimed.

"All the better to claim you with," said Ambrose with a wolfish grin. He poured some more oil and greased his shaft. "I am going to take you now, Daniel," he said huskily, "and I will make you mine. You will never give your body to anyone else, do you hear?"

"Yes, Ambrose, I hear you. I promise. Now make me yours."

With infinite care, Ambrose brought the tip of his shaft to that puckered hole and pushed in slowly. He had only penetrated an inch or two when Daniel moaned. Ambrose paused, the sweat gathering on his brow. Gently, he tried to push in again. This time he was able to go in a little further before he heard Daniel's cry. He paused again, rubbing comforting circles to the small of his back. "I am fine," muttered Daniel. "Keep going."

Ambrose tried a third time, pushing slowly but determinedly inside until his whole length was sheathed in Daniel's body. He paused again, this time to try to compose himself. It was too good. He was not sure he could hold out for very long. "You feel divine, my love," he whispered into Daniel's ear.

Nuzzling his face into the back of Daniel's neck, he wrapped his arms around his chest, surrounding him like a blanket, and began to move—small little plunges at first, then longer and more powerful thrusts. "Ah," cried Daniel.

"Yes, my love, take me." He thrust powerfully again. "You are mine, Daniel."

"Yes!"

Ambrose was losing his mind, losing himself in the heavenly heat of Daniel's body. They were one, not two separate entities, but one body, one soul. He began a punishing rhythm, plunging in and out, in and out, delirious with pleasure, desperate to reach that hallowed peak. "Daniel," he grunted. "Oh, Daniel." Those were his last coherent words as he quickened his pace, feeling his cock swell, and with a harsh cry, he emptied himself into Daniel's warm body.

It took several moments for sanity to return. He stayed impaled inside Daniel, not wishing to part from him just yet. "Talk to me, love. How do you feel?" he asked urgently.

Daniel's voice was dazed as he breathed, "I feel claimed. I feel yours."

Ambrose kissed the back of his neck. "That you are," he murmured. His hand reached for Daniel's erect shaft, wanting to give back some of the pleasure he had just taken. He took out the bottle of oil from his pocket and poured a few more drops, then began to stroke Daniel's thick length. "Let me please you, my love," he urged, stroking rapidly up and down, grip firm on Daniel's cock.

"It won't take long," said Daniel throatily. "I am nearly there."

Ambrose's spent cock, still buried inside Daniel's body, pulsed with renewed desire as he heard Daniel's moans of pleasure. "Go on, my love," he urged. "Spend your seed into my hand."

Daniel gave a loud groan as sticky jets of his spend spurted from the tip of his cock. "Oh you clever, clever boy," crooned Ambrose, raining little kisses to the back of his neck and the side of his jaw. Slowly, excruciatingly, he pulled himself out, pleased at the rush of his seed as it dripped out of Daniel's hole.

Then, it was time to clean the mess. He pulled out his handkerchief and wiped his cock, then re-arranged his clothes. "Stay here, darling," he told Daniel. "I am going to wet this in the lake so I can clean you."

Quickly, he went outside, dazzled by the bright light after the dimness of the cabin, and wet the handkerchief. He was back presently, wiping Daniel as clean as he could. "There you go," he whispered soothingly as if to a babe. "Let me help you dress." With tender care, he assisted Daniel, who seemed to be in a strange, dreamy state. Once dressed, he sat him down on the bench and nestled his long body into the crook of his arms. For a long time, Ambrose held Daniel, stroking his hair, stroking his arms, dropping sweet little kisses.

When finally, Daniel spoke, it was to say these three words, "I love you."

"And I love you," murmured Ambrose.

"That was… that was incredible," breathed Daniel.

"It felt amazing to me too."

"So, I think your rule about us not being lovers has already been broken," remarked Daniel dryly.

"Yes," said Ambrose ruefully, "at least while we are here and nobody can find us out. But darling, I fear it would not be quite so easy back in England."

Daniel took Ambrose's hand and kissed it. "We will work it out," he promised. "As long as we love one another and can be honest, we will find a way."

They left the cabin and walked slowly back towards the house, reluctant to leave their little oasis of love. As they neared the edge of the woodland, Daniel stopped and gave him one last ferocious kiss. "I shall need sustenance to keep me going until tonight," he explained.

"Tonight?" queried Ambrose.

Daniel's expression hardened. "You will come to my room tonight, Ambrose, else I shall pay a visit to yours. I too can be commanding and forceful when it comes to us."

Ambrose did not put up a fight. "Very well," he said quietly. "Wait and I shall come to you when I am sure the coast is clear."

For the rest of the day, Ambrose floated in a dizzy cloud of happiness. His logical mind pointed out to him at odd times that this happiness could not last, that things would once again become complicated when they returned to England. He was too happy though to listen to that voice for long. There would be time enough to deal with whatever was to come next. At dinner, he felt himself being observed closely, first by the Earl of Stanton, then by his lady. Each time he encountered those observing eyes, however, he was met with bland smiles. He was not sure what to make of it.

At last, they all retired for bed. Ambrose washed and put on his nightshirt, then read until the house went quiet. Then, pulling on a robe, he tiptoed silently to the room next door. He did not knock this time, merely turned the handle and went in. Daniel lay in bed, a candle casting a golden glow upon his beautiful face. On seeing him, he lifted back the covers in invitation, and Ambrose got into the bed after casting off his robe and nightshirt. The two of them came together then, naked skin on naked skin.

Hours were spent in kisses and explorations of each other's body. There was no repeat of the occurrence in the cabin, yet each of them through loving touch spent their seed in pleasurable satisfaction. Afterwards, they got themselves clean then returned to bed, holding each other and talking quietly into the night.

"When was it you knew of your feelings for me?" Daniel wondered.

"I was struck dumb the moment I first saw you," confessed Ambrose. "But if you meant to ask when it was that I fell in love with you, I think it was the morning after your grandfather died and we got drunk together in my study. I remember seeing you curled up, asleep on my settee. You gave a soft sigh as I covered you with a blanket, and my heart stopped. I knew then."

Daniel groaned. "It was the same for me. When I woke up from sleeping on that damned uncomfortable settee and saw you asleep across from me, I realised what I felt for you was not just lust but love." He sighed softly. "How much time we have wasted! We could have been together from that day."

Ambrose could not fully agree. "I think there were still too many obstacles in our way then. I was not ready to acknowledge the true nature of my feelings even if I felt them strongly. And I had no way of knowing then that what you felt would stand the test of time. I was convinced that you would soon move on to greener pastures."

"But I did not. I think, Ambrose, that perhaps you misjudged me at the start."

Ambrose consoled him with a quick kiss. "I may have done," he conceded. "However, instead of ruing the time we lost, maybe we should appreciate the greater knowledge we came to have of each other over all these years, for it is with a certainty that I can say to you now that you own my heart and always will." So saying, he took Daniel's hand and placed it on his chest, close to his heart.

Daniel reciprocated the gesture in kind, taking Ambrose's hand and placing it on his chest. "And you own mine," he said softly. Then he smirked, "Although it did not take me long to find it out. I knew it all those years ago."

Ambrose decided it was time to distract his lover with a kiss. They did not come up for air for a very long time. Much later, Ambrose murmured, "I shall want to pay a visit to Benjamin and Sarah tomorrow."

"And get them out of their marriage bed? They shall not thank us for the interruption to their loving," remarked Daniel in amusement.

"Please, darling, no," Ambrose shuddered. "Do not put disturbing images about my sister into my mind. It was bad enough when Lexie spoke of some such things to me the last time we met."

"Lexie," said Daniel flatly, his body stiffening. "You know, Ambrose," he went on coldly, "that if I am to promise fidelity to you, then you must do so too. Please end your affair with her."

Ambrose laughed softly, kissing Daniel's stubbly cheek. "It has been done already. Do you think I could lie with anyone else after what happened with us that day we kissed? Of course not."

Daniel blew out a long breath, his body still unyielding. "I am very fond of Lexie," he rasped softly, "but do you know, Ambrose, just what level of jealousy the two of you caused me?"

Ambrose brought his face to Daniel's chest, peppering it with little kisses and nuzzling the curling hair, then whispered,

"And visions of your depravity at Tremayne's will haunt me forever, so I suppose we are even." After a while, he added, "In any case, I had no plan to arrive at my sister's house unannounced. I will send them a note in the morning letting them know that we shall visit in the afternoon."

Daniel ran his fingers through Ambrose's hair, holding him to his chest. "You shall see the house I built," he said with a touch of pride.

"Is it well built?"

Daniel's hand slid from Ambrose's head down to his cheek, giving it a punishing tap. "This hand, Ambrose, can do many things," he growled. "It can caress. It can punish your insolence. It can also build a magnificent house. You will see."

And indeed, he did. Their visit, the following day, went a long way towards allaying Ambrose's worries about Sarah's future. He was secretly impressed with the house that Daniel had built in such a short time, but he would not say so, as Daniel's head was already big enough. Of course, it would need more furnishings and decoration on the inside, but he felt sure that Sarah would soon put her talents to making the house feel like a welcoming home, as she had done with Ivy Cottage. It brought a momentary and unwelcome reminder that he would live alone in that cottage from there on, but he pushed the melancholic thought aside.

Later, they went for a stroll in the meadow outside the house, and there, Ambrose was amused to see both Benjamin and Sarah chatter excitedly about the workshop that would be built there, just as soon as they could break ground in the spring. It would be a place for Benjamin to tinker with and invent new machinery, such as a steam plough with an improved design that he had in mind and which his papa had promised to try out on the Stanton lands when it was ready. Sarah was determined to assist him in this work, having already proved herself an able assistant when together, they had fixed a leak on the steam plough that Daniel had purchased for his lands in England.

That night in bed, after a bout of loving, Daniel kissed the top of his head and murmured, "Those two are like two peas in a pod."

"I think they are well matched," agreed Ambrose. "Even though I am glad to see Sarah so happy, it will be hard to say goodbye." He turned his head to look into Daniel's eyes. "Soon, I must return to England," he stated firmly. "Quite apart from the estate requiring my attention, there is also Emily. I have never been apart from her for so long."

"How is the little rascal?" chuckled Daniel.

"That madam has us wrapped firmly around her little finger," replied Ambrose. "She has asked about you, several times. Where's Uncle Daniel?"

"I have missed her too." Daniel sighed. "Will you give me another two days here with you? Then, we shall all return to England, Isabella too, unless she wishes to remain here."

Ambrose buried his nose in the warm crook of Daniel's neck, inhaling his essence. It was fast becoming one of his favourite places to be. "Once we leave," he murmured, "things will be different."

"I know."

"I—I love you Daniel," he said haltingly, "but I cannot risk anybody finding out about our love."

"I know."

"We shall have to agree… on some boundaries."

Daniel gathered Ambrose to him and kissed him soundly. "We shall draw up a contract," he said. "Tomorrow, we will sit together and write down the terms."

And so it was that after breakfast the following morning, Daniel took Ambrose to his father's study and sat him down across from his desk. He withdrew a blank sheet of paper and wrote with a flourish at the top: "*Agreement between Daniel Stanton and Ambrose Cranshaw*".

He glanced up at Ambrose. "Number one, absolute fidelity. Do you agree?" Ambrose nodded, and Daniel wrote it down.

"Number two," began Ambrose. "No overt signs of affection between us. In front of others, I will continue to address you as 'my lord'."

Daniel thought about it then nodded and wrote it down. "How about physical love?" he ventured. "Are we to remain celibate as monks?"

"I would like to see you try!" teased Ambrose. Then, turning serious, he went on, "I do not think I can resist you, my love, but we shall have to be very careful and very discreet. There are too many eyes and ears at Stanton Hall, so I will not feel right doing anything more than kissing in your study when we are alone there."

"How about Ivy Cottage?" wondered Daniel.

Ambrose considered the matter. "Once Elsie leaves the cottage in the evening after her work is done, then I shall be alone," he said slowly.

"Then may I visit you there?" asked Daniel.

"You cannot do it every day, or it will raise suspicion," decided Ambrose. "How about twice—no three times–a week? Come after dusk and stay for a few hours."

"If I must," said Daniel sombrely, writing this down. He looked up again once he was done. "Now I have some conditions of my own," he said in a firm tone.

"What are they?"

"I will employ an assistant estate manager who you will train in all the responsibilities of your work," stated Daniel.

"Whyever so?" demanded Ambrose, affronted.

Daniel huffed, "It is not any disparagement on your work, Ambrose, merely a strategic consideration. Only think, if there is someone to look after the affairs of the Stanton estate, then we may both absent ourselves from it."

"Where would we go?" Ambrose wanted to know.

"I am a rich man, my dear," retorted Daniel. "We can go wherever we want, abroad where nobody knows who we are. You do know, countries on the Continent that have adopted the Napoleonic code have no laws outlawing sodomy."

Ambrose took a sharp breath. "I... I am aware of this, yes," he murmured.

Daniel eyed him severely. "Then this is my condition. We shall travel abroad and spend at least two months of the year together, sharing a bed."

Ambrose touched a finger to Daniel's pursed lips. "Very well, my love," he whispered. The condition was duly written down.

Daniel looked up enquiringly. "Is there anything else we need to add to this agreement?"

Ambrose hesitated. "Have you considered, Daniel, what will happen if you do not marry?"

Daniel's expression became mulish. "I will never marry, Ambrose, and I can write that now into the agreement. I do not care much about my title, but it will pass on to Benjamin and his children after me. I will ensure Benjamin's eldest son inherits the estate, as well as provide for you and Emily in my will should I predecease you. Do you have any objections?" Ambrose shook his head, and this was duly written down.

Daniel put the pen down and rose to his feet. He folded the contract and slipped it into his pocket, then came round the desk to stand before Ambrose. "Then we are in agreement, my love," he said softly. "Kiss me now and seal our bargain." He drew Ambrose to his feet and took him into his arms for a celebratory kiss.

Epilogue

Christmas Eve, eight years later

Daniel lifted the bedcovers, careful not to disturb Ambrose, who was sleeping soundly, his breaths punctuated by soft little snores. Of course if asked, Ambrose would deny strenuously that he snored, but there it was, the incontrovertible proof. Not that anyone else was here to report on it.

Daniel smiled to himself as he got out of the bed and dressed quietly. This was now a familiar routine, established many years ago after he and Ambrose hammered out their agreement. Several times a week, he arrived at Ivy Cottage after dark and slipped inside with his own key. There, he spent his evenings with his love, talking, bickering, occasionally playing backgammon, concluding with both going to the bedroom to strip off their clothes and bring pleasure to one another.

They had become more adventurous in the bedroom, learning the ways to please each other. Sometimes, it was Daniel that did the claiming, driving himself into Ambrose's quivering body. And though the feeling of having his cock tightly sheathed in Ambrose's hot passage was exquisite, he found himself missing that feeling of being taken, of being possessed. So, more often than not, it was Ambrose that penetrated him. There was something indescribable in seeing the transformation of Ambrose from the meek, gentle man he was in public to the possessive and commanding presence he was when they were alone.

Then, when they were sated, they held each other for a long, peaceful time until Ambrose drifted off to sleep. Much as he wished he too could sleep in that warm bed with his love, Daniel knew he could not. So, in the darkness of night, he dressed and readied to go. Just before leaving, Daniel pulled a small wrapped box from the pocket of his jacket and deposited it on the pillow beside Ambrose. "Happy Christmas, darling," he whispered, brushing a final kiss on his forehead, then silently left the room and made his way out of the house.

He walked along the deserted avenue to Stanton Hall, habituated to this lonely traverse back to his home. He was thirty-seven years old and still vigorous enough to do it. What he would do when he reached an age of decrepitude, he did not know. Perhaps by then, he would have convinced Ambrose to spend more months of the year abroad with him—that lovely farmhouse on the outskirts of Amsterdam maybe, or the villa in Bordeaux. Or else, they could go further afield and explore the delights of Constantinople.

He reached Stanton Hall and let himself in through the side entrance, using the key he kept in his pocket for this very purpose. The few servants he kept were of course aware that he went out for long hours in the evening and returned late at night. They were too well trained to ask questions and too well paid to gossip. He made sure of that.

Once inside, he removed his coat and hat, hanging them on a hook by the door. Quickly, he went up the stairs, eager to reach the comfort of his bedchamber. Only as he crept along the darkened corridor, he saw a light streaming from below the library door. *Curious.* Changing course, he directed his steps towards the library, opening the door softly and peeking his head round.

Benjamin sat in an old armchair, sipping on a glass of whiskey. He raised his brow on catching sight of his brother. "So, you are back from Ivy Cottage," he remarked.

Daniel strolled into the room, closing the door behind him. He went to the sideboard and took out a glass for himself, pouring a small shot of whiskey. Drink in hand, he came to sit opposite Benjamin. "You are up late," was all he said, taking a warming sip of the liquor.

"I went down to place the presents under the tree," explained Benjamin. "On the way back up, I felt an impulse to come sit here, in this very armchair where I first met Sarah." He smiled ruefully. "It is Christmas Eve, and I am feeling nostalgic."

Daniel laughed softly. "Yes, I have been feeling nostalgic too. Probably to do with the fact that we are all here together this Christmas. I wonder if or when we shall ever be able to do that again."

Benjamin set down his glass on a side table. "Ma and Pa are not getting any younger," he agreed. "I am just glad they managed to come with us this time." He stood and stretched. "I had better get back to bed before Sarah sends a search party," he yawned. He took a few steps towards the door but was stopped by Daniel's next words.

"Are you happy, Ben?"

Benjamin turned to face his brother with a crooked smile. "Now what kind of question is that to ask in the middle of the night?" he enquired.

Daniel shrugged. "A spur of the moment thought. So, are you happy?"

Benjamin retraced his steps towards his brother and took a seat once more. "Yes, I cannot complain about my lot. There have been difficult times, but overall, life has been good. How about you? This thing between you and Ambrose. It cannot always have been easy. Has it been worth it?"

"Yes," replied Daniel unequivocally. "I would wish sometimes that the world were different, more accommodating of our kind of love, but I have no regrets. Ambrose is… he is everything to me."

Benjamin nodded. "I see it. And I am sorry that this world is not kind." They were quiet for a moment, then Benjamin got to his feet once more. "I think it is past time our aging bodies were put to bed," he declared. "Goodnight, brother."

Daniel finished his drink and set it down. "Goodnight, Ben," he murmured, rising to his feet. "Do not expect me to wake before ten," he added with a yawn.

Both brothers made their way to their rooms, Daniel to an empty bed, and Benjamin to his wife, Sarah. She stirred as he joined her under the covers. "You were gone a long time," she mumbled sleepily.

"I had a little chat with Daniel in the library," Benjamin explained, kissing her cheek. "Let us catch some slumber," he added. "It won't be long before the little horrors come storming in here."

She nestled into his body. "G'night," she slurred, already half asleep. Benjamin was not far behind in finding blessed slumber.

Over in the next room, the occupants were not asleep. Frank was a light sleeper these days, and the sound of his sons' footsteps in the corridor outside his room had wakened him. As he stirred, so did Charlotte. "It is late for them to be still out and about," she grumbled to her husband. He grunted in reply and gathered her to him. All was quiet, though neither of them had gone back to sleep.

"Do you ever miss this place?" wondered Charlotte.

"No, my love," replied Frank, tenderly brushing hair off her forehead. "Home is in Ohio. This grand palace has never felt like home to me, even when I lived here as a young man."

"Is it a home for Daniel then?" she asked worriedly. "I sometimes think it must be lonely for him living here all alone — even with Ambrose close by at Ivy Cottage."

"Hmm," replied Frank noncommittally. "It is not what I would choose for myself, nor for him, but he seems content."

"It is the way of the world, is it not?" mused Charlotte. "Your life is not at all what your father had planned for you. And who could have imagined the paths each of our three children decided to take in life?"

"It is their lives to lead, not ours," replied Frank philosophically. "I once told Daniel that what matters most to me is that my children are safe and sound. Everything else is a minor consideration."

Charlotte dropped a kiss to his shoulder. "I have not always liked this life that Daniel has chosen to lead, but you are quite right. In the end, what matters most is that he is safe. I do not ever again want to go through the agony of worry we suffered over Benjamin during the war."

"That boy has taken years off my life," concurred Frank. He reached to the bedside table and opened the drawer, pulling out a small wrapped packet. "Seeing as you are awake, my love, here is your Christmas gift."

She took it from him and tore off the paper. Inside was a leather bound volume of the complete works of Plato. "I saw this at Hatchards when we were in London last week, and thought you would like it," rumbled Frank, watching his wife closely for her reaction.

"How lovely! And so beautifully bound. Thank you, dear," exclaimed Charlotte throwing her arms around Frank.

He drew her to him, capturing her lips for a kiss. It was meant as a gentle gesture of affection, but soon, as was often the case with them, it deepened into something more. She moaned softly as his tongue slipped into her mouth. "Frank," she breathed.

"Seeing as we have been rudely awakened," he grunted, "there is one way to help ease us back to slumber." His hand reached down to the juncture of her thighs and unerringly found the small nub that brought her so much pleasure. He stroked her there all the while his mouth continued its plunder of hers.

"Oh," she breathed, "I believe that is an excellent idea."

In answer, her husband positioned himself above her and drove his erect cock into her welcoming heat. It had been nearly four decades since that first time he had made love to his glorious Charlotte in a secret tryst in a rented house on Charles Street. And in that time, he had never tired of this, nor of her. Their bodies had got older, aches and pains had beset them with age, but still they found pleasure in each other's arms. When they were done, he held his Charlotte close and whispered goodnight.

"Mmm," was her sleepy response.

"Merry Christmas," he murmured. And then he too slipped into satisfied slumber.

Next day at luncheon, a large group of people gathered to break bread together. Daniel looked around him in satisfaction. Here he was with all his loved ones, celebrating Christmas in the year of our Lord, 1873. Life was good. He should not complain.

Under cover of the table, he reached for Ambrose's hand and squeezed it gently, sending a message of affection to the love of his life. Ambrose was in the process of teasing his lovely daughter, Emily, about her dislike of Brussel sprouts, but on feeling the touch of Daniel's hand, he glanced sideways at him and gave him that divine, ambrosial smile that had captured his heart all those years ago. Lord but he was beautiful. Smoky grey eyes met burning black ones. A current of understanding passed between them. *"Just you wait until I have you to myself,"* said the grey eyes. *"I cannot wait,"* replied the black eyes.

Afterword

Dear reader,

I hope you enjoyed **The Viscount's Forbidden Love**, the fourth and final book in the series, **The Stanton Legacy**, which follows the lives and loves of the Stanton family. However, fear not, as it is not the last you will hear of some of the characters you have encountered. If you would like to read some more about Lexie Forbes and Mr Templeton, then do check out **Mr Templeton Finds Himself a Wife**. And if you were wondering if Isabella Stanton is to have a story of her own, then do read **Miss Stanton Meets her Match**, an age gap romance between Isabella and her tenant at Netherwick Hall, Mr Wilson.

Please do consider subscribing to my newsletter on **mmwakeford.substack.com** to get latest authorly news, book recommendations and freebies.

May I ask you for a small favour?

Reviews are the life blood of independent authors. Please could you help spread the word about this book by submitting a review on Amazon, Goodreads or any other book reader platform. Thank you!

M.M. Wakeford

About the author

M.M. Wakeford lives with her husband and son in a London terraced house that gathers dust while she loses herself in her writing. A lifelong reader of romantic novels, she writes in many genres including contemporary, sci-fi and historical romance. All her stories strive to capture that heady feeling of falling in love, with authentic characters whose journey to a happily ever after is lined with dilemmas to overcome. If you're looking for a page turning romance with high emotion and a good dose of spice, you've come to the right place.

MY CAPTIVE DUCHESS
Book 1 – The Reeves of Reeves Hall

"You cannot leave Reeves Hall again. Here you will remain."

Recently widowed, Jane, Duchess of Coleford, has moved to an isolated part of Cornwall with her young daughter. There she meets her nearest neighbour, Brook Reeves, a man with a seemingly permanent scowl on his handsome face who soon makes it clear that he wants her gone. Despite his many offers to purchase the crumbling house she inherited from her late husband, she stubbornly insists on staying.

It is not long before the two become adversaries, both determined to ignore the attraction that has flared between them. Until one day, Jane ventures uninvited into his domain and sees things she must never tell the world about. There is solution. At Reeves Hall she must remain, his captive

or's note: My Captive Duchess is a slow-burn yet steamy ance set in Regency England with a science-fiction twist. It ook one of a four-part series, The Reeves of Reeves Hall, set ound the mysterious Reeves family who are not what they eem. However, this book can be read and enjoyed as a standalone.

Praise for My Captive Duchess:

"Absolutely outstanding writing... Original story with uncompromising storytelling that you will have difficulty putting down once you start reading. Highly recommend." Goodreads review

"I applaud the clever plot in this story. I adore both Regency and Sci-Fi, but never expected to see a combination of my two favorites! Well done!" Goodreads review

"I found the story so engaging I couldn't put it down." Goodreads review

"A strong start to the Reeves of Reeves Hall series, and left me wanting to read more in this series." Goodreads review

"I couldn't put this book down! It was a good story with steam and great characters." Goodreads review

"Excellent writing with a thought-provoking sub-plot… Loved the juxtaposition of high-tech future tech to the age just before the industrial revolution." Goodreads review

"The most fascinating story I have read in a long while... All in all, a wonderful read!" Amazon review